Allegro

Cassandra Frew

This is dedicated to my fellow 'Sommersett'

High inmates 1982-1987, most especially

my best friend Jason, who was the

inspiration for Michael.

And, as always, to my late husband Chris -

my Lorien.

Without your love and support, this series of

books would never have eventuated.

Commenced 14 December 2009
Completed 7 March 2010

The characters in this book are fictitious. Any similarities to persons either living or dead are purely coincidental.

Allegro - Copyright © Cassandra Frew 2020 - ISBN 978-0-6488635-2-6

TABLE OF CONTENTS

PREFACE 1

TERM 1 2

    Translated from Sanskrit 2

    From Boys to Men 22

    Aftermath 36

    The First Small Step 49

EASTER 68

    The Bay Long Weekend 68

    Saturday 83

    Easter Sunday 108

    Home Again, Home Again 132

THE BAND 148

    The Epitome of Matty 148

    1, 2, 3, 4 160

    5, 6, 7, 8 170

    Burning Down the House 179

THE BIGGER PICTURE 202

    The Bitter Pill to Swallow 202

    The Debt We All Pay 222

    Happy Birthday to Me 238

    Here Comes the Bride 273

EPILOGUE 287

GLOSSARY OF AUSSIE SLANG 290

About the Author 297

PREFACE

THE SCHOOL YEARS slip away so quickly. In eleven months, high school would be over, and we'd be expected to become part of the real world. I wasn't sure I was ready for it, but Lorien held enough excitement for our futures. He couldn't wait to get his teeth into life.

We both wanted to teach music and were happy to travel to do so if it meant we could be together. He still held the idea of forming a band at the centre of his options, something he'd been planning for over a year. The catalyst would be he and his twin Elijah's eighteenth birthdays, which were in a few short weeks…Valentine's Day. He figured when we were all eighteen, we could start the pub and club circuit, but he'd not moved with the speed he had hoped. A drummer still needed to be found and he had a few more songs to write before the compilation was complete. His dream was still alive though, and I loved him so much for it.

TERM 1

Translated from Sanskrit

"You better hold on tight, this ride means business,
I gotta new life and I want you in it.
For 24 hours, the sky's the limit.
And if I say pleeeease...?"

L Standish, 'Skulling Champagne'

WE'D ONLY BEEN BACK AT SCHOOL for two weeks and Lorien and I were already ditching classes together. Only one or two so far, but we weren't setting a great example for ourselves to follow for the rest of the year. The worst temptation was in knowing his home was only across the road. We'd disappear through our lunch break and just didn't bother going back unless we had History as one of the last two periods. His mother was the teacher.

My best friends Michael and Bree were not thrilled about it either. Michael complained that we had all weekend and evenings to spend with each other. "You're encroaching on *my* friend time when you're doing it during school hours." If the teachers didn't notice us missing from classes, Michael and Bree certainly did.

We were currently sitting in what was both our favourite class, Music. It was not only due to our shared love of music, our whole relationship started in this very room, back when we were in Year 11. It was during lunch, in the music room, we first got together. We were interrupted when class started but continued to flirt silently with each other until the bell rang, then racing across the road to spend the final period of the day wrestling on his sofa.

To pay homage to that special day we always had our secret game at the ready, which was becoming more obvious to our Music teacher, Mr O'Dowd. On the few occasions we'd been caught, his prime weapon was to put us on separate sides of the room from each other. This didn't prevent anything - we still had eyes. Today had been one of those days and Lorien was at my side like a flash as the bell rang for lunch. "Let's go to my place." His eyes were sinister, his breathing slightly hurried.

"We can't keep doing this Lorien - we should be taking Year 12 more seriously. *You* might be some form of genius, but I need to study to keep my grades up."

"You get my grades up all the time," he said, his dark eyes scorching as he pulled me to him at the hip. "Pleeease Ash? Elijah can bring home the Maths work with him this afternoon. Please...!" How could I say no? I didn't want to say no. I sighed dramatically and said,

"Only if you say please."

He laughed, knowing he had his way and took me by the hand, racing me through the quad. His parents had been aware for some time we were having a physical relationship. They had raised their twins masterfully however and respected both them and the girls with whom they chose to have their relationships. We were also nearly adults, myself having turned eighteen last July.

My car was already parked in their driveway as I'd spent last night with him. I rarely bothered to move it to the school parking lot anymore; I just came and went from Lorien's when I wasn't staying overnight. "Wait,"

I said as we reached the northern side of the house, our most secluded point of entry. He looked at me quizzically. "Are you sure Cara has a lesson scheduled for the next two periods?"

"Positive," he answered quickly and then grabbed me, pressing me up against the outside wall.

We both knew the first connection we made for the day was sure to be quick and fulfilling, passion and desire throwing us into the epicentre of the storm. He leant his chin against my forehead and took a deep breath, then lowered his face to mine, slowly, gently, trying to maintain a steady pace. It was a pointless gesture; within thirty seconds of the first playful kisses, we were recklessly stumbling through the back door. Our fingers worked at each other's buttons and zips, stripping the clothes from our backs. We were naked by the time we'd even reached the lounge area and urgency prevented us making the short trip up the stairs to his room. He straddled my hips around his with my back to the dividing kitchen wall, slowly gliding himself against me, separating and teasing me to the arousing heights I had only for him. "Baby girl," he muttered, his lips against my throat, the friction doing no end of good to him also, "you are always so *ready* for me," he groaned. "Oh... ah... that's it...," he breathed as he eased inside me.

Our kisses were shameless and searching, feeding off each other in a vampiric frenzy, our moans verbalising the intrinsic aching of our bodies. He was just getting a good rhythm on when the toilet flushed upstairs. *Crap!* he mouthed at me, our eyes wide. We dislodged instantly and scrambled for our clothes, running into the back bathroom. "Who would be home?" I whispered.

"I have no idea, the car's not here so it can't be Dad, and Mum has lessons scheduled. It can only be Eli." We waited, listening for another sound. A few minutes later we heard a girl laugh.

"Keren," we whispered in unison.

"Damn him," Lorien added. "Or not to damn him, that is the question," he whispered in my ear as he leant in, aligning to me from behind. His hands grazed across my back, starting to knead tenderly.

"Listen Bard, you can dream on," I said, turning to him. "I'm not making love in the bathroom with your brother and his girlfriend only a few metres away." The whimsical lullaby version of Bobby Darin's 'Dream Lover' hummed into my ear. "Lorien." He laughed and continued, singing softly. "Lorien!" He drew me closer against him, rocking me gently in his arms. "Lorien," I sighed, nuzzling my back against him. He knew how to play me and *always* get his way. He finished, turning me to face him and kissing me sweetly.

My passion had abated for the moment, thrown from my body in fear no doubt, but the soul searching was still there - shared between us through the magical kisses that took me away from the problem of what was outside this door. The sex with Lorien was always like a bonfire, but the stand-alone kisses were something else entirely. His hands were talented as to be expected, all the instruments he played were strummed, plucked, or stroked, but the most amazing part of this skilled musician's body was still his lips, and he didn't play any brass or woodwinds. "I think we'd better get you a saxophone," I murmured. He drew back, smiling.

"Where did that come from?" he laughed. "Have you been having illicit thoughts about me again?" he crooned into my ear, holding me firmly against him.

It was embarrassing that I still had daydreams about him. It had been happening since we were first together and was even now the case. *Most* embarrassingly, it included when we were being intimate. Even consumed with him I *still* fantasised about him. "Ash, what's wrong?" he asked as he pulled his boxers on, sitting on the closed toilet seat and settling me onto his lap. I told him and he laughed again. "Ash, it's fantastic I not only have you in my arms but I'm also in your head at the same time. Can't you see how special that is? It's not a problem, it's a gift." He drew my face gently to his shoulder, "My bashful little Angel," he whispered against my ear, stroking my back soothingly. It made me feel a lot better.

I then realised I was still sitting on him naked and moved to put some clothes on. "Where are you going?" he asked pulling me back to his lap.

"To get dressed."

"But..." I put my finger to his lips to shush him, which he slowly sucked into his mouth.

"Lorien, listen." He did. We could hear panicked whispers coming from the next room; they knew someone else was also home.

"This will be *so* great," he laughed quietly, knowing that the mood was severed now. He allowed me to stand and dress this time, and we moved to the door, waiting.

A few seconds later, there was a slight knock and Elijah asked, "Dad?"

"What are you doing home son?" Lorien answered in an all-but perfect mimic of his father.

"Ah, I forgot a textbook," he spluttered out.

"I think you've got your little girlfriend here," Lorien said and threw the door open, laughing.

"Lorien, I'm going to kill you!" Elijah launched himself at his twin and wrestled him to the ground.

"Hi Keren," I said.

"Hey Ash." We watched our men tussle for a few moments and then Keren said, "I thought *we* came here to do that Eli?" This refocussed their attention.

"Great," I said. "We were hoping to get the Maths off you tonight. I'll have to call Bree later and get it off her. Looks like it's a night home for me."

"Let me grab a uniform for Monday and a few clothes, I'll come with you." I was hoping he'd want to. He slept in the spare room at my place. My parents were fairly cool and were certainly not idiots, but we played it their way until they went to sleep.

"Don't you think you should put something on now?" Keren asked. Lorien was still standing in his boxer shorts.

It was still a little weird at times, as Keren and I had initially gone out with each other's twin for a few months until we ended up being wrongly suited. Although Elijah had always been Keren's first choice, it irritated her in a small way that I had been his. In all fact, I had made this life changing decision for all of us. It was through what I considered an ill-fated dream at the time that ended up making my world whole, with Lorien at my side.

We pulled into my driveway and Lorien grabbed his clothes off the back seat as I unlocked the front door. No one was home, a definite blessing, as we hadn't figured in the time difference and school was only just letting out now. He dumped his bag at the dining room table and ran up the stairs to hang his clothes in my wardrobe. Everything else he would need was already in a drawer I had emptied out for his use.

I upended my bag onto the table, sorting through the books I needed to complete my homework before going into the kitchen to make coffee. Lorien announced his return by sliding his hands around me from behind, leaning me into him. "No one's home?" he asked, kissing softly behind my ear.

"No, it must be Mum's afternoon rostered on at the Doctor's surgery."

"Hmmm," he breathed, turning me to face him.

"Homework to be done, Mr Intensity." I smiled then kissed him, draping my arms around his neck.

"But we only just got started before Baby," he complained. "How can I concentrate on anything else but you?" He grazed his hips against me, trying to remove all discussion of any other possibility from my mind. It wasn't going to work this afternoon however as I had a heap of homework to get through and would have to ring Bree to get the Maths work we missed when we decided to skip class.

I kissed him again, his hands working their way down my back and coming to rest on my rear, pulling me close. When I felt him against me, I drew back, stopping the onset of the inevitable before it could build any further. "Ash," he groaned, still holding me tightly, "please."

"Begging is *not* going to work this time," I said and pulled away from him entirely, picking up the two mugs and taking them to the table. He sighed, resigned to the fact that there would be no afternoon delight and came to sit next to me, pulling books out of his bag.

"Aren't you going to ring Bree?"

"She won't be home yet; I'll give it half an hour."

I flipped open my history binder and started to summarise the last fifteen pages of handwritten notes. I endeavoured to pay special attention to the history homework, as this was the class Lorien's mother taught. "What else have we got?"

"Today's Maths and the English essay, plus I want to get summaries done for all my subjects. I haven't done a scrap of study notes in over a week." He smiled at me, knowing he was to blame for this. A small part of me insisted I share the blame.

"Who are you going to write your essay about?" he asked, thumbing through the pages of his binder to find the next vacant page.

"Being biographical, I thought I would write about you," I smiled at him. "You're the most interesting person I know."

"Then it is you I shall also write about, my gorgeous girl," and he left me to concentrate for the moment.

I checked my watch as I closed my history binder, it had been nearly half an hour and Bree would be home by now. I found my mobile phone among the litter on the table and rang her. Michael answered. "Hey Ash, how's it going?"

"Hi Michael, what are you doing there?"

"Getting our homework out of the way. What are *you* doing?" His inflection was obvious, as he knew Lorien would be with me and he *adored* giving me a hard time over my romance with him, casting lewd aspersions whenever he had the opportunity.

Michael and I were chronically single prior to the Standish's moving to Sommersett eighteen months ago, and although he delighted in my discomfort when he chose to tease me, it was Michael who had finally played the trump card that got Lorien and I together after my breakup with Elijah. We were all sure Michael would come out of the closet one day, but when he'd comforted me at the movies after I saw Lorien and Keren kissing, it made not only Elijah, but also Lorien, jealous. I loved Michael with all of my heart, and I had a sudden pang, missing him terribly. "Why don't you all come over here? We can study together and you can stay for dinner," I suggested.

"Hang on." I could hear him mumbling to no doubt Bree in the background and then came back to the phone.

"OK, we'll be there soon." He hung up. When I sat back down Lorien said,

"Since its Friday do you want to do something with them when we've finished studying, after dinner?" One of the many things I loved about him was he knew our friends were special to me, to us, and he was aware we didn't spend as much time together as a group as we once did.

"I'll ask them when they get here. Do you want to ring Elijah too?"

"Let's see what we come up with first." I smiled at him and started on my English essay, looking at his to see if he'd finished.

My eyes nearly fell out of my head when I read the title - 'Ashlyn Mercy's Mind and Body: How It Affects Me', the subtitle making it even worse, 'The Biography of an Erotic Princess'. "Lorien!" I cried, snatching up the binder and starting to read. He'd gone into graphic particulars on *his* reaction to running his hands over me, using his lips and fingers to then delight in seeing me aroused by his actions. He explained our passionate lovemaking in explicit detail and, for good measure, threw in a few future fantasies involving him watching me pleasure myself whilst he sat and viewed it all from a chair sitting opposite me.

He reached up and slowly drew down the elastic holding my ponytail, running his fingers through my hair to fluff it out and pressing his face into it, deeply breathing in its perfume. I would never have admitted that reading this turned me on, but I couldn't help but laugh when I reached the part including the use of a hand-held camcorder. "It's not meant to be funny Baby," he whispered in my ear, moving my hair from around my face to run his lips down my neck as his hand eased over my breast, working his thumb against my hardening nipple through my shirt.

"You can't hand this in!" I said, exasperated.

"It's perfect in grammar and punctuation, is it not?" he murmured, drawing my shirt up so he could lean down to kiss my stomach.

"Well yes," I stammered, falling into his trap as the heat started to build. I pulled myself together enough to continue, "I don't want Mr Mills reading this about me though."

"If he gets a hard-on, I've been successful then, haven't I?" He moved back up to play light kisses at my throat, his fingers at the buttons of my shirt.

"I don't want him thinking of me like this at all," I breathed as he eased a breast out of my bra, taking it slowly into his mouth. He teased gently, moaning,

"Hmmm…"

"Lorien…" I forgot what I was going to say.

"Hmmm?"

"I..." His hand dropped down and snaked between my legs to caress at the edging of my briefs, pulling them aside and working his fingers against me.

"Hmmm!" He knew he'd caught me in his web once again, no intention of stopping now.

"But..." He dipped a finger into me, slowly and deeply, working his thumb around me externally. Each time I spoke, he moved this into a more delicious level. I wasn't sure whether I should be silent or babble on incessantly. I wanted him so desperately now and the living room floor would more than suffice. However, I found myself laying backward further, drawing my legs up and apart to make his exploration easier. A car door slammed.

"God *damn* it!" He stopped, sitting up. "That's twice in one day; someone is out to get us." He grazed his lips once more across my nipple, groaning in dismay. He started to do my buttons up, and then leant in to kiss me for the final seconds we had left before there would be a knock at the door.

"It's open," I called, and Michael came in, followed by Bree and Simon. I got up and went to greet them, kissing and hugging Michael and Bree. Even though I saw them at school every day, our social interactions had been sadly lacking. I felt guilty.

"Hi twin," Michael said to Lorien and handed him a gift. "I know your birthday isn't for another week, but I thought you'd prefer I gave this to you when your family isn't around." I could just imagine what it was. Lorien tore off the wrapping and turned the book over in his hands so he could read the cover. He smiled widely at Michael and turned it around so I could see - 'Kama Sutra, 100 sexual positions and tips on lovemaking'.

"Thanks Michael!" I said, laughing.

"No need to thank me, he needs to thank me, and he will in a few weeks no doubt," he said, gesturing to Lorien.

"Thanks Michael and I *do* mean thanks!"

He started flipping through the pages and I went to make more coffee, Bree and Michael following me into the kitchen. I could hear Lorien from in here muttering, "Done it, done it, want to do it, *really* want to do it, oh yes Baby!" I tuned him out.

"Has anyone heard from Cyndi and Frankie?" I asked, pouring the boiling water into the mugs. They'd not come back to do Year 11 at Sommersett High last year, instead opting to go to TAFE and complete their courses; shortly thereafter they moved in together. They'd been at Michael and Bree's eighteenths, but I hadn't seen them since.

"They're coming to the twin's birthday, aren't they?" Bree asked.

"I'm pretty sure. Lorien?" I called out to get his attention.

"Busy Baby," he said, continuing his murmurings. I smiled at Michael saying,

"You're never going to see me again until we work our way through that you know." He grinned, raising his eyebrows.

"You'd think it was *your* birthday," he teased.

We took the mugs back to the dining table as Simon broke into braying laughter. "Jesus Standish, you aren't seriously going to hand this in, are you?" Lorien's English binder was in his hands and he'd read the biography about me. Lorien looked up at Simon and then at me, an 'oops' expression on his face. "You gotta hear this!" I made an unsuccessful swipe at the binder and he proceeded to read it aloud to the rest of us, holding it out of my reach. I went purple and Michael was laughing, no problem with him being honest in his emotions. Bree looked angry and said to Simon,

"You don't write things like that about me."

"*No one* writes stuff like this. You should send it into Penthouse, they'd publish it in a second. Whew!" Simon looked at me strangely and Bree punched him on the arm.

"Get your head out of the gutter mister, the only carnal thoughts *you're* allowed to have are about me!" Lorien came over, hugging me to him.

"I'm sorry Ash, I didn't realise what he was doing - I was too wrapped up in the book." I knew this, but was still angry Simon had helped himself, not that much could be done about it now.

"I know what we're getting you for your birthday," he said, winking at Bree. "You're a deviant Standish." Lorien sat down and lowered me onto his lap, his arms wrapping around me. When I felt the shift in his face against my back, I could tell he was smiling, full of pride at his conquests and knowledge of me no doubt, or maybe he agreed with Simon, he *was* a deviant.

Mum walked in around 6.00 pm and we were almost done with our homework. "Hi kids," she greeted us. "Do we have you two at home for the weekend?" she asked as she came over to kiss me on top of the head. Lorien got one too. He grinned at me; he loved being around my family as much as I loved being around his.

"Yes, I've also asked everyone to stay for dinner. I hope that's OK."

"We're getting pizza when your Dad gets home so it's no problem at all. Just let me get these groceries away and I'll get out of your hair."

"I'll give you a hand Anna." Lorien stood to help her; he'd finished over half an hour ago.

It was amazing I'd managed to get anything done since. He started flipping through the pages of Michael's book again. Every now and then he'd nudge me, facing the page he'd been looking at to me, a lecherous grin on his face. After the third instalment of this, I sat on the other side of the table, not that this disarmed him. He flicked paper at me and ran his feet slowly up my legs. When I threw him an angry glare, he wiggled his fingers at me before sucking them into his mouth. I knew where those fingers had been and I blushed, making him smile.

I could hear him and Mum discussing his upcoming birthday; my parents were also invited to attend. They were having a family-only affair at the Standish's first so their relatives could come for an afternoon with the boys before the party started at Sommersett Golf Club at 7.00 pm. Some would go home, and some would stay for the festivities. I'd argued with Lorien about my being at his home with their relatives, thinking I should allow the extended family a little alone time with the twins. However, he insisted I be there as I *was* family. Cara and Nick voiced this also when Lorien told them what I'd been thinking, and it was settled.

I'd tortured myself over his present, I knew what I wanted to get him but was afraid to go out and actually buy it alone. It wasn't the kind of thing I could ask a friend to accompany me to buy either; it was personal between Lorien and me. I eventually plucked up the courage and bit the bullet, knowing it was well worth the embarrassment, as I *knew* he would love it.

We had a great night all together again, deciding to watch some old favourite movies, one of which included 'Grease' of course. Bree and

Michael were hooked on it. Lorien, Simon and I laughed most of the way through as they recited it word perfect, including singing all the songs with the three of us joining them at times, especially through 'Summer Nights'.

We also picked three classic horrors currently on offer, 'Jaws', 'A Nightmare on Elm Street', and 'The Texas Chainsaw Massacre'. "Which one do you want on first?" I asked, scrolling through the horror titles.

"'Jaws'," said Simon. 'Jaws' it was. I went to the bathroom whilst I was up, and when washing my hands, thought of the sexual frustration we'd experienced all day. And, here I was about to add to it, slipping off my bra.

"Who wants drinks?" All four hands rose. When I brought them in, Bree and Simon had moved off the sofa to join Michael lying on the floor. All six of their legs were waving in the air. They looked like kids and I laughed. "Nothing," I said when they looked at me curiously.

Lorien was sitting in the armchair, furthest from the little group on the floor. I curled my legs up onto his lap, my back facing the TV. "You don't fancy 'Jaws'?" he whispered as I traced my tongue around his ear.

"I fancy *you*," I exhaled. "I can't wait until we get to bed...It's been a rather frustrating day."

"It still is," he breathed, angling his head so I could continue to trail my lips across his jaw and down his throat, running my hands under his shirt and moulding them to his chest. "You're driving me crazy woman," he murmured.

"You're both driving *me* crazy. A woman is about to get eaten over here too!" We all laughed. Michael was a classic. I Looked at Lorien, smiling. He leant forward and gave me a soft kiss and I nestled into his arms to watch the devouring of Chrissy.

About halfway through the movie, Lorien shifted slightly and I felt him open a few of my buttons, sliding his hand inside to caress me slowly. *No bra!* he mouthed. I smiled up at him and arched into his palm. He lowered his head to my chest, easing his face inside my shirt, flicking his tongue across my hard nipple. I grabbed his head and lifted it, mouthing *no!*

No? I smiled which he took for a sign of consent as he chuckled and started to lower his lips again. I grabbed his head, bringing his face up to mine, frowning at him.

No! He licked the tip of my nose playfully. I drew him down to kiss me. He pulled away.

"No," he whispered, grinning down at me and shaking his head.

"No?" I smiled, knowing it would be yes. Then he kissed me, his fingers creeping back under my shirt.

We must have been getting right into it as after a few minutes in trance-land Bree said, "Can you keep the snacking noises down please?"

"It's better than watching the movie!" Simon said. Had he been watching? You never knew with Simon. When they'd averted their eyes again, Lorien whispered to me,

"I want to take you right here and now." He ran his hand under my skirt and up my outer thigh, tickling lightly with his touch. Michael sat up, pausing the movie.

"I am going to take you now..." he took me by the hand, guiding me to the sofa, "and put you right here."

"Michael!" Lorien groaned.

"I'm trying to watch people get slaughtered here which is extremely difficult to enjoy whilst you two are rooting around all over the place behind me." Bree and Simon laughed. Lorien got up.

"Where do you think you're going?" Michael asked.

"Toilet."

"Good, let the little buggers swim for their lives," Michael said, and Simon laughed loudly, rolling around on the floor - Michael telling him to shut up as he restarted the movie.

When Lorien came back, I gestured him over and he quietly climbed onto the sofa, lying across its length with his head on my lap so I could play my fingers through his gorgeous dark curls. I loved his hair. Michael scowled at him. "I promise I'll behave." He turned around dubiously and Lorien did behave, well for most of the time.

When they left, we turned everything off and raced upstairs to find the light was still coming from under my parent's door. "We're not meant to make it through this day, are we?" he groaned, standing at my bedroom door.

"Come in for a kiss at least for now," I whispered.

"I'll wait until they're asleep. If I come in there, I won't be able to leave." I pouted at him. He smiled and blew me a kiss, closing his door.

I checked every five minutes to see if the light had gone out and finally, after nearly an hour, it did. I waited ten more minutes to make sure they were asleep then quietly opened Lorien's door. I stripped off and climbed in next to him. He was already naked and appeared to be sleeping peacefully as he didn't move to embrace me.

I ran my hand softly across his chest, the feel of him still delighted me; so firm and well shaped. I traced the contour of his abs down, feeling his muscles contract under my touch. When I reached my destination, he grew hard in my hand. I teased my fingers up and down his length then pulled the covers back to allow him to stand straight up, lowering my mouth to him. His breathing started to deepen, and he mumbled my name as his fingers trickled through my hair. If he hadn't been awake, he certainly was now. "Baby," he moaned as he tugged my hips towards him. I moved one leg over his body, and he pulled me to his mouth. After a few minutes of this dual intimacy, he said urgently, "Ash, stop." When I didn't, he raised my head from him. "I'm not ready yet Baby, I want to be *inside* you when this goes off, not half cocked." I had to smile; it was anything but half cocked. "Turn around." He pulled me forward, his arms circling me from the back of my thighs. Using his fingers, he splayed me, giving his tongue a better range of the playing field. I moved my hips slightly back and forth and effortlessly sailed into my long-anticipated climax. After being teased all day I found my release and as always, it was so worth the wait.

Now I wanted him inside me and obviously so did he as he quickly lowered me onto my back, thrusting the full length of himself into me and drawing all the way out before thrusting back in. He repeated this tortuous movement for several minutes before getting to his knees, raising my lower body off the bed at an angle. Groaning softly, his stroke became faster and more intense as he coated his thumb in my dew and teased it against me, bringing me immediately to orgasm again.

When he couldn't restrain himself any longer, he lay down with me, kissing me deeply as his fingers found my breasts, his hips moving at a dazzling speed. "Oh... God... Ash..." he moaned quietly, his body flexing. I held his hair from his face as he smiled, slowing his pace, working off his ebb. He collapsed beside me, laughing into the pillow, "I feel so much better now," he said, rolling over and drawing his arms around me. "I thought that one was going to blow my head off." I knew how he felt.

Wednesday morning period one, English with Mr Mills and I was squirming around, uncomfortable. We were getting our marked English essays back today and I was already inwardly churning as to what Mr Mills' reaction would have been to Lorien's biography. "Morning class," he said as he entered, reaching into his briefcase to remove a wad of our English essays. He proceeded to walk around the room, handing them back. "I was astounded to find although the dux of English each year since his commencement at Sommersett," Oh God, he was referring to Lorien, "he'd managed to weave an intricate and absorbing tale about one of your fellow students." He paused in front of our desks, placing my essay in front of me before continuing. Lorien smiled at me widely and I put my hands to my face, waiting for the worst. "This tale was perfect in not only it's grammar and style, it also made me take more notice of Miss Mercy than I had, seeing her in a whole new light." He put Lorien's paper in front of him, saying, "Well done Lorien, it was a wonderful story and I enjoyed reading every last word." A large red A+ was scrawled in the top right-hand corner of the page and I slumped further into my seat. With that, Mr Mills went back to the front of the class and resumed the lesson.

I could see Lorien writing a note, which he placed inside his paper before handing it to me. *Do you think I'd ever do anything to hurt or embarrass you my bashful little Angel? I love you, read it...* I was confused as I picked up his essay, starting to read.

The title was not the one I expected, instead now called 'The Effects of Ashlyn Mercy – Biography of a Princess'. As I continued to read, I found myself falling deeper in love with him. The way he described me and the mental images he created were so beautiful and well written, it was hard to believe it was me being described in his near prose-like passages. I knew this is how he did truly feel and was blushing due to the flattery he'd bestowed in his words of adoration.

When I'd finished, I looked at him, a slight smile on my face. *I love you*, I mouthed, and he reached up, stroking my cheek with his fingertips. "We all realise the depth of your feelings for each other Mr Standish and Miss Mercy, but if you could do your best to remember you're in English class we'll all be able to get some work done." Lorien smiled at me as the classroom laughed, lingering his palm on my cheek for a few moments more before sneaking it under the desk to take my hand. *I love you too*, he mouthed back.

From Boys to Men

"They can steal the ruby of your lips
or the pearls that are your smile,
They can mine obsidian from your hair
but not the diamonds from your eyes."

L & E Standish, 'Ashlyn's Song'

KEREN AND I formed part of the receiving line as their guests started to arrive the following Saturday afternoon. Lorien's arm never left my waist for even a second as the introductions took place. Nick was an only child. With the exception of his mother Betty, all the other family members were Cara's: her younger brother Howard, older sister Marie and her brother-in-law Steven. Marie and Steve had three children, their cousins Peter was fourteen and twin girls, Julie and Casey were nine.

His Nanna was the last to arrive and Lorien stooped down to plant her cheek with a kiss. "Hi shorty," he said and rested his elbow on her head. She was tiny.

"Don't you shorty me," she said. "I will smack your bottom for you."

"Do it Nanna," Elijah said, making her laugh. Nick led her out onto the verandah to join the rest of the family.

Lorien hugged me from behind and lowered his mouth to my ear, "Let's sneak upstairs for a bit."

"A bit of what?" I asked, not intending to disappear with him at the onset of his family gathering.

"I mean a moment of time, not a bit of this," he said and pushed himself against me.

"Lorien, play nicely in front of your family," I warned.

"They can't see anything from out there," he said, checking over my shoulder.

"No, but we're standing right here," Keren interjected.

Nick came back in and took three bottles of champagne from the fridge. He poured several glasses, handing one to each of us. I'd never tasted champagne before. It was fizzy and quite sour, however I felt very relaxed. It must have been high in its alcohol content.

Lorien led me outside, his arm around my waist, as Nanna was in the process of pulling photos of the twins out of her purse and handing them around. "This one is my favourite," she said, passing it to me. Lorien and Elijah were about four and stark naked, a pulsing sprinkler frozen in the background. "They never had Mr Winky out of their hands did they Cara?" Cara laughed and came to look at the photo over my shoulder. "Elijah has the poor thing stretched out so far I'm surprised it didn't come off."

"Nanna!" Elijah chastised her and the whole crowd laughed appreciatively. Keren whispered something in his ear, and he hugged her to him, smiling.

"Is seeing me naked doing anything for you Ash?" Lorien asked, working on making me blush. I ignored him, handing the photo to his Aunt Marie. "Nothing at all?" he stressed, turning me to face him, his arms around me. I smiled at him and shook my head. He grinned and moved down to kiss me. I pulled back; I couldn't kiss him so openly in front of his family. "My bashful girl," he laughed softly and drew me tightly against him, which *was* acceptable. He nibbled at my lobe, exhaling softly into my ear, teasing me. I moved slightly away, and he pulled me back, whispering, "Do I get that kiss now?"

"No," I said and turned around.

He ran his hands lightly across my stomach, knowing it was one of my erogenous zones. To all facing me it would have appeared to be a sweet act of affection, to Lorien and me, we knew it was foreplay and it was stirring me, as he was well aware. I took his hands in mine, preventing them from any further motion when all I wanted to do was to turn and kiss him like no family member should witness their relative be kissed. I needed to get away from him for a few moments and went inside to see if I could do anything to help prepare. He followed me. "Lorien, I came in here to get away from you!" I moved behind the island bench so he couldn't reach me.

"I want that kiss Baby and I'm coming for it." He started to dart around the corner, and I ran the other way. It was a tactic from him however as he reversed his stride and caught me neatly around the waist. "Kiss me."

"No," I laughed.

"Kiss me!"

"No!" I frowned at him playfully. He picked me up and sat me on the bench, moving his body between my legs.

"Kiss me..." he sighed, then kissed me. My arms and legs encircled him, holding him to me as I kissed him back.

Finally parting, we looked at each other, wanting more. "Let's go upstairs," he said. I was about to rebuke him when Julie and Casey started singing,

"Ashlyn and Lorien sitting in a tree, K.I.S.S.I.N.G." Lorien chased them out the door, the girls laughing as they ran from their cousin. It had at least averted his attention; I may not have been strong enough to continue fighting off his advances.

"Need any help?" Peter had joined me in the kitchen.

"No, not really," I smiled at him. He took a seat on one of the stools.

"Ashlyn, that's a ... pretty name."

"Thanks, I like it."

"So, what do you like to do Ashlyn?" I looked at him curiously. Was he hitting on me? He threw me what he possibly considered an alluring smile.

"I like hanging out with your cousin, Peter."

"Didn't you used to go out with Eli too?" Oh God, was he lining himself up as number three?

"For a short while."

"I can see why they both went after you, you're a fox." I couldn't help myself and I laughed aloud.

"A fox? I didn't realise people still used that word."

"I'm not like most people," he said, actually winking at me.

"No, you're not. Get out of there Pee Wee," Elijah said from the door. *Thank you*, I mouthed, and he winked before closing the door behind his retreating cousin.

I was feeling a little out of it after my fourth glass of champagne and decided I would have no more. I went outside to my car and grabbed a few breaths of fresh air whilst I took the twin's birthday presents from the boot. I wanted to get them upstairs before anyone realised I was missing and managed to slip up the stairs unnoticed. I left Elijah's on the desk and hid Lorien's under the bed, moving to the door to check if it could be seen from this angle of the room. The door opened behind me and I turned in surprise; if it was Peter, I was going to deck him.

"Why the surprised look Baby?" Lorien asked as he kissed me, trying to shuffle me toward the bed.

"I thought it was Peter," I said, breaking free from his embrace.

"Has he been giving you a hard time?" he laughed and then pressed himself against me, emphasising his choice of adjective.

"Behave yourself!" He wasn't sober either and I could picture us writhing around on the bed, his entire family standing in shock at the doorway after coming to find us.

"I don't want to behave myself." He came at me again and I moved away. "Just one little kiss Ash?" He put on his best puppy dog look. "Just one?" I kissed him lightly on the nose.

"There." He grabbed me and kissed me deeply, his legs moving us toward the bed again.

"We're cutting the cake Lori!" Cara yelled up the stairs.

"Damn it!" he laughed and took me by the hand, leading me back downstairs.

We played out the same tradition as last year; the twins smeared the icing up Keren's face and mine before licking it off. Their poor mother had been the receiver of this, albeit with no erotic undertones, up until their seventeenth birthdays when Keren and I came on the scene. However, alcohol had not been involved last year and it was fairly innocent. This time, after Lorien had licked my face, he went in for the deep kiss and I pushed him away. "No." He smiled at me, leaning in to try again. "Lorien..." I warned.

"If you have to do that son, take it around the back please." Lorien took me by the hand and said,

"I have Dad's permission."

"You also need mine," I laughed and allowed him to lead me to the northern verandah. Rounding the corner, we heard Marie say,

"You can hardly blame him; she's such a pretty little thing."

"Come here pretty little thing," he growled, safely out of eyesight. When we finally came up for air, I rubbed my hand against him gently and whispered into his ear, "I have an extra present for you when we get home. I'm going to lather *your* candle in icing and lick it..." I ran my tongue across his lips, "and suck it ..." my mouth now to his earlobe.

"Boing!" he said, laughing quietly as I felt him harden instantly under my fingers. He draped my arms around his neck and moulded himself to me. We stood there pressed against each other, getting lost in each other's eyes.

I heard the toilet flush inside, and soon after, the door behind us opened. His Nanna said to Cara, "Don't they make a beautiful couple? Oh, to be young and in love again."

"Come on Betty," Cara said, directing her around to the other verandah to leave us our privacy. Lorien smiled at me, drawing me to him for another kiss, letting the heat ignite and burn itself under its own intensity.

"Hmmm Baby, let's fuck!" he purred into my ear. I pulled back in surprise; I'd never heard Lorien swear. He was smiling at me, taking in my expression.

"Later Sweetheart," I blushed. His profanity had sent a flush through my body, realising I liked it.

"I can guarantee that." He pulled me to him for another kiss as I heard running feet, and Julie called out,

"They're doing it again Casey, come and see!" Lorien sighed as he drew away from me and we resigned ourselves to walk slowly back to the other verandah to sit with the family - Lorien finally behaving himself.

Keren and Elijah were now missing so I motioned the girls over and whispered to them to go and find out where they were. "You're nasty Ash," Lorien laughed, and we twisted around to watch over our shoulders, waiting for the impact. Sure enough, within two minutes Elijah was chasing them down the stairs.

"Ashlyn told us to," Julie said defiantly when Elijah had one girl under each arm.

"Thanks Ash!" He laughed though, and Keren came through the door behind him. We all stayed and visited with the family for the rest of the afternoon. No one was game to attempt a sneaky retreat; we were being too well watched.

We farewelled all the family around 6.30 pm. Nanna was the only one coming to the Golf Club for the adult party. "You boys need to slow down," Nick said, taking in his slightly inebriated sons.

"It's all good Dad!" Elijah told him, filling his glass again. He took Lorien's from him and filled it before turning the bottle towards mine.

"None for me thanks," I said, and Keren passed on it too. I'd had enough for the moment, although I felt more centred than a few hours ago.

The function room had been booked and most of our friends were already on the dancefloor when we arrived. I scanned the room for

Michael, Bree or Simon, unable to see them anywhere in the crowd. Nick went to the bar, getting drinks for his mother and Cara as they took a seat at one of the vacant tables. We found my parents and sat with them for a few minutes before Lorien took me in his arms and swept me onto the floor. I was a little concerned his balance would give way, but he managed to keep us upright.

When 'The Hustle' started Lorien said, "Hang on Ash, I have to find Nanna." The twins swooped, dragging her onto the floor. Nick and Cara joined them, as did my parents, which charmed me no end. I took a seat with Keren and saw Michael, Bree and Simon enter; we waved them over.

"Go the oldies," said Simon, enjoying the show. Michael went to the bar, bringing back several schooners of beer.

"Who are they for?" Keren asked.

"Whoever wants them. I think the twins will want one when they're finished out there."

The boys performed the actions to the letter, as did their parents, revealing it was probably they who had taught the line-dance to their sons. Nanna was having a wonderful time and when the song finished, Lorien continued to lead her gracefully around the floor. She could barely reach his shoulder. "Hey gang," Elijah said as he sat down next to Keren.

"Happy birthday!" said Michael and handed him his present. "Thanks Michael," he said, and started to unwrap it. I was expecting it to be the same book he'd given Lorien but was surprised to see it was some surfer's biography. I noticed the images were familiar as Elijah flicked through the pages; Michael had put a different dust jacket over it so it would be appropriate to give to him in front of his parents. It only took

Elijah a few seconds to realise that the pictures didn't match the title and then he *really* looked at it.

"Thanks mate!" Elijah said when he'd finally worked it out and showed it to Keren, who blushed. I laughed, as it was usually me on the receiving end of Michael's playfulness. He passed Elijah a beer, which he downed quickly. "It's hot out there," he said and reached for another. Bree and Simon had a gift for him too.

"Fantastic!" Elijah said, as he unwrapped the Arnette surfing sunglasses and the actual biography the dust jacket had originally come off.

"Where's Lorien? We have something for him too." Simon smiled knowingly at me and I was immediately nervous as to what they'd bought. As if he heard his name called, Lorien was on his way across the floor to us and took a seat next to me. He leant over and kissed me before greeting our friends.

"Hey guys!" Michael passed him a beer. "Thanks mate!" He drank, but not as quickly as his brother. About to drape his arm around my shoulder, Simon interrupted him,

"Open this first Lorien." I looked at Simon and found all three of them were smiling at me. Surely it couldn't be too bad if Bree was also involved.

Lorien burst out laughing as he removed the wrapping paper, turning the box to show me. It was a hand-held camcorder. "It's second-hand but works fine," Simon said, still smiling at me. "Now we'll want to see all those home movies kiddies." We all laughed, with exception of Elijah and Keren who hadn't been there at the time of the reading of the

English essay, thank God. Elijah's eyebrows drew in, not getting the joke and Lorien took great pleasure in giving him the highlights.

Everyone eventually joined the dancers on the floor, leaving Lorien and me alone. I was watching Elijah dance with his Nanna. "When did your grandfather pass away?"

"Pop died about six months before we moved here. Another reason why Mum and Dad chose Sommersett instead of the myriad of other towns around; fate obviously meant for us to be here." He smiled at me warmly, kissing me softly.

"What about your other grandparents?"

"I never knew them. They died when Mum was only fifteen and Aunty Marie took over the household to keep the family together."

"That's so *sad* Lorien." I looked up at him with sorrow in my eyes, "Cara is an orphan."

"Don't be sad Baby, Mum met Dad and the rest is history, including her choice of job." He laughed at his own joke then leant down to kiss me again. Lorien took my hand, "Come on hottie, they're playing our song." I laughed and followed him onto the floor; this had been his excuse for every song we'd danced to that night.

Mum and Dad said their goodbyes a few hours later; it was getting on past 11.00 pm. "Enjoy the rest of your evening Darling," Mum said as she kissed me goodbye.

"Looks like you'll have your hands full Ashlyn," Dad said, gesturing towards the twins. Elijah could barely stand up, Lorien was not much better. I laughed,

"They're Nick and Cara's problem, not mine." Little was I to know...

About fifteen minutes later Elijah stumbled over, "Heersh my violin playin-girl, my liddle fiddler," he slurred. I was neither of these things to him. "Cannav a birthdey kizz?"

"Elijah stop it, they'll throw you out if you keep this up." I pulled a chair out for him. "Sit," I ordered. He slumped onto the chair.

"Cannav a birthdey kizz?" he asked again.

"You're drunk." He lifted one eyelid and scanned the room. "So's Lori but you kizzim."

"He's not acting like an arse."

"Wanna shee my arsh Babe?"

"No, but how would you like me to kick it for you?"

"You're funny," he chuckled. He then sighed deeply and turned to me, "I luvuu Ash, alluz did, alluz will. But you don't lumme, uluv Lori. No one loves Eli. It's sad, sad, sad."

"Keren loves you Elijah," I offered warmly. It didn't give me any joy to hear him talk this way, drunk or not; possibly what he said *was* true, probably not. Now was certainly not the time to argue semantics with him.

"Keren's great," he grinned up at me. "I thing I pizzed her off tho', she's crangy wimme."

"She'll be OK tomorrow."

"You nevah get crangy wimme, nevah did, nevah do."

"I care for you Elijah and I always will." He reached up with his arms and stupidly I went to him to let him hug me. The hug turned into an unbreakable grasp, his arms wrapped around my hips, his hands running themselves over the curves of my rear. He pulled his face against my stomach, nuzzling into me, kissing me.

"Elijah, stop it," I said as quietly yet forcibly as I could. I didn't want anyone else witness to this scene. He dragged me down onto his knee.

"Kizz me Ash, nowunce loogin."

"Elijah, *stop* it!" I was getting a little scared and I had no idea how to get out of this situation. As he moved in to kiss me, I moved away, pushing his face with my free hand. I didn't want to hurt him, but I wanted him to stop, so I slapped his face.

"Oooh, feisty." He went in for one last attempt. We both ended up on the floor, him and the chair on top of me, and I whacked my head a beauty in the process of the fall. Thankfully Nick appeared, pulling his son and the chair off me.

"You sit!" he ordered Elijah, putting the chair back upright. Nick stooped down. "Are you OK Honey?" He helped me to my feet and looked at my head gingerly, trying to see if the skin had been broken. Fortunately, it hadn't, but I was going to have a great lump to show off tomorrow.

"I'm OK Nick, he was just being stupid."

"I know what he was being..." We both turned to look at Elijah; he had passed out in the chair. "Thank Heaven for small mercies, if you'll excuse the pun Ashlyn."

"We small Mercy's are great at breaking other people's falls." He laughed with me. I winced.

"You'd better sit down too Ashlyn. Where's Lori?"

"I don't think he'll be much help," I said, pointing him out through the crowd. He was hugging his mother on the dance floor, possibly even asleep on her shoulder. Nick gestured to Cara and she came over, Lorien at her side.

"Hello Baaaaaaby." He sat down beside me, nowhere near as drunk as his twin but still pretty ripped.

"Cara, can you get Michael and Simon over here to help me get this mess into the car."

"Oh dear," she muttered, and went off in search of them.

"My brotherz dead drunk!" Lorien said, lifting Elijah's head by the fringe and dropping it.

"You're not far off either young man!" Nick said. "What is it with you kids? The second you hit eighteen you have to write yourselves off." Lorien drew his arms around me, pulling me to him. "Before you go assaulting Ashlyn you need to know she's already hurt."

"Wotappend?" He scanned my face, looking for the tell-tale signs of pain.

"Your brother knocked her off a chair, she banged her head on the floor and Elijah landed on top of her. You behave yourself Lori, or so help me you'll get it from me tomorrow!"

Nick was out of patience and the charge under his arm was not making life any easier. At that moment, Elijah opened his eyes, leant forward and vomited all over the floor. I heard Nick curse fluently under his breath. Thank God the cavalry arrived shortly after. Cara had found Michael and Simon, and between them and Nick, they carried Elijah to the car. "Make sure he's finished being sick before you drive him home!" Cara called before coming to sit with Lorien and me. "Are you going to be sick too?" she asked. He'd turned a light shade of green and his face was wrinkled up.

"Don't think sho…"

"Ashlyn, can you take him outside whilst I get someone to clean this up." Her wish was my command as I was feeling a little off-colour myself.

Out on the balcony he took several deep breaths, "Thas a lot bedda." He came to me, wrapping his arms around me. "I luv you sooo much Ash… hmmm," he sighed as he started to run his fingers lightly through my hair. I winced. "Wotappend?" he asked, drawing back, my face between his hands. He had not taken in his father's prior explanation.

"Nothing to worry yourself over Sweetheart, your brother is just very drunk." I kissed him softly and pulled myself back against him before continuing, "He grabbed me and toppled us and a chair over, me being the break-fall unfortunately."

"He grabbed you how?" His face darkened as he drew back from me again to look into my eyes.

"Let's talk about this tomorrow, OK? I haven't had a decent kiss from you since we got here," I said, tactfully changing the subject. It worked; he hugged me fiercely, saying,

"I'm not gunna have any more to drink coz I don't wanna spew like Eli and I don't wannu cranky wiv me." He had obviously picked up on Keren's current disdain for his brother.

"I'm not cranky with you Lorien; I love you, even when you're being silly."

"I love youuuu Baby and I'm gunna let you make a man oudda me tonight!" I highly doubted this, he'd be lucky to make it home without falling asleep. The icing of the candle would have to wait.

Aftermath

"And of all the lessons I have learnt whilst seated at your side,
The most important one of all is holding onto pride."

L Standish, 'Tripping over Hurdles'

WHEN I WOKE I could smell something fishy cooking downstairs. It was horrible. Lorien was still asleep so I tied my robe around me and went down to see what was going on. Nick was in the kitchen frying something over the stove. "What on earth is that?" I asked.

"Kippers," he smiled. "They're both going to eat this and then drink these." He pointed to the condiments on the island bench then proceeded to put vinegar, olive oil, tomato and Worcestershire sauces in a glass each, stirring. When the eddy had slowed, he broke a whole egg into each one and sprinkled the top with cayenne pepper. "Prairie Oysters they're called, a top hangover cure in my day." I couldn't wait to see this. "Want some kippers Ashlyn?" he asked.

"Ah, no thanks Nick, I'm not really much of a fish eater at the best of times."

"Feeling a little green too are we?" he smiled.

"Not really. I don't like fish for breakfast, especially *that* fish, ugh. Where's Cara?"

"In our room with Elijah, we slept in his bed last night. I think she's feeding him ice, but I can guarantee it won't stay down for long." He was enjoying this. "How are you feeling about last night?" he asked, changing the mood. I wasn't sure if he knew exactly what had been going on before Elijah and I took the fall.

"He was drunk," I said, shrugging.

"He may have been drunk but he was also being anything but a gentleman."

"Yes." I didn't know what else to say.

"Does Lori know?"

"I don't think so. He started to ask about it last night but I changed the subject."

"Good girl. As long as you're OK with it there's no need to upset Lori. He loves you and his brother very much and this would hurt him a great deal. I will speak to Eli and I assure you that he'll then come and speak with you."

"It's really not necessary Nick, I'm OK and OK with it; he was just being an idiot."

"He won't be getting off Scott-free I assure you, and you also got hurt in the process," he reminded me. I rubbed the back of my head, the lump fit nicely into my cupped palm.

"I think I'll go and get something to dull the pain a bit."

"You know where everything is, help yourself."

I got up to climb the stairs and heard a door open. I turned straight back around and took a seat again; I wasn't going to miss this, and Nick smiled at me knowingly. It was Lorien and I felt a little sorry for him considering what was about to unwind. "Where's Eli?" his father asked, knowing full well where he was.

"I dunno." He rubbed his eyes and plonked down on one of the stools, looking somewhat miserable. He glanced up scratching his chin and noticed me, "Morning Ash." Coming to sit next to me, he put his arms around me, complaining, "Why is it so much fun at the time and the next day so painful?" He lowered his head to my chest, and I rubbed his back gently.

"That's life son," Nick answered.

"Got any juice Dad?" he mumbled.

"Oh no, I have something *much* better for you boys today. Sorry, I mean men. Now go and find your brother." Lorien looked at me with his eyebrows raised. I did not intend to spoil Nick's surprise for them, and I raised my eyebrows back at him innocently. How could he not already smell it? Perhaps Nick ate this regularly and they were used to it, yet I'd never known this aroma in the house before.

Lorien was halfway up the stairs when Elijah and Cara came out of the bedroom. Cara looked down at Nick with a frown on her face, she was not as happy about what was about to transpire as he was. "Morning son," called Nick and crashed a few pans around.

"Dad..." Elijah croaked, unable to raise his voice any louder. He looked like death warmed up.

"OK family take a seat; Daddy has prepared you something special this morning. And what a *be-you-tiful* morning it is," he smiled at me. The twins took a chair and looked at each other dubiously. When their father put the plates in front of them Elijah bolted for the bathroom and several seconds later with nowhere to go, Lorien took off into the side garden.

"Nick," chastised Cara, thinking he was taking this too far.

"Honey let me be, I know what I'm doing. This is a long-standing Standish tradition, and I will not be robbed of the opportunity." She looked at me and shook her head, taking a seat next to me to watch the fallout. Lorien came back in first.

"This is so unfair! I was nowhere *near* as maggoted as Eli so why do I feel as bad?"

"A wicked mistress is that of lady alcohol," Nick grinned. "Here," he said, handing Lorien a glass.

"What is it?" When his father told him the name, he put it down again.

"Now there isn't really an oyster in it son, it's just the name of the hangover cure." I delighted in the fact Nick had also forgot to mention what *was* in the drink. Lorien sniffed it cautiously then raised the glass to his lips. "Down in one gulp," Nick instructed.

"Drink it over the sink please Lori, I don't want it all over my tiles," Cara said. Lorien looked at his father with distrust.

"It will do you the world of good if you can keep it down Lori, give it a try." He went outside and far enough around the verandah where we could no longer see him. I heard the bathroom door open, and Elijah called out,

"Are those stinking things off the table?"

"Yes Honey, come on," answered Cara. She took the plates and scraped them into the compost bin.

"Hey!" Nick cried, "I would've eaten those." Elijah returned to the table not looking much better. "Try this son." He handed him his Prairie Oyster. "Down the hatch."

"Over the sink please Eli," Cara said. He went to the sink and took a big gulp, bringing it straight back up.

"I think I'll go and see how Lorien's doing."

He wasn't on the side verandah, so I continued around to the back and there I found him lying on one of the wicker lounges; he appeared to be sleeping. I sat down on the other lounge, watching him. His glass was empty, and colour had returned to his face. Perhaps the Prairie Oyster had done the trick. His eyes fluttered open, and he saw me sitting there, smiling at him. "Hey Baby." He opened his arms, and I went to him, lying against him as gently as I could.

"How are you feeling?"

"So-so, I managed to keep it down at least. Eli must feel like hell," he laughed, then groaned.

"Poor Lorien," I soothed my hand across his forehead as he nestled against me. "Did you enjoy your party?" He nodded, saying,

"What I remember of it." He sat up a little and reached up to draw me to him, feeling the lump on my head. He opened his mouth to speak, and I silenced him,

"Later, OK?" Energy levels low, he let this ride a little longer and lay there in my arms, content for the moment.

Cara came to the door and told us she had some real food if we were hungry. "Come on Lorien, you have to eat something," I said, taking him by the hand and leading him inside. She'd made toast with vegemite, a tradition from her family apparently and it was a lot easier to handle than the kippers. Both twins managed to get a few pieces down along with some juice. Elijah was still a horrible colour.

When we'd finished Lorien said, "I need more sleep. Will you come with me Ash?"

"Of course," I smiled at him.

"You and I have some business to attend to," Nick said to a confused Elijah as I led Lorien up the stairs.

I pulled the covers back to let him slide in unhindered then drew them over him; I was enjoying pampering him I had to admit. I climbed in next to him and he rolled over onto his stomach, draping his arm across me. "Oh Ash, make it go away," he laughed.

"Do you feel better at all?"

"A bit. I need something to take my mind off it, but I don't think I can write or play anything at the moment." He sighed deeply.

"I may be able to help you there," I hinted. "You still haven't seen your present." He opened one eye and looked at me. "I'll be back in a second." He watched me reach under the bed to take the box I'd hidden there yesterday, then went into the bathroom to change.

I'd bought two sets of lingerie and considered which one I should put on first. One was a black satin corset with suspenders, stockings and split panties; the other a beautiful maroon flowing babydoll with matching G-string, completely sheer with exception to the ribbon that ran under the bust and around the neck. I decided on this one, as it was my favourite.

When I peeked through the doorway, he was lying with his eyes closed again. I stepped out and stood there, knowing he'd check on me at some stage. Sure enough, he soon sat upright, his eyes wide. "Holy crap!" I smiled and blushed. "Come here to me this instant!" he growled. I grabbed the box from the bathroom before sliding the door shut behind me. I sashayed across the room, feeling a little ridiculous but doing it for him; I knew he'd love the lingerie and me modelling it for him. And, it *was* for his eighteenth birthday... not to mention Valentine's Day. "Oh my God Ash," he breathed as he knelt and drew me to him, sampling my body with his hands, "I love you in red." I shoved him back onto the bed and worked his boxers down, Mr Winky saluting me throughout the process. I crawled over him and my hair feathered across his body as I leant down to torment his nipples with my tongue. He loved it when I took control, as difficult as it was for me at times, and I was sure this being one of the main reasons he enjoyed it so much. Straining against me, attempting to connect I kept him just a tiny fraction from me, letting him barely hit the target before moving my hips away. I wasn't the lead player for very long. He rolled me over onto my back, running his hand over the sheer covering of my breast; teasing with his lips and tongue, he tasted me through the wispy material. "Hmmm Baby, you're the best girlfriend in the world," he murmured. He was doing exceptionally well for someone who had very little appetite until now.

Not long after however, Lorien pulled back laughing, a slight grimace on his face. "What's wrong?" I asked.

"I don't think I can do this now, not with the hangover still lurking. I'd hate to be running to the bathroom mid stroke...a bit of a turn off?" he suggested. I laughed.

"It's OK, get some more sleep. I'll be lying right here when you wake up."

"Just to make sure," he drew me alongside him and spooned into me, "I'm going to hold you close," he sighed against my back. We both slept.

I woke to feel Lorien hard against me. His hand was definitely awake, leisurely rubbing the back of my thigh, up and over my hip and back again. "I feel a *lot* better now," he purred as he moved his hand into the top of the G-String; easing it down to my knees, playing light kisses to my shoulders as I kicked it to the floor. He lifted my top leg slightly, sidling in closer and better angled behind me. "Just need to make sure the engine is oiled before we start the ignition," he murmured, slipping a finger between my legs to caress me, his lips back at my neck. "Baby," he whispered into my ear, slowly sliding into me, "you make me *so* horny when you're this aroused." It was nearly impossible to *want* to stop him now we'd gone this far, but I wanted him to see the other outfit before it was too late to interrupt this growing heat. He had the wonderful ability of intensifying me immediately when inside me.

"I have more for you," I teased.

"No, I have more for you!" he growled, flipping me onto my back. This reminded me I'd been in the wars too and my head still hurt. I didn't want him to be aware of this so moved into a slightly different position. He'd find out or remember soon enough; best-case scenario he wouldn't find out at all.

"Don't you want the rest of your present?" I asked, attempting to wriggle out from under him.

"You mean this isn't it?" he asked, smiling lazily as he pushed himself deeper into me. As I pulled away the smile faded, realising I was going to get out of bed. "Can't it wait Ash?" he groaned, reaching for me, trying to pull me back against him. He knelt behind me, kneading my breasts between his supple fingers as he kissed around the nape of my neck - trying all the moves that usually made me succumb to him instantly.

"Nuh uh," I shook my head, reaching down for the box at the side of the bed. "This is your Valentine present," I said, looking down at the babydoll, "this," I said, standing as I handed him the box, "is your birthday present." When he removed the lid, he licked his bottom lip slowly.

"Hmm, hmmm! Look who's a lucky birthday boy…" He jumped out of bed and stood with me, slowly graduating the babydoll up my body in a chiffon caress. "I love you so much," he whispered as he dropped it to the floor, his hands moving down my back, pulling me against him as tightly as possible. He kissed me deeply and I knew he wasn't going to see the other set of lingerie on me today, so I surrendered to him, winding my arms around his neck. He surprised me by exhaling into my ear a few minutes later, "Let's get this baby on my Baby."

He sat on the bed to watch me dress, his arms around me. I passed him the panties, stepping into them as he held them to my feet, slowly drawing them up as I hooked the corset around me. His eyes were on mine, dark and intense. He took the stockings out of the box and threaded first one and then the other over my feet and up my legs, pressing his lips to my stomach as he reached around to attach them at the rear suspenders. I loved him so much and he drove me *crazy* with wanting him, wanting him *all* the time. Even though we'd been going out for over twelve months, it was still like the first day. "Ash," he whispered as he pulled me closer to him, "you're so *seductive* you fiendish girl." He kissed at the split in the panties, they separated, and he was directly against me, brushing gently with the tip of his tongue. "I could just eat you alive," he moaned and then proceeded to do so.

When he knew I was getting close, he stopped and looked up at me smiling. I was flustered. "What…"

"No way are you going on your own, you're taking me with you, and I want to watch you, *all* of you." He stood and kissed me again as he eased my breasts further out of the bodice, so my nipples were unrestricted. He ran his lips across them lightly before positioning me over his lap. I gasped as I sunk onto him. Holding my forearms, he lowered me gently backwards. I was a little tentative as I didn't want him to drop me, but he was strong and he assured me, "It's OK Baby, I won't let anything happen," and we both started to move against each other. At this angle, Lorien was able to direct my body in an almost weightless motion and he filled me so deeply. His gaze first locked on mine and then ran the length of my body, taking in his own handiwork at the connection of our union.

My breathing had quickened to become erratic, on the brink, and when I threw my head back, he pulled me to him for the final quick strokes, his mouth finding my breast. He bit lightly as our two bodies solidified into one. He was a true gentleman and always waited for me. "Oh God Lorien," I panted in his ear as I started to wane, holding his upper body firmly to mine, "I love you so much." He looked up into my eyes, holding my gaze; his breath still racing as he ground my hips quickly against him, setting off another instant explosion. I bit my bottom lip between my teeth, not wanting to alert the whole house as to what was happening upstairs. We fell back onto the bed, satisfied for the moment.

Tender and gentle now, he brushed soft kisses over my lips as he traced his fingers around my jaw. My hands moved down over his warm, firm back, loving the crevasses and plains, fitting my hands to the roundness of his perfect curves. "I love you Ashlyn Mercy, and you're so damn sexy," he murmured.

"No, *you're* sexy."

"No, you." We played this game for several minutes, finally winning by shutting him up with my lips.

We couldn't stay cloistered in his room all day and eventually got out of bed. He was looking a lot better than before and nearly one hundred percent when he'd taken a shower. I ignored his protests to join him, it being way too obvious if we were to walk downstairs together with wet hair. I also needed to wash mine carefully and the less he thought of my cracked head the less likely he was to ask about it.

Sitting in his pappadum chair, crossed legged, he was waiting for me as I exited the bathroom. "Now we still have to go back downstairs together with wet hair."

"They would've heard the shower stop and start," I said.

"I'll tell them we did it for effect," he smiled.

"Will you now? Well go ahead." I waved him toward the door; he didn't move.

"Come and have a quick cuddle," he said, patting the chair as he moved over to let me on. When two people sat in a pappadum together, there was little choice but to be intimate. He hugged me to him, his cheek to my forehead. It was my happy place and I nestled into him, nowhere else on Earth I'd rather be. He ran his fingers through my hair, and I winced.

"What happened to you anyway, you still haven't told me," he said. This was actually not true, he'd been told twice but I chose not to correct him.

"Nothing really, I took a tumble with Elijah. He was drunk and stumbled, pulling me with him." I felt a little guilty about the heavily edited version I was telling him, but I agreed with his father, there was no point in his knowing.

"I can't believe Eli did this to you. I knew he was blind drunk, but this is pretty serious." He sat up and checked out my head, gently moving the hair with his fingers.

"I'm OK Lorien, honestly. It looks a lot worse than it is." Another white lie.

"Are you sure? Do you want to go to emergency?" I shook my head.

"No Sweetheart, I'm great."

"The greatest." He lowered his lips back to my forehead, at ease. I struggled to get out of the chair and pulled at him.

"Come on Lorien." He sighed and rolled himself out gracefully.

"You're a hard task-master Ash."

"I have a present for Elijah and I want to give it to him."

"A cricket bat to the back of the head would be a good place to start," he smiled, then saw the box. It was a similar size to the one I'd given him. "He'd better not be getting the same gift as me," he exclaimed, reaching behind me, trying to grab the box to check.

"Don't be silly, I got him a surf-pack for his board." He grinned and kissed me once more before we re-joined his family downstairs.

"You look a lot better," his mother said as we descended the stairs. He shot me a sly grin before replying,

"Sleep fixes everything." Elijah was lying across the sofa watching a game on mute. Lorien flicked his legs off and sat next to him, pulling me onto his lap. "Come on bro, Ash has a present for you." Elijah was still pale and miserable. I saw Nick look over his shoulder from the verandah and I smiled at him. He smiled back, coming in to see what I'd bought for his undeserving son. No one else other than Nick and I were aware of what happened last night, with the possibility of Elijah, if Nick had his chance to speak to him.

"Ash, I owe you an apology," he said, looking up at me with guilt-laden eyes.

"Later Elijah, open it." He checked his twin and Lorien was grinning at him.

"Well come on," Lorien said. He lifted the lid off the box and pulled out the backpack.

"Quicksilver surf-pack, awesome!"

"Dude!" Lorien and I chimed in, laughing. Elijah leant over to kiss me and hesitated, so I pushed my cheek against his lips instead. His father had obviously spoken to him.

"Thanks Ash, it's great." He looked at me humbly, like a mangy dog wanting a morsel; I smiled at him, giving him his canine treat.

"*She's* great," mumbled Lorien, drawing me closer to him. We had a little private interlude, which we *tried* to prevent when in their company. Sometimes though, it was out of our control. Elijah broke the bubble when he asked,

"What did Ash get you Lori?" We looked at each other and burst out laughing, unable to stop ourselves.

"I don't think I want to know…," said Nick, returning to his paper on the verandah. Other than the bumped skull, I was so deliriously happy.

The First Small Step

"If someone had told me yesterday that all our tomorrows were stark
I would have taken the time to repeat our crime,
To make sure it won't stop at the start."

L Standish, 'Turn on the Light'

LORIEN HANDED ME a roll of manuscript during lunch, and I opened it eagerly. "You're finished?" He was grinning at me, his eyes excited.

"It's more than that, I'm meeting with a guy this afternoon who plays drums *and* has a van which will solve the problem of getting our gear to the gigs."

"I'm so proud of you!" I hugged him to me, kissing him.

"This one's for you to sing." He rifled through the pages and found the one he was looking for, passing it to me. Its title was 'Merciful Mayhem', a play on my surname no doubt. I followed the tune in my head against the beat; it felt good, a wonderful song.

"When are we rehearsing?"

"This afternoon if it's OK with you; Eli's already on board."

"Definitely Lorien, I can't wait!"

"What have we got after lunch?" he purred into my ear.

"I can wait!" He laughed with me. We were *trying* to stay focussed, at least during school hours, although we still tended to lapse on occasion.

I found it impossible to relax when we got back to his house. I couldn't wait for the drummer to get here so we could hear the complete sound. "Ash, you're making *me* nervous," he said. "Come and tune up, it'll take your mind off it. If you're a good girl I also have something for you," he waggled his eyebrows at me, pulling me to him for a cuddle. We were both excited and for once, it didn't involve hormones.

"What?"

"No, you have to be good."

"I'll be *very* good later Lorien," I promised, making it about hormones again. He laughed then ran up the stairs to his room. Elijah walked in, just home from school.

"Hey Ash, where's the virtuoso?"

"Upstairs getting something." Elijah laughed,

"Is it for you?" I nodded. "You're just going to love it."

"You know what it is?"

"You'll find out soon enough," he said, hearing Lorien's door close. He took the stairs two by two and jumped over the last few, a box in his hand.

"Here Ash," he kissed me lightly and sat down to watch my reaction. I could tell by the sliding sensation it was clothes but surely not anything like the birthday present I'd given him, not with Elijah in the room. "Well, are you going to open it?" I tore off the lid. Inside was a sexy electric blue dress with what appeared to be a high midriff connected to the skirt by thin straps under the bust. It was very short and had a rather low neckline by the look of it. Inside the box was also a matching choker and a pair of black fishnet stockings and although I loved it, and would love to wear it for him, I was a little unsure why he was giving it to me now. "It's your costume Ash," he said, smiling at me. I looked at Elijah and he laughed.

"I knew you'd have a fight on your hands Lori."

"Lorien!" I was actually speechless. There was no way I could wear this in public and perform on a stage.

"It matches your violin Baby." He was right. The electric-blue, electric violin the Standish's had given me for my eighteenth birthday was the exact colour of this dress, not that it meant I was ready to jump into its tight skin. "Just try it on Ash, please?"

"OK, but *you* stay here." He laughed and pulled me to him, kissing me again before I went into the bathroom to change. If he came with me, we were likely to be in there for hours.

I had to admit, it looked great. It was more flattering than flirty but still definitely sexy. I checked myself out as well as I could in the bathroom mirror. Hearing their voices in the lounge room I stepped out boldly with a loud "Ta Daaa!" not realising the new drummer had arrived.

"So, you're the violin chick?" he asked, eyeing me off appreciatively. Lorien introduced us, a rueful smile at his lips.

"Ashlyn, this is Matty." He moved forward to take my hand, shaking it slowly.

"Great to meet you," he said, sizing me up. He was about twenty-five years old, skinny and scruffy. I hoped he was a better drummer than he looked.

"Want some help getting your drums Matty?" Elijah asked, refocussing his attention. Lorien darted up to me.

"I'm sorry Ash, I didn't get a chance to let you know; normally I'd have to drag you out of the bathroom in an outfit like that."

"Why did you get it for me if you didn't think I'd wear it?" I smiled at him as he took me into his arms.

"I hoped you would." He leant in, his lips to my ear. "You look so incredibly gorgeous Ash; we may have to consider calling this rehearsal short."

When I heard Matty and Elijah come back through the door, Lorien didn't break the kiss. He was staking his claim on me, letting Matty know I wasn't up for grabs. "I should get changed," I said, eventually drawing away from him.

"You'll have to get used to it sooner or later." Lorien smiled and kissed me again.

"Maybe! But it doesn't have to be today does it?" He shook his head and let me go, leading me to believe he didn't particularly want me looking like this in front of Matty on our first meeting either.

I was in my school uniform when I came back out, just a normal girl again; Matty checked me out regardless. "The school-girl look works fine too Ashlyn," he smiled lazily, and I ignored him. He had his drum kit set up and they were only waiting on me to start. Matty took a seat on the stool, waiting for instruction.

"OK, give us a drum roll," said Lorien. He rattled it out perfectly. "How about we start, and you come in when you're ready?"

"Works for me." Lorien counted us in, and we broke into 'Tears of an Angel', one Lorien had written several months ago which we all knew well.

The sound of the bass and electric guitars paired with my violin was a fantastic sound and when Matty came in after the first chorus, we *were* a band. I was amazed at how professional we sounded but should have known better - Lorien was a talented musician and songwriter. "That was pretty good," Matty commented when we'd finished. "You wrote all these songs we're going to perform?"

"Over the last few years, yes." Lorien said.

"No keyboards?"

"That's my preferred instrument, but we don't have a lead guitarist so it can wait until we find one."

"I think you've got something kid." Lorien prickled. "Your voices are passable too." I didn't like Matty, and the twins didn't seem to be in love with him either. "What's the name of this band?"

"Listening at Keyholes." Matty raised his eyebrows and nodded. "So, are you interested in the job?" Lorien asked.

"What are you offering?"

"Same as us. Twenty five percent each after expenses and an extra twenty dollars to you for the use of your van. More if we need to travel further." Matty looked at me before replying.

"I can work with that. You need to know you're not the only band I play with, so you'll have to give me notice when you want to rehearse... I might be able to get us a few gigs too."

"How's Tuesday and Thursday afternoons?" Lorien asked.

"Fine. Do you want me back again tomorrow?"

"No, I think Thursday will do. Eli and Ash have to learn the last few songs and you don't have to hang around today either, we'll call it a successful audition." Lorien grinned at me and took me in his arms.

"Whoo hoo, young lovers..." Matty said as he started to pull his kit apart. Elijah helped him and Lorien did too, obviously wanting him out of the house as soon as was possible.

"Would you rather us come to your place for rehearsals to save you carting your drums around?" Lorien asked.

"Doesn't worry me, if you want to that's cool."

"Come here on Thursday and we'll come to you after term break."

"OK, no need to bring your amps or anything, just the guitars. I have all the equipment you'll need at home."

I stood at the door and watched as they loaded his kit into the back of the van. Matty stopped and lit a cigarette, smiling at me. I ignored him - he was creepy. When it had burnt down far enough he said, "Ash!" and tapped his cigarette, the ash falling to the ground. I was glad when he finally left.

"I don't like him," I complained to Lorien when I was back safely in his arms.

"Don't worry, if he doesn't work out, we'll get rid of him. This is *our* band, not his, and we call the shots."

"I agree with Ash," Elijah said. "What a dick!"

"At least we're all agreed then," Lorien said, smiling.

I practised the final three songs with Lorien until I had them down pat. Thursday was upon us and we were all excited during lunch. Keren, Michael, Simon and Bree were all coming this afternoon to watch us rehearse. "Tell me more about this drummer you love so much," Michael asked.

"You'll find out for yourself soon enough," I told him, scoffing.

"Are you going to wear the new outfit?"

"I suppose so; I brought my boots with me just in case." Lorien had been at my place last night and he encouraged me to bring them, citing that they were the perfect accompaniment for the dress, me citing he was oversexed. He was listening to Michael's and my conversation; how could he not with me perched on his lap.

"She looks hot!" Lorien growled at my ear.

"Must be early menopause," Michael grinned. I kicked out at him playfully. I was on such a high.

Mrs Standish, as I called her during school hours, was not as excited as the rest of us. We had a double History period as our last classes of the day, and we were all squirming and fidgety for most of the lesson. Finally, at 3.10 pm she let us out, five minutes early. "Thanks Mum." Lorien pecked her on the cheek as we dashed out, running across the road to his house.

"What time is Matty getting here?" I asked, wanting to be already changed when he arrived.

"4.00 pm. We have heaps of time." Elijah said.

"Go on sexy boxers, go and slip into the barely there," Michael teased, and I went into the bathroom to change. Before coming out this time, I made sure there were no strangers present.

Lorien was setting up the equipment in the rumpus area and was outside the door when I came out. "Hey sexy boxers," he laughed, pulling me to him and kissing me.

"Let's have a look then," Michael prompted, and I twirled for them. Simon whistled.

"It's a beautiful dress Ash," Bree said. "Can I borrow it sometime?" I looked at Lorien for the answer as he'd bought it for the band.

"It's your dress Ash. You can do with it what you like." I went to him and kissed him in thanks. "What I would *like* you to do with it is let me rip it off your body," he whispered throatily in my ear.

"Let me wear it first Lorien, OK?" Bree laughed.

We sat around drinking coffee waiting on Matty to show. "I think we'll start with 'Merciful Mayhem' Ash. Are you ready to fly solo Baby?"

"Not first up, please Lorien."

"No biggie Ash, I'll throw you in the middle somewhere, OK?" I smiled at him; he understood I didn't want that spotlight shining straight on me.

It was just after 4.00 pm when we heard the van in the driveway. Lorien and Elijah went to help him bring in his kit.

"Hi there Ash," Matty said. "Always nice to see you." He looked around and noticed four new faces, especially Bree's. "A groupie, excellent."

"She's my groupie bud," Simon told him, possessively putting his arm around her.

"OK, I hear you, no need to get all bent out of shape." Keren, Michael, Bree and I looked at each other as he went back to the van, shuddering and squidging up our faces, mouthing *Ewww*! He was simply hideous!

As soon as the drums were set up Lorien wanted to start, getting this underway and over with as quickly as possible. He passed Matty the song list and he clicked his sticks together, counting us into the first of ten songs.

We played three straight off, one into the other without stopping. At the end of this small set Simon, Bree and Michael were clapping loudly.

"You guys are *great!*" Michael enthused. "You're going to make a fortune!"

"What would you know about it, poof?" Matty's comment sliced through our joy like a hatchet. Michael was many things: muscular, handsome, bronzed and tall. He was not however one to take a shot like that without loading his guns and firing back. He slowly stood to his full 190 cm and walked over to Matty.

"What's a poof?" he asked, appearing to be unaware of the term. Matty sniggered and said,

"*You* know, fag, arse bandit, queer... homosexual!" Matty thought he'd put Michael in his place, but he had *no* idea. He'd just been set up a beauty.

"I see," Michael said moving closer. "You call me a poofter yet it's *you* who seems to be familiar with all the terms. Care to tell us why, or more importantly, how you came by them?" Michael's question was pregnant with poisoned barbs. Matty was flustered and sputtered around, looking for the elusive quick comeback that didn't come. "Are we going to have a problem shorty?" Michael asked finally, lowering himself down to Matty's face level.

"OK, enough break, let's get back to it." Lorien said, looking for an end to this. "You're up Baby."

'Merciful Mayhem' sounded great and when we were done Bree, Michael and I clung in a tight circle and jumped up and down like little kids yelling, "Yay!" I think Michael was just daring Matty to have something to say, but he showed more smarts than I'd given him credit for and wisely kept his mouth shut.

We finished around 6.00 pm, and with the exception of Matty, it had been a great rehearsal. We helped the twins push the furniture back into place and unhooked the equipment, Bree then following me into the kitchen to make coffee. "Seriously Ash, you guys are great! I'd also forgotten what amazing voices the twins had, you being no slouch either." She smiled at me broadly.

"Well thank you Miss Swain," I said in my most haughty of voices.

"I can't wait to hear you guys play for real. Have you got anything lined up yet?" Lorien came into the kitchen and was able to answer the question I didn't know the answer to.

"Not yet. We need some more rehearsal first, although after today I don't think it'll take as long as I expected." He had to bend down to kiss me - I'd taken my boots off. "You were wonderful, Gorgeous," he said, smacking me lightly on the bum. I beamed at him.

"That guy is class 1A, prime dick!" Michael said, joining us in the kitchen.

"Hey, that's pretty close to what I called him!" Elijah said. We laughed and headed out onto the side verandah.

"Anyone got any plans over Easter?" Michael asked. We all looked around at each other a little dumbfounded as no one had really said anything about the school holidays up to this point. "I'll take that as a collective no," Michael said, laughing. "Want to spend four fun-filled days at Wally's weekender at the Bay? I thought I'd ask Cyndi and Frankie too."

Wally was his mother's boyfriend of about twelve months now. Michael was aware this man could possibly be his stepfather in the not-too-distant future, and he'd learnt to live with the idea. None of his mother's other boyfriends since her divorce had been quite so lucky. "Excellent!" Elijah and Simon chorused.

"Now there's one problem..." we waited for him to continue. "There are only four bedrooms and I'm not sleeping on the lounge room floor. I'm happy to take extra mattresses with us, but you'll have to flip for it.

"Frankie and Cyndi can have it, they're outvoted!" Simon decreed and we were all in agreement. "Surely they'll be over the passionate encounters now they've been living together." Lorien and I looked at each other, knowing this could never be the case for us. Even though we spent all day, every day and every night together, it was never enough. It made me curious about his and Bree's relationship. They'd been going out since Year 7, wow, going on five years I realised, but I'd never really spoken to Bree about it. I knew when she'd lost her virginity and when extra special things happened, especially when we were younger, but I really had no idea of what they got up to behind closed doors these days. I wondered whether Michael had ever asked her about it.

"You're mighty deep in concentration there, pretty one." Lorien whispered in my ear. I smiled at him and shook my head.

Cara walked through the front door just then, juggling a stack of books. Her boys ran to help her. "We're off to Nanna's for dinner. Are you boys coming?"

"Do you mind if we stay here and get take-away?" Elijah asked.

"No, just remember it's a school night. When your father gets home we're leaving, and we won't be back until tomorrow. Your Dad's off all day and I don't have a class until just before lunch, so behave yourselves!"

"Yes Mrs Standish," we all droned. She laughed and her husband came in the door behind her, grabbing her around the waist.

"Nick," she chastised.

"Yes Mrs Standish?" he grinned at her. This was also the grin of his sons.

"Go and pack," she told him, a little flustered, "I've got to pick up dinner for the kids."

"Don't worry Mum, we'll order Chinese, they deliver," Elijah said.

"OK, if you're sure." She went upstairs to get her clothes together.

Around 9.00 pm, a car pulled into the driveway. I was surprised to find that Bree's Dad had come to pick them up, assuming I'd be dropping them home. I was glad though as it was a fifty-minute round trip to Gracey and then Woodbine to drop the three of them off. We waved them goodbye, and Elijah left with Keren to walk her home. "Let's take a bath!" Lorien suggested, his eyes dancing.

"I didn't know you had one."

"Come with me lassie," he said in a really bad Scottish accent, leading me up the stairs.

I'd seen his parent's room when I got the original tour of the house with Elijah, but I hadn't gone in as I was afraid of the white carpet. Although I'd seen inside this room on a few occasions, it never failed to take my breath away. Lorien guided me through to the far wall and opened the door to their ensuite. It was as beautifully decorated as the bedroom and in the centre was a round spa bath, more than big enough for two. "I've never been in here before," I said, looking around. Lorien started to fill the bath with water and came over to undress me. I was transfixed for the moment on the filling tub; water was coursing in from four different taps. I'd never seen anything like it before. "Exactly how much allowance do you two get each week?" I asked, knowing his parents had money.

"Enough to feed a family of three. Want to try for one?" I laughed, refocussing my attention back to him.

When I looked into his eyes, the heat of them burnt into mine as we slowly peeled off each other's clothes. Lorien climbed in and I followed, sitting in front of him. He reached over and pressed a button, sending the jets into their pulsing action. "This feels great," I sighed, leaning back against him.

"Hmmm," he sighed, bringing his hands up to cup my breasts, "Great…" I eased around slightly so I could reach up to kiss him and ended up on his lap instead. "Much better," he mumbled through the kiss as his hand lowered to torment me softly. Although totally enjoyable, I was curious why his usually eager fingers weren't on a more thorough search.

"Bath versus shower Baby, two different things. I can do this," he resumed his teasing, "but not this." As he worked his fingers to separate me further, I understood his point. The water, especially in moving water, diluted any and all lubrication instantly, making it slightly abrasive.

"How do you know about this? You've only slept with one other person."

"I told you and Nanna confirmed it, I never had Mr Winky out of my hands from birth up until, well pretty much up until I met you." I knew this was not necessarily true. He'd told me about the fantasies he'd had before we were together about me, and over that period, how much he'd enjoyed his showers.

"So, sex is out of the question in a spa?"

"If you want sex Baby, just tell me and I'll rip the plug out now." He returned to the earlier caresses, moving my whole pubic region as one. "Stay right there," he stood and reached over to the vanity, bringing back a washer and razor.

"What are you up to?" I asked, smiling.

"Let's draw, you first." He sat on the edge of the bath, allowing me full access to his pubic hair.

"You want me to shave you?" I asked, a little unsure of his intention.

"Not the whole area," he laughed. "Draw me a picture Baby, sculpt me."

"You're sure that thing won't go off?" I asked teasingly, Mr Winky at eye level to me as I crawled over to him.

"Scout's honour." He drew a cross over his chest and formed the Scout's salute, his palm towards me, fingers straight with his pinkie captured down by his thumb.

"You were never a Scout," I scoffed, and he grinned at me.

I thought about it for a few moments whilst lathering him up, then went to work. It didn't take long and when I was finished, I sat back and admired my work of art. "Aw Baby, it's beautiful." I smiled up at him and I agreed it was cute. I'd shaved him into the shape of a heart. "Your turn."

He wiped all the loose hair into the washer and went to the basin to rinse it as I positioned myself on the edge. "No peeking now," he said as he lathered me up. "I may need to take a bit more off you to get *my* design right. Is that OK?" I smiled down at him and nodded.

He was at it for several minutes, pausing every now and then to play a finger against me. There was no water here and he was taking full advantage, looking up to catch my reaction when his fingers 'slipped'. I was giddy when he'd finished sculpting; it was hard work to stay upright on the ridge of a bath whilst someone was working you in the most intimate of ways. He wiped me off and threw the washer into the basin, then cupped his hands into the water to rinse me off properly. "OK, you can look now."

"It's a 7?" I asked, uncertain.

"It's an L," he laughed.

"Not from where I'm sitting." He hugged me to him and laughed with me. "And what does the L stand for Standish?" I asked defiantly, knowing what it would be. He moved back down my body, his cheek pressing against my inner thigh.

"Lorien..." he darted his tongue out to tease me, "Loves... Lapping... his Luscious... Lover's... Lips..." With each word, he massaged me more intensely, raising me to an incredible pitch.

"Luscious lover loves being lapped," I sighed, but knew it wasn't going to work with me perched on the edge of the tub - I couldn't relax enough.

"I want more love in the tub first," he said when I told him, sliding me back into the bath. He reached behind, grabbed a loofah and some body-wash, and gently scrubbed me all over. It was wonderful and I was now *very* relaxed.

When I went to do him, I asked, "Can I get your hair wet?"

"You can do anything you want to me, whenever you want to Ash." So honest and open was this statement I knew it to be true. I moved aside so he could lower his head into the water before sitting back up. It was hanging straight and halfway down his back.

"I love your hair so much," I said and ran my hands down his hair, straddling across him so I could kiss him intimately. We could've been anywhere in the world sitting in this tub and I was nearly ready to get out of the bath, starting to ache for him. I broke the kiss and ran the loofah slowly over his chest, arms and shoulders, admiring for the thousandth time his sexy body. I raised his arm to bring the loofah down his sides and into his armpit. He flinched it back down. "I didn't know you were ticklish!"

"Aren't you," he teased, raising my arm to give me the same treatment. I was. I turned him around and worked the loofah across his broad back, rinsing him off before running my lips across his shoulders. He turned around and I stared into his eyes.

"Lorien..." I exhaled. He pulled the plug, the water draining as quickly as it had filled.

We dried off slowly, sensuously and quickly tidied up before running down the hall to his room. Once there, we were free again to explore and entice, to lust at each other with wanton abandon.

He laid me across the bed, my arms above my head as he lightly traced his fingers over my body. "Not ticklish now?" he whispered.

"Nuh uh," it was electric. "Why do I always get the special treatment?" I sighed, complaining in no way. He was always so attentive, at times even discouraging me when I went to pleasure him solely.

"I love you Baby, and I love it when you love what I do to you. We both know that I'll go off like a cracker each and every time, but for you, I want a rhapsody," he finished softly, returning his tickle work back at my altar. "Oh, and I can feel you love it, Miss Moist!"

"Have you been reading your birthday book?" I groaned.

"Yes," he leant down and kissed me, working his fingers more forcibly against me and then into me. "Haven't you noticed?" he teased, in both verbal and action.

"I thought you were always adventurous," I whispered. He chuckled lowly as he eased his tongue from my collarbone to my breast, taking it into his mouth slowly. "The problem is... my mouth gets so jealous of my fingers and I just can't control it," he said breathily, moving further down my body to nuzzle at my stomach. "If you didn't taste so good...it wouldn't be a problem..." His jealous mouth fought briefly with his fingers and when finally victorious, he fed.

I looked down at him as I started to reach the heights and his eyes were already on mine, sending a rip through my body. He slipped a finger back into me as my breathing conveyed my urgency, holding his face tightly as my body tried to repel him. He put his arms across my stomach and legs to keep me still, making my body take my own pleasure to its maximum, and laid out flat, barely able to move, my whole world rolled in and out of focus. Every part of my body felt this climax, from my toes to my eyelashes; I throbbed and burned under him, so totally and utterly abandoned. "Hmmm, that was a good one," he breathed, and reached under the pillow for the never-ending supply of condoms. The box he pulled out was empty. "Damn it, I'm out." He knew my period hadn't long finished, that was when we enjoyed our shower sex. I quickly counted back the days.

"Don't worry Lorien. It will be fine, I promise." He groaned and laughed softly.

"Ash, we shouldn't." However, we did.

He flipped me over and entered me from behind, hard and deep, so filling every part of me with every part of him. Soon after, his breath was hot on my back and his hips gained speed; kneeling backward to change the angle, he forced into me harder, deeper, and cried out softly.

He collapsed next to me, pulling me over to kiss me tenderly, his breath still racing. "We don't do it that way very often." I said.

"I can't see your beautiful face," he puffed, tracing his finger over my lips as he smiled at me. He'd made me blush. "That was called classic doggy in case you were wondering," he laughed quietly. "Come on, let's shower."

"Why? We don't always after sex and we just had a bath."

"No condom," he reminded me, and I agreed with him. I didn't want Cara to find the residue all over his sheets.

When back in bed I continued my previous thought. "There must be something you'd like me to do for you, or to you?" I asked smoulderingly. "Whether it's in the book or not."

"Trust me Ash, I'll be showing you a few pages every now and then to get your input… but there's something you *could* do for me…" I looked at him with a smile on my face, waiting for him to continue. "I want to watch you play with yourself," he whispered.

"I don't think I can Lorien." I was glad the lights were off, knowing from the heat of my face I was blushing again, furiously.

"Why not Ashlyn? I love you so much and it would make me *so* hot."

"I don't know why. I'm not the confident person you are, nothing worries you."

"Can I help you try?" I nodded, not knowing where he was going with this. "Are you OK to go again?" I smiled coyly. I was always ready for him.

He placed his hand between my thighs, circling softly. As my breathing started to deepen, he stopped, taking my hand and placing it where his had been. Covering my hand with his, he moved me against myself. He alternated his pressure, at times leaving me to my own devices, then coming back to join me. He went to manoeuvre one of my fingers into myself and realised that the well was dry. "You're not letting yourself go are you Baby?" he asked softly, running his lips over mine.

"I can't get past my own self-consciousness. I'm sorry Lorien, there's nothing I wouldn't do for you, but this seems to be something I *can't* do for you."

"No need to apologise for it Ash," he drew me to his chest. "If it never happens, so be it; I enjoyed trying though." He smiled at me. "Mind if I have another go at it?" I laughed and told him to go right ahead.

EASTER

The Bay Long Weekend

"My girl don't want diamond rings or chains of gold,
It's chocolate!"

L Standish, 'What I Buy for my Baby'

WE DECIDED TO TAKE THE TWIN'S CAR as it had more room. Elijah drove with Keren sitting up front with him, and Lorien and me sitting on the back seat. It was nearly impossible to cuddle in a car when you were both strapped into seatbelts so were content holding hands. There would be plenty of time for other such enjoyable encounters once we arrived.

The trip took forever. The traffic was abysmal, and Keren and Elijah started to argue as we neared our destination due to the road directions and the fact she had programmed the wrong 'Bay' into online maps. I looked at Lorien and rolled my eyes; he smiled and leant over to kiss me. "I can't wait to get there," he purred, causing Keren to turn around and ask,

"Are we even going to see you two over the weekend or do you plan to spend the entire time in the bedroom?" What was it to her anyway?

"That will depend..." Lorien replied, "on whether my mistress of the night unties me at some stage." I laughed and smacked his leg lightly, unaware of what the next few days had in store for us.

"You wish!"

Michael, Bree and Simon were already there when we arrived and were unpacking the car. Elijah looked around at the water. "I don't know why I brought my board, it's dead flat."

"There are other places than right here to surf," Michael told him.

"I don't know why I even bothered to come," Keren barked. I was beginning to agree with her. I saw Lorien look to his brother and Elijah shrugged his shoulders back at him. Whatever was eating her, he was not yet aware of the issue. I had no doubt he'd find out soon enough.

Lorien grabbed our bags and his laptop from the boot, and I followed him into the house. Before choosing a room, we asked Michael which one he wanted. "My room is the first one down the hall. You can have any of the others; no one has staked a claim yet." We picked the furthest room, not only to be as far away from everyone as possible but also to avoid having footsteps constantly walking past the door.

The rooms were simply decorated, a weekender it was indeed, but each room had a double bed, dresser and wardrobe. Lorien put the bags on the bed and his laptop on the dresser. "Why did you bring that?" I asked him.

"You'll see," he said. As I started to go through my bag, I heard the door snick shut.

"What are you doing?" I asked, smiling at him.

"What do you think I'm doing?" he said, dissolving the space between us.

"Don't you think we should be a little social first, or do you want Keren thinking we *will* be in here all weekend?"

"I'm feeling *very* sociable right now and I don't give a damn what Keren thinks." He leant down and kissed me lightly.

"What was that all about anyway?"

"I have no idea and it doesn't seem Eli knows either. Chicks..." He laughed and dodged out of the way as I tried to smack him.

"I don't do that to you, in fact I don't think we've even had a fight have we?"

"Wanna wrestle?" he asked, waggling his eyebrows.

"No, I want to unpack and then go to the supermarket for supplies. I don't want to be running there every fifteen minutes when we need something." He sighed dramatically and opened his bag, pulling out his toiletries and a few other things, putting them on the dresser. He upended the rest of the contents straight into a drawer.

"Finished." He smiled at me as if he'd won some kind of award.

"You're a grub!" I told him and laughed.

"Come on Ash, we have all day to do that..." His arms worked their way around me from behind as he moved in to start kissing the nape of my neck. He exhaled softly in my ear and rubbed his hands slowly across my stomach.

"It's not going to work Lorien." I did my best to pull away from him, but he wouldn't let me go. I turned around in his arms and noticed one of the things he'd put on the dresser was the camcorder Simon and Bree had given him for his birthday. I looked at him and raised my eyebrows.

"What? We're on holidays, are we not?" I wasn't that naïve.

"Go and put it to good use then and let me have ten minutes please."

"Yes Ma'am!" He saluted and took the camcorder off the dresser. "Act 1, Scene 1 - Ashlyn unpacks."

"Lorien..."

"Yes?" he drawled. When I didn't respond, he continued his narrative, "Come on hottie, strip for me."

"Will you get out of here!" He laughed and put the camera down, coming over to kiss me quickly before leaving the room.

"Lorien," I stopped him. As he turned back around, I pulled my shirt up and flashed him.

"Baby, I didn't have the camera on," he complained. I pushed him out the door, laughing, closing it behind him.

No one bothered with groceries - Michael and Simon went to the bottle-shop instead and brought back two cartons of beer. After they'd stacked it in the fridge Simon cracked one open, handing it to Bree. "Anyone else?" He passed one to Michael, Elijah, Lorien and I. Keren declined. Everyone spread out all over the floor or in one of the several beanbags scattered around. Lorien and I took the sofa, not paying much attention to the conversation going on around us.

Lorien took a swig from his beer then took mine from my hands, putting them both on the floor. He sidled against me, nuzzling at my neck, his hands working their way slowly up and down my sides. "Hmmm, succulent," he said, drawing his lips around my throat, dragging them and his tongue down my neck. He rolled so he was nearly on top of me, and my hands found their way into his hair, holding his head against me. The rest of them were shouting random numbers and I briefly wondered what weird game they were playing now. I'd certainly made a lot of progress with the public affection affliction; it rarely worried me around our friends anymore. Lorien rolled back, bringing me with him, lying across the sofa with me now on top of him. Our kisses were deep, and our breathing became soft groans. "Ash," he exhaled, his hot breath at my neck, "you make me so *hard*." Making sure I was paying attention, he lowered my hand to him, using our bodies as a shield.

"Fifty!" I heard Michael call out, laughing. We continued to ignore them, Lorien's hands now on my rear, squeezing me gently before slipping them down the back of my shorts.

"Fifty-five!" Called Elijah, "No, sixty!" It was getting a little annoying, disturbing my concentration. I ended up breaking the kiss, turning to face them,

"What the hell are you guys playing?"

"We're pre-empting your ardour shuffle, five points for every one we get right." Michael passed me a sheet of paper and on it was written many lines, ticks against the ones we'd already performed.

Mouth on throat action

Tongue visible

Twin runs fingers through Ash's hair

Ash runs fingers through twin's hair

Twin says Ash's name

Ash says twin's name

Body rolls or any other major change of position

Dirty talk

Groaning

Lippy kisses

Full on pashes

Hand relief

Blowjob

Sticky fingers

Sticky face

Hands out of sight

Hands on arse

Hands on tits

Hands on cock

Hands on jixie

Spanking

Writhing of any kind to any part of the body

Loading the bullet into the gun barrel – bonus 50 points.

"You guys need to get out more often," Lorien said as he sat up and read the list over my shoulder.

"You had this already prepared"?" I asked incredulously.

"Spanking," Lorien laughed.

"What the hell is a jixie?" I asked.

"You're sitting on it," Michael said, grinning.

"Let's give them the bonus fifty-pointer now Baby." Lorien leered at me and started to lower me back to the sofa. I laughed, knowing he wasn't going to 'load the bullet into the gun barrel' in front of them. He started to ease my shirt up, kissing my stomach and sneaking his hand under, reaching for my breast.

"Sixty-five!" Simon called.

"Lorien, what are you doing?" I said, trying to sit up. He was taking this joke a little further than I expected.

"Giving them what they want, it's the only way to get them off our backs," he said, his tongue circling around my navel. "Hmmm," he groaned, and worked his fingers at the button on my shorts.

He sat up abruptly, smiling at all the wide-eyed and slack-jawed faces staring back at him. "I really thought..." started Bree, not knowing where to take this statement. No one had much to say for a few moments, bewildered still at the thought of what was assumed they were going to see.

"Nice to see you all ran from the room." I chided.

"We were in shock and so were you," Bree laughed.

"I would never pass up a live sex show!" said Simon.

"I'll tell you what twin," Michael said, standing to get more beers. "I'm going to fine you a dollar every time I'm forced to bear witness to any of your lewd carry-ons." Lorien reached into his pocket and pulled out his wallet, fishing out a twenty-dollar note and flipping it to Michael.

"Let me know when I need to give you more," he winked.

"Thanks twin," Michael said primly and tucked the note into his pocket. Keren got up and walked out of the room, Elijah followed her.

"I'm setting up the camera in a second," Lorien said lowly.

"Nuh uh!" I shook my head, smiling at him.

"Yes uh," he told me, nodding, his eyes shining.

"Nuh UH!

"As soon as Eli and Keren come back out, I'm *so* in there, and when I'm done, I will come and find you..." I ran my fingertips lightly across his lips and moved my mouth to his ear,

"Nuh uh," I whispered. Our little verbal foreplay was loaded with promise, him provoking me and me saying no in return when we both knew it was yes. The toilet flushed and Elijah walked back in alone.

"Where's Keren?" I asked.

"She's having a sleep." I looked at Lorien and grimaced. After the prelude on the sofa we were both ready to get right into it, but now we'd have to wait. *Too bad for her!* Lorien mouthed, and got up, leaving the room.

A few minutes later Lorien called down the hallway in a singsong voice, "Ashlyn..." All eyes were upon me as I surveyed the smiling faces, from one to the next.

"*What?*" I asked them.

"I think Lorien has something for you," Bree laughed.

"Oh... Ashlyn..." I heard again from the hallway.

"Go get him tiger," Simon prompted. "Show him what you're made of!" I pulled a face at him as Lorien continued to call,

"Do I have to come out there and get you Baby girl?"

"Just go will you. His voice is driving me crazy," Michael said, coming over and pulling me off the sofa. "See you tomorrow."

"Michael, it's like 2.00 pm!"

"I'm sure you'll be able to keep yourselves active for the next eighteen hours or so," he laughed, shoving me into the hallway. Lorien was standing at our doorway and held his hand out, grinning from ear to ear.

"Come to me Baby," he said, standing only in his boardies. "I'm ready for you." As I started down the hallway to him, trying not to smile, he pulled his shorts open and slid them down his legs, kicking them off as they hit the ground. He certainly was ready for me!

I was a little constrained at first knowing a recording eye was on me, but I relaxed soon enough and all-but forgot it was there, becoming less inhibited than I'd ever been. For over a half an hour we made love, changing positions, using our voices, hands and mouths – hot and heavy, as all great sex should be.

As soon as we'd finished, we watched it back and I now understood why Lorien had brought the laptop. In fact, I did more than watch it - I couldn't tear my eyes from it if a swarm of terrorists had come screaming through the room. A few times one of our bodies was in the way but the majority of it was pure and utter sexual eroticism, and surprisingly, I wasn't embarrassed at all. I loved it!

When it had played through Lorien looked at me, his eyes wide, a crooked smile on his lips. "Wroof!" he said. "Let's watch it again!" This time he added his own personal narrative to it, pausing and back scanning at times to get the full effect. "Watch your nipple the second I touch it, oh yes. Own it Baby!" I laughed quietly. When I was about to reach my first orgasm he back-scanned again, "Look at your face Ash, here you go, you're just about to…" There was a light knock on the door. *Crap!* we mouthed to each other, scrambling for our clothes. It had a déjà vu sensation about it…

"It's just me," Elijah said. "Are you decent?"

"One second," Lorien answered as he pulled his shorts on. I couldn't find my shirt anywhere so jumped back under the covers, nodding to Lorien and he opened the door.

"It took you long enough," Elijah said, then spotted me. "I see," he grinned at his brother and then me. He moved slightly to the left and said, "I *do* see!" I followed his gaze and realised the laptop was still humming away and our little show was now at the point of penetration. And, not just your everyday run of the mill penetration, I was on top of Lorien who was sitting forward, his lips and tongue grazing from one breast to the other as his hands held my hips, helping me maintain my rhythm. My head and body were angled backward; supporting myself on his thighs, I ground against him at a frenzied pace.

Lorien slammed the laptop shut as I groaned and rolled over, hiding myself under the covers. I couldn't look at Elijah standing there, grinning at me. "You're *so* lucky it wasn't Simon or Michael that came in here instead of me. Atta boy." He lightly punched Lorien on the arm.

"OK, knock it off. What do you *want?*"

"I'm taking Keren home, I thought you both may have wanted to come... but I see I'm *way* too late for that." He laughed and left us to our humility.

Lorien came to sit beside me on the bed. "Are you OK?" I pulled the covers back down and saw him trying to hide a smile.

"Could it have been any worse?" I whined.

"Yes, Simon or Michael could have come in and they probably wouldn't have waited as long." I had to laugh with him. Oh well, we were like family now, so chances are we'd be busted in a real-time version eventually. "Now, are you getting up or am I climbing back in there with you?" I only had to think about it for a second before I whipped back the covers, inviting him in. His shorts were already halfway off.

We were dressed and making the bed when Michael started clomping up and down the hall, banging two pot lids together. "Bring out your dead... bring out your dead!" I laughed and opened the door.

"Come in you idiot." He walked in and threw himself across the bed. "Hey, we just made that!"

"Is that a fact?" he smiled up at us deviously. "I didn't think you were in here taking a nap, sister!" Bree and Simon came down the hall, a dictionary, paper and pens in her hand.

"Are we playing in there?" she asked.

"Methinks there have already been several games played in here," Michael said, moving over to make room for us all.

"What's the game?" I asked, sitting next to Lorien at the head of the bed, his back against the wall again, mine aligned to it this time as well. I looked at him and smiled, and he smiled back, leaning over to put his hand to my jaw, drawing me to him for another kiss.

"That's another dollar you owe me twin!"

"No way, I'm still nineteen in front," Lorien laughed.

"It won't take long for that to dwindle." Michael said. "OK Bree, hand out the pens and paper."

Michael explained the rules of the game and it was pretty simple. He went first, picking a word from the dictionary of which no one knew the meaning. He wrote down the correct answer and we all had to write down what could be a feasibly correct answer. If someone picked your answer, you got a point. It didn't sound all that exciting, but it ended up being one of the funniest games we'd ever played, and I was not usually into the Michael version of games. "Right," he said, flipping through the pages of the dictionary. "The word is 'carminative'." I thought for a while before writing 'the effect of the breakdown of mortar in brickwork through erosion and time'. It sounded plausible enough to me.

When everyone had finished, we handed our paper back to Michael and he read them through a few times to get it right before reading them aloud, doling out fresh paper so we could work our scores against the answers. "OK, one of the five answers is correct, is it a) the act of coming in," we all laughed, and I knew that would be Simon's, "b) medicine to remedy flatulence…" we laughed again, this was going to be harder than I thought! "c) the effect of the breakdown of mortar in brickwork through erosion and time, d) to have a calming essence or e) the inner lining of a golf ball." I had no idea!

We silently started to write, and I ended up picking in order of the alphabet: Bree, Simon, Me, Lorien and Michael. "OK, the answers are Simon, correct answer, Ash, Bree and twin. I had none right other than my own, and three out of four of us picked Lorien's answer as the real one and he leapt ahead. He'd picked mine however, so at least I had one point. This was fun. "Your turn Ash." As I was thumbing through the pages, Elijah stuck his head in the door.

"I didn't know what was going on in here!" He laughed and came to sit on the bed with us, Michael moving over to make room. Elijah caught my eye and grinned at me. I felt my face flush and dropped it down, breaking the eye contact.

"Here twin," Michael handed him a piece of paper and told him the rules. "OK Ash, what have you got for us?"

"The word is 'invigilate'." I wrote down the correct answer, 'to supervise examination candidates'.

After a few minutes, they handed me back their papers and I started to read them through. When I got to Lorien's, he'd written *I want to run my tongue...* I snapped the piece of paper shut.

"Sweetheart, I can't read this out. Want to try again?" Simon snatched it out of my hands.

"I'm so glad we aren't in the room next to yours," he laughed, reading it.

"Great," sighed Elijah, he was.

"Don't worry twin, it'll be just like home," Michael said in mock sympathy.

"We at least have a bathroom between us there." He obviously hadn't mentioned the X-rated movie he'd seen earlier; otherwise, we would've been copping it big time by now. I reminded myself to thank him later, when I could pull myself together enough to do so.

Lorien handed me back his paper, now reading 'the act or practice of orally stimulating the female genitalia'. Not much better but it was possible at least someone else had written it. "Is the answer a) to supervise examination candidates, b) to bathe with hot lotions, c) an allusive remark, d) to lick someone's tonsils..."

"Lorien!" Bree and Michael cried. He smiled and shrugged his shoulders.

"e) skilled in the art of horse riding, or f) the act or practice of orally stimulating the female genitalia?"

"Lorien!" they cried again.

"You're going to have to pick one, he can't have written them all." They handed back their papers and I announced the results. "In order it goes correct answer, Bree, Elijah, Simon, Michael and Lorien." No one had any of them right.

We played the game for hours and didn't realise the time flashing by. "Let's eat, I'm starving!" Simon said and we all climbed off the bed to walk down to the take-away shop, still not having been to the supermarket. Lorien and I were voted to do this first thing in the morning. I walked down the street arm in arm with Michael as Lorien hung back with Elijah to find out if everything was OK with him and Keren.

Later that night when we were all in bed, I asked Lorien what the problem was. I lay across his chest and reached up to kiss him lightly before finding the crook of his arm again. "You!" he said, smiling.

"How can it be?"

"Apparently she's so hot-damn jealous of everything about you."

"Why? And what *things*?"

"The way we are when we're together, the fact that you and Eli are close, the band, your grades, the things I give to you…"

"You gave them to her too, didn't you?"

"No, not really Ash. Keren and I were obviously a couple at the time but in no way like you and I are. She feels overshadowed by you every time she turns around apparently."

"What can I do about it?" I asked, leaning up to look him directly in the eye.

"Nothing, and that's what Eli told her too; this is a monster Keren created and now has to deal with." I wondered briefly when exactly had Keren and I lost the ability to talk to each other.

"She's jealous she and Elijah aren't affectionate like you and me?" He nodded. "And your brother is like my brother?" He nodded again, tracing his finger around the shape of my face.

"That I'm smarter than her, just?"

"Uh huh," he whispered, running his lips across my temple.

"That you buy me gifts?"

"Yes Baby," he said and kissed me softly.

"It's ridiculous! How can I change any of that? Why would I *want* to change it?"

"You don't Ash. As I said it's something *she* needs to get over. I don't think Eli can even help this time. He is what he is, and that's not going to change either."

"Do you think they'll break up?"

"I doubt it, it'd be a pretty stupid reason don't you think?" I agreed with him. I sat up to get out of bed, needing to use the bathroom before I went to sleep. "Where are you going my little electric blanket? Not in to console my brother I hope." I smiled at him.

"Don't be silly, I'm going to the bathroom."

"Hurry." I did.

When I came back, he moved over to let me slide in against him. "Goodnight Baby," he whispered, kissing me gently.

"Goodnight Lorien," I said, kissing him back. We fell asleep in our favourite position, in each other's arms.

Saturday

"Unless you're holding all the pieces
you can't complete the jigsaw's face."

L Standish, 'Juxtaposition positions'

I WOKE TO FIND LORIEN GONE and sat up bleary-eyed as the door opened softly, and there he stood with two cups of coffee in his hands. "Hey Gorgeous," he whispered, putting the cups on the dresser and coming over to kiss me good morning. I certainly didn't look gorgeous, but he did, dressed only in board-shorts and a smile.

"What time is it?" I asked.

"Just after 7.30 am," he said sitting on the bed, handing me a coffee.

"What are you doing awake at this time on a Saturday?" I smiled as I blew gently over the hot liquid before taking a sip.

"What are *you* doing awake at this time on a Saturday?" he asked back, grinning.

"I love you..." I leant over and kissed him again, wanting him to get back into bed with me.

"Is that a reason to be awake?" he laughed softly, as the rest of the house was still asleep.

"Yes, I have a morning woody." He laughed, louder this time and quickly adjusted his volume.

"I thought that only happened to guys?" he said, as I nuzzled my lips against his neck. "Baby girl..." he sighed, allowing me to have my way with him for the moment.

When I had him horizontal and the heat of the kisses became more urgent, I slid my hand into the warmth of his boardies, "Hmmm, what do you have for me today?"

"Ash," he groaned, "if we start this now, we won't get out of bed all day." He sat up, taking me by the shoulders, "Priorities woman!" I pouted at him. It was a rare occasion neither of us got our way when it came down to making love. It was only a few breathy sighs, or chosen words and actions, which turned a no or maybe into a yes! I sat thoughtful, Lorien asking,

"Dirty thoughts again lover?"

"No, I was just thinking you've never said 'no' to me."

"No, that can't be right," he smiled.

"I mean without being playful..." I continued to think back, not finding one instance with exception to my long-anticipated deflowering.

"I love you Ash, why would I ever say no?"

"You just did without using the actual word!" I pouted again, making my point clear.

"That was meant as a 'later' not an outright 'no'. Let's shower Baby..."

He took my hand and we crept to the bathroom, trying to keep the noise down. After five minutes of lather, rinse and repeat I finally got my way; the hot water cascading over our fused faces, my back pressed against the tiles of the shower wall. "You're a wicked temptress," he whispered, once our mutual satisfactions had been reached, "I love you so much Ash."

"At least we got out of bed." I smiled up at him, and with my hands slowly tracing his curves, I pulled him to me, "Sexy boxers!" He laughed and turned off the taps.

"Your 'L' has nearly grown out," he noticed as we dried off, then looked down, "and my heart."

"Were you itchy?" I asked.

"Very," he laughed. "We won't do that again for a while. Agreed?"

"Agreed!" I answered and had to have a quick scratch thinking about it, making Lorien laugh.

It still didn't appear anyone was awake when we came out of the bathroom. "Are you hungry?" he whispered.

"I can wait until they're all up." He nodded and picked up a note off the kitchen bench. It was from Michael and he'd listed a few extra items, including more alcohol.

"Looks like it might be a big one tonight," he said, unlocking the car.

"Every night's a big one when you're with a Standish."

"You just love the gutter these days, don't you missy!" he chastised playfully. "And what exactly do you mean by 'with a Standish'? Don't you mean 'with a Lorien'?" He had his eyebrows raised at me, the key in the ignition ready to turn.

"You *are* twins…" I hinted.

"Do we look identical?" I laughed and shook my head. "So, there are other obvious differences then?"

"No, not really," I grinned at him. Lorien knew Elijah and I hadn't gone anywhere near as far as I had with him. In fact, on day one with Lorien, we'd gone as far as Elijah and I ever had, and I loved to tease him about it.

"Well fill me in Ash," he said, backing out of the driveway, "you've always been rather elusive on this subject and I don't think you've ever given me a full answer to your history with my brother." I laughed,

"I've seen it."

"Felt it?"

"Lorien!" He smiled patiently, waiting on my answer.

"Only against me," I laughed.

"Now *that* I can believe." He tilted his face toward me so I could kiss him without him taking his eyes off the road.

"Do you know where we're going?"

"Michael said last night to turn left and drive." Sure enough, a shopping complex was nearing in the distance.

We parked out the back and walked through a small valley of second-hand clothes, bookshops and porn outlets before we got to the supermarket. After checking everything off on the list, we went into the adjoining alcohol section, getting another carton of beer and two bottles of vodka. "Michael's crazy," I said, taking the bottle in my hands to read the label.

"No drinking games for you?" Lorien asked as he paid the cashier.

"I don't want to end up like you and Elijah after your birthdays," I pointed out.

On the way back through second-hand row, Lorien turned the trolley into a sex shop. "What are you doing?" I asked him, hands on hips.

"Just window shopping…" He took my hand and led me in, nodding to the guy behind the counter.

"Looking for anything in particular mate?" he asked.

"Not really," Lorien said, and he went back to reading his paper. A few minutes later, we were in front of the accessories. "Hmm hmm hmm, like a kid in a candy store. What do you reckon Ash?"

"About what?" I was almost completely behind him, hiding I realised, but why? No one knew me here and who really cared anyway.

"Anything take your fancy?" I actually stepped out from myself and decided to have a good look around; it's not as if you were in this kind of shop every day. I picked up a silver ring, turning it over in my hands.

"What is it?" I asked, trying to open it.

"Trust you to find that," Lorien laughed, putting his arm around my waist and drawing me to him. Although the clerk had appeared not to be paying attention, he answered before Lorien had the chance.

"That's a cock ring. You put it under the balls and over the dick before your guy gets hard, increases the staying power."

"I see, thank you." I stammered, my face hot and I knew would also be flaming red. Lorien's whole body was moving and when I looked up at him, he was laughing silently.

"At my expense, thanks a lot!"

"Baby, you're the world and all it contains. There is so little enjoyment I get from anything but you." He took it from me and swapped it for a larger one. "This will be a better fit," he winked at me. I blushed again. "And we'll get two of these," he said taking some fur-lined handcuffs off the display. "Hmmm," he mused, reading the label, "I thought it was illegal to hunt acrylic these days. Whoa, some of this definitely," he said, grabbing the milk chocolate body paint. I started to giggle. "Not into shopping today Ash?" he asked as if we were browsing through Myer. I pointed to the massive dildo perched haughtily on top of the display. "You want that? I don't think I can reach it, he'll have to get a ladder ..." he turned to call to the clerk for assistance and I smacked him on the bum. "Oi lady, keep your hands off the merchandise."

He hummed lightly and proceeded to flick through the DVDs, selecting two at random. "Here's something for the girl who loves Johnny, and a multi award winner!" he said, showing me the cover, 'Pirates Collector's Edition'.

"I don't think he was in this trilogy." The other DVD in his hand was called 'Teachers' and he put it back; possibly realising it was a little too close to home. He handed everything to me and pulled a length of fabric from a hook. He smiled at me before putting it over my eyes and tying it at the back of my head.

"Can you see anything?" he whispered at my ear. I shook my head. "Great, we'll take two of these as well." I started to laugh,

"Two? How would we find each other?"

"It's always handy to have a spare. Anything else Baby?"

"No, let's get out of here."

We dumped it all onto the counter and I spotted some XXX fortune cookies next to the register. "Let's get these for everyone else." He grinned at me and grabbed a few boxes, sitting them with our pile. Lorien handed over a credit card, adding his driver's licence to it when the clerk asked for ID.

"That will be $246.99," the clerk said.

"Lorien!"

"What?" I wasn't going to argue the price with him in front of the clerk, so let it go for now.

As soon as we were on the way to the car I said, "How could you pay that much for all that stuff?"

"It can be our Easter present to each other, especially the chocolate paint. Hmm hmm, and I have *such* a sweet tooth," he said, loading everything into the boot.

"Just make sure no one sees inside this bag please!" I said.

"I promise." He sidled over on the front seat to kiss me.

"You're ready to use all this right now aren't you?"

"Aren't you?"

"Holy whips and chains, Batman," I laughed, and he laughed with me, and then prompted me again for my answer. "Maybe..." I said softly. I definitely wanted to cuff him down and eat the paint off his body. I shuddered in delight at the thought, which he noticed and leant in to kiss me again.

I brought Elijah and Keren up again on the way back. "Do you think they're having sex?"

"I'd say so Ash, they've been together nearly as long as we have. Eli may have been a slow starter with you, but I can pretty much guarantee they'd be bumping uglies by now." I laughed at his analogy.

"You haven't really given me any details about your and Keren's past either you know."

"You already know we never had sex."

"Yes, but what *did* you get up to? You can't tell me you were as much of a gentleman as Elijah was with me, considering how quickly *our* relationship moved from one level to the next."

"It was completely different with Keren; I didn't love her."

"I wouldn't have thought that would matter to a sixteen year old at the time."

"Well, it did to this sixteen year old. I was in love with you, remember?" I lowered my face, smiling. When I got past my private little la-la moment, I continued.

"You must have done more than kiss."

"Not really."

"A handful of boob?"

He laughed. "Once or twice."

"Mouthful of boob?"

"That would be tasting and telling."

"You asked me about it with Elijah!"

"I asked whether you had his dick in your hands, not your mouth around it." He was right.

"Lorien, you're keeping secrets from me," I said.

"My mouth never went south from her neck and my hands didn't venture past her waist. How's that for a direct answer?" I was satisfied with it.

When we pulled into the driveway, Elijah was sitting outside in his boxers drinking coffee. He got up to help unload the car. "I'll have that one," Lorien said, taking the brown paper bag out of his hands. Elijah looked at him curiously and continued to grab the other bags.

"Jeez, get enough?" he laughed. They had to make a second trip back just for the alcohol. I took our special bag inside, pulling out the body paint to read the ingredients as I waited for Lorien to come in.

"I knew I'd find you in here with the toys," he said, closing the door behind him. "Shirt off!" he ordered.

"Now?" I asked, my eyes wide. He raised the shirt to my underarms, waiting for me to lift them so he could pull it over my head, reaching around with one hand to unhook my bra. "My, you're getting the hang of that aren't you?" He waggled his eyebrows at me and sat on the bed, unscrewing the cap off the bottle.

"Come to me Baby, Lorien wants his breakfast." I stood in front of him, and he dipped the brush into the semi-viscose liquid, applying it gently to my nipple. "Ooh, pointy," he purred as he lowered his head. A short time later, he drew back from me, smiling as he licked his lips.

I could hear doors opening and closing, the rest of the crowd was awake and active. I grimaced at him, knowing we'd have to put this on hold for a while. "One more, you don't want to feel unbalanced all day, do you?" he asked cheekily before painting the chocolate to my other nipple, this time running the edge of the brush further around, leaving more to be ingested than before.

I held his head to me, not wanting to stop now. He circled the brush around my navel then dotted his way up my body, finally running it over my lips. When we broke from the chocolate kiss he smiled, "You have it all over your face." He kissed and licked it off me.

"Lorien..."

"You know we'll get interrupted..." I knew it. I sighed deeply, but was content to wait for our next opportunity, and with a great deal of enthusiasm, I had to admit. As we went to walk into the lounge room he whispered from behind, "And don't think I've forgotten about the birthday candle you promised me ..." I didn't have a chance to reply as he shunted me forward, bringing us both into full view of the just woken uppers. I thought he'd forgotten about that...

"Morning young lovers," Michael said from the kitchen. "Coffee?" He added two more cups from the cupboard.

"Where is everyone?" I asked.

"Out on the front verandah. Here, carry these will you, they're Bree and Simon's." He handed ours to Lorien and he took his and Elijah's. We passed them around and I took a seat in the corner. Lorien sat at my feet, his arm wending up the inside of my calf, draping his hand over my knee. Each time I went to drink, he'd flex, dragging my knee toward him. *Stop it*! I mouthed, smiling down at him tenderly. He shook his head. *No.*

Michael enlisted Bree's help in the kitchen, and they went in to make breakfast as the four of us started a challenging and vilified game of Uno. Simon and I needn't bothered to have played as the twins hammered each other as hard as their cards would allow at every opportunity. After three rounds of this, Simon turned on Elijah as I did to Lorien and it evened out again, in fact too well, as they turned their attacks back on us in their now unified collaboration. Twins!

Bree held the door open for Michael as he carried out two large plates holding a total of ten bacon and egg rolls, going back in for a tray of glasses and a bottle of juice. I thought he'd gone overboard but Bree and I ate one each and the boys managed to put away two... all gone.

"Come and help me with the dishes," I said to Lorien, standing to take him by the hands, yanking at his arms to get up. He twisted in my grip. Taking hold of my forearms, he pulled me into his lap, cocooning me in his arms. He smiled at me, looking deeply into my eyes, as he poked his tongue out and waved the tip at me.

"Give me some tongue action first Baby," he growled. I laughed and knew it was pointless arguing with him; he had me securely and there was nowhere I could go without his say-so. I leant down and kissed him lightly. As I drew back, his hands made their way into my hair, pulling my face back to his, turning it into a long, slow kiss. We were floating somewhere in the rip of the time and space continuum, oblivious to our surroundings until I heard Michael say,

"After downing two rolls how the hell can he still be hungry?" It broke the mood, and I drew back smiling, my forehead pressed to his, looking back into his eyes.

"Dishes?" he said quietly, and I nodded, standing.

"Let's play this inside," Michael said to the others, "otherwise there'll be no dishes done."

It didn't take us long - there were only two plates, six glasses, mugs and a few assorted kitchen implements and we were soon ready to re-join the Uno championship. We pulled two beanbags up next to each other and were dealt into the next round. "Right O, fresh game, all in, new scores from hereon in. Now... what will the punishment be for the loser?" Michael asked. He tapped the pen against his teeth for a few seconds and then proceeded to tear a piece of paper into strips, handing us each one. "Everyone write down a punishment and the loser picks one at random at the end of the game. Finish time will be..." he looked at his watch, it was 11.30 am now, "4.00 pm. The clock is running people, start writing."

I had no idea what to put, knowing I could possibly be drawing mine out again at the end of the game. I finally wrote 'wear what you sleep in for the rest of the day'. If I managed to lose and get my own punishment, I could at least live with this one. I was sure not everyone else was as concerned with my welfare, especially since there were 'no friends in Uno'. I handed it back to Michael and the game commenced.

It was fairly close for many hours with exception of Lorien and Elijah who made sure they sat next to each other to continue their earlier dual hammering and were a good 500 points behind the rest of us who were closely grouped in scores. Unfortunately, I had Michael on the other side of me, which counterbalanced the fair play Lorien had given without question, thwarting my every move.

At 3.30 pm, it wasn't looking good for me, I wasn't getting any decent cards, and when I had something to play was forced to play it to Lorien, not Michael. Miraculously Lorien lost the next hand with a fistful of 50-point cards. This cycle repeated itself for the next few rounds and suddenly Lorien was at the top of the scores. I realised what he was doing, throwing the game so he'd lose and not me, making me love him even more for his selfless concern. I wasn't the only one to pick this up however and Michael made comment after the very next round when Lorien lost again.

"You're throwing the game twin, aren't you?" he asked, eyebrows raised.

"Why would I do that?" he answered in apparent honesty.

"To save your lady-love from the dragon's fiery breath I imagine," Michael countered.

"If my watch is correct Michael, it's dead on 4.00 pm, game off and I lose." Lorien looked at me and smiled. *Thank you*, I mouthed. He shot me a wicked glance, mouthing back, *you owe me big time!*

"Reach into the bag and pull out your destiny, twin," Michael said, holding the bag out for him to pick a slip of paper. *Please be mine, please be mine, please be mine*! I prayed. He read out the paper 'wear what you sleep in for the rest of the day' and I was relieved.

"Come on Ash, let's go."

"Hang on, you need to change first," Michael reminded him.

"She's what I sleep in," he winked at him, dragging me to our room through a chorus of laughter. I wasn't concerned about wanting to go back to our room; Lorien was not compelled to perform any of the other tasks waiting deviant for him in the bag.

He closed the door and came to lie next to me on the bed, rolling onto his side to face me. "Hello," he said.

"Hi."

"What's your name?"

"Ashlyn Standish."

"Oh, that has a nice ring to it... I think I love you Ashlyn Standish."

"What's *your* name?" I asked.

"Lorien Mercy," he said, laughing.

"Well, I think I love you Lorien Mercy."

"I may need some proof."

"Proof! You can't handle the proof!" He laughed loudly at this, telling me I was one of a kind.

We lay like that for the couple of hours we were sequestered away, playful banter and soft kisses co-starring in our movie roles; we were happy just being alone together. Eventually there was a soft knock at the door. "Dinner's ready." It was Bree and we heard her scurry quickly back down the hall. Lorien grabbed the fortune cookies on the way out the door.

After we'd eaten, Michael was eager to get into the drinking games he had planned for us, opting for 'I have never' as the icebreaker. "The name of the game is if you *have* done what is outlined, you drink. Which means every time you drink, you've actually done what is being stipulated, even though the opening statement is 'I have never'. For example, if I were to say 'I have never attended Sommersett High School, we would all drink, got it?" We all nodded. "I'll go first... I have never... touched Ashlyn's naked boobs."

"Michael, are you going to make me the centre of this whole thing?" I whined, knowing how this was about to unravel.

"No. I have never...touched Ashlyn's naked boobs!" he asked again and laughed when both Lorien and Elijah drank.

"This will be a great way of getting some information about you Baby, Eli's going to dob you right in," Lorien said quietly.

"I have never..." Michael started.

"You've had your go pal!" I told him. He ignored me and continued,

"I have never... given Ashlyn an orgasm." Everyone burst out laughing when both twins drank again; they seemed to be enjoying Michael taking the lead role. With his shot down, Lorien looked at me and raised his eyebrows, smiling. He was obviously not expecting Elijah to have drunk to that one.

"I have never... tasted Ashlyn's vaginal juices."

"Michael!" Lorien was trying not to laugh, and then shrugged his shoulders at me before drinking.

"I'm going to end up blind," he laughed as Simon refilled his glass. "You didn't drink bro?" he asked Elijah. He laughed and shook his head. "I'll have more questions about that orgasm then later."

"Lorien!" I looked at Elijah and he winked at me. "No more about me!" I told them.

"OK, OK..." Michael said as I stood up to go to the bathroom. When I came back, they were all laughing. I could just imagine what I'd missed.

"I have never..." started Simon, "had sex with Ash." They all drank, including Bree, and I had to laugh. I glared at Michael and he pointed at Lorien,

"It was your twin!" My hands on my hips, I looked down at him, frowning.

"It had to be done Baby!" he exclaimed. "How else could I put a stop to it?" You could drive a van through the holes in that excuse! He reached up and pulled me onto his lap, kissing it better.

"I'm sorry Baby, forgiven?" he asked as he passed me my drink.

"I *suppose* so," I sighed, and he laughed, kissing me again.

"Hmm, vodka makes me *randy!*"

"Fresh air makes you randy!" Michael stirred. "Ash hasn't had a drink yet, I need one for her..." he thought for a second and started, "I have never... sucked..."

"For God's sake Michael!" I said, cutting him off.

"OK, I have never kissed a boy, how about that?"

"Are you going to drink?" Simon asked.

"Not this time," he winked at him, leaving us to make whatever we chose from that remark.

"Does my brother count?" Lorien asked.

"Depends on how deeply you've kissed him I suppose," Michael said. Lorien didn't drink. "Come on ladies, down the hatch!" he urged Bree and me. We drank.

"I have never... seen a Standish cock," Michael asked next.

"Is that anything like a Cornish game hen?" Elijah said, and we all laughed. Everyone drank except Bree.

"How does that work?" Bree asked.

"I own a Standish cock, so I've definitely seen one, three in fact," Elijah answered.

"And guys all shower and piss together," Simon added.

"Not always at the same time," Michael said, and we laughed again. "Now Ash, do you need to sink two shots for that one?" I glared at him and he laughed, letting it go.

After several rounds, I was feeling pretty wasted and my stomach hurt from laughing. Michael had managed to embarrass everyone successfully in turn; I was actually thankful he'd picked on me first. As Elijah leant the bottle over to refill my glass, I said, "I don't think I can drink any more of that." I had a horrible taste in my mouth and my throat was on fire. Lorien got up and went to the fridge, pulling out a beer and showing it to me. I nodded and he grabbed one for himself too, coming back to sit in one of the beanbags. He put his hand up to his face and waved me over with his finger and I went to him eagerly, spreading myself over his lap.

All politeness was gone in lieu of the drunken crowd and we kissed passionately, his hands running slowly over my back and thighs. "Aren't you playing anymore?" Bree asked.

"Mmph," we mumbled back, escalating into light moans as we attacked each other's faces with our mouths.

"Isn't it like something out of a fairy-tale?" Michael mused, regarding our carnal feasting. "So sweet and romantic..." Lorien pulled back from me, taking my face in his hands, he stared into my eyes. Our breathing was in sync, hot and urgent.

"Let's..." I hadn't even finished the thought of going to bed before he was standing. He held his hand down to help me up and took me into his arms, our mouths once again fusing to each other's.

"Nighty night!" they called as he carried me to our room.

He threw me onto the bed and ripped his clothes off in a flash before coming to assist me with the removal of mine. "I'm sorry Ash, this might be quick, I'm ready to explode!" he said as he entered me, never before had he seemed this hard. Sure enough, in less than a minute, his speed quickened, and he groaned, ending his torture. "Oh Baby," he said as he rolled to lie next to me, "what you do to me." He laughed quietly and said, "I should've used the ring, you know, to increase the staying power." I laughed with him, thinking back to the explanation the clerk gave me. "Hmmm," he sighed deeply and got out of bed.

"Where are you going?"

"Your turn..." he smiled at me as he went through the bag, pulling out the cuffs and a blindfold. "Are you OK with this?" I nodded quickly and he sat next to me, drawing me forward to kiss me tenderly as he tied the blindfold gently around my head. He straddled over me and shifted me into the centre of the bed, taking my right hand and clicking it into the cuff before attaching it to the bed frame. "Not too tight?" he whispered. I shook my head, my body already thrumming under him as he cuffed my other hand. I was now completely at his mercy. I felt him shift off the bed and heard the light go on, although I still couldn't see anything. After a few minutes I said,

"Lorien...?"

"Shh Baby, it's OK... I'm just setting up the camera. Is that still alright?" I smiled; it was OK. We'd become a rather kinky couple indeed this weekend.

"Lorien," I whispered a few minutes later, "this is becoming maddening." I could hear him chuckle lowly from the other side of the room.

"Patience my love," he crooned and finally I felt him climb back on the bed. He ran his hands up and down the underside of my arms lightly, my back arching, wanting his hands and mouth on me. He surprised me when I felt his lips nuzzling into my armpit, having no idea how sensitive they were as he purred, "So hard," running one hand gently over my breast, the other lowered between my spread legs, circling slowly, "so wet," he said at my ear, his lips at my neck. "Hmm Baby, you like this?"

"Uh huh!" I breathed, feeling myself starting to rise.

"Me too..." He feathered his lips over my nipple, teasing gently as he slipped a finger inside me. "I'm going to have to dry you off you wicked girl, before I can coat you in chocolate." He moved between my thighs and licked slowly, thoroughly, stopping each time I was reaching orgasm.

"Lorien!" I complained.

"Not yet Baby, I just can't seem to keep up with your fluid supply." He separated me with his fingers and buried his face deeper into me, working his mouth noisily. "Hmm, it's better than chocolate..." He shifted a few minutes later, my head was reeling and my body aching, screaming for release. I heard him unscrew the cap from the paint bottle and felt the brush lightly against me as he applied it.

"Oh God, Lorien…" I moaned about ten seconds later and this time he let me reach my Nirvana. I found myself wrenching in the cuffs, wanting to hold his head to me, to run my fingers through his hair. But I couldn't touch him. It was infuriating.

He crawled back up my body, kneeling on either side of me, drawing his thumb across my bottom lip, which I sucked greedily into my mouth. "Hang on," he whispered, and I heard the clink of the brush against the glass bottle again then felt his fingers at my mouth, easing it open as he slid between my lips, tasting of chocolate.

"Hmmm," I moaned as he rocked his hips slowly back and forth, his breathing starting to increase in its intensity. And, all of a sudden, he was gone with a popping noise as he pulled out of my mouth. I heard him ripping open a condom and before he could come back to me, I said, "Free my hands." I wanted to be able to touch him. I was starving for his warm, smooth skin. He uncuffed my right hand and I pulled the blindfold off, finally able to look at him and touch him. "Come here you," I growled when both of my hands were free. As he slid into me, I ran my hands slowly over his marvellous broad back, absorbing its texture.

Our breaths raced and the power once again took us to become a duet. I dug my nails into him, scratching down to his rear and up to his shoulder blades. He threw his head back, crying out loudly, too loudly. I started to laugh. "Bugger them, they know what's going on," he chuckled as he collapsed next to me, taking me into his arms and playing light kisses across my lips. "I love you so much Ashlyn Mercy, my life would be over without you."

"It's going to be difficult to keep topping these erotic encounters," I said, kissing him back.

"There's no such thing as bad sex, well not with you anyway." He leant on his elbow and smiled down at me. We could hear laughing from the next room, not concerned it had anything to do with us - they were still having a good time.

Sometime later Lorien asked me if I was sleepy, I wasn't. "Do you want to go and join them?" he asked. It sounded like a plan and when I looked at my watch, it was only 9.30 pm. "I'm going to feed you more vodka," he said and smiled lecherously at me.

"And I'm going to drink it," I laughed as he flicked off the light and closed the bedroom door behind us.

"Well, if it isn't the fornicating duo!" Michael greeted us. They were all a lot merrier than they'd been when we left the room. I was therefore expecting bawdier comments, and naturally, they did not disappoint. Lorien looked around for the beers he'd left next to the beanbag before our hasty retreat and Elijah told him they'd drunk them. He went to the fridge to get more.

"Or do you want vodka Ash?" he asked me before twisting the lid off the beer. I nodded.

"Vodka makes my fanny sore!" Michael and Bree brayed in laughter, leaving Simon to explain the old joke to us, confusion evident on both our faces. I looked at Lorien, smiling, and he laughed and sat on the floor next to the coffee table, filling my glass for me.

"What have you got on your face?" Bree asked, looking at Lorien. He wiped his hand down the side of his mouth and saw his fingers held traces of body paint. He grinned at me and stood up,

"Better wash my face," he said and disappeared into the bathroom. They all looked at me and burst into laughter.

"What have you been up to in there?" Simon asked and I was terrified of him rummaging through our room.

"Nothing that concerns you!" I said and he let it drop. Lorien returned and sat beside me on the floor, smiling at me widely.

"Sorry to have left you alone with the vultures," he apologised.

"I can handle these idiots," I told him. "Have been for several years now..." I looked around the room at all the people I loved so dearly, shaking my head.

We partied on for a few more hours before I felt Lorien rousing me gently. "Time for bed Baby." I'd fallen asleep with my head in his lap. The last thing I remembered was him running his fingers through my hair, which no doubt assisted in sending me to sleep.

I snuggled into his embrace when back in bed and he came out with the question I'd been waiting for him to ask. "So, are you going to tell me about this elusive orgasm that I've only just learnt about?"

"It was no big deal Lorien..."

"I hope you don't think that about the ones *I've* given you." I looked at him to see whether he was kidding and the grin on his face seemed to confirm this.

"Stop teasing me!"

"I still want to know. Especially since Elijah didn't drink to the oral stimulation question of Michael's. I'm guessing he administered it digitally?"

"Like through his watch?" I laughed.

"You know what I mean..."

"Well no, he didn't."

"How else is there?" he asked confused. "Did the sight of him alone make you so excited you fell into an orgasmic frenzy?"

"Sure, why not."

"Ashlyn..." he admonished.

"What do you want me to tell you Lorien? If you're so curious, ask him."

"He would tell me to ask you."

"Well, you're in the midst of a rather annoying catch-22 situation then aren't you?"

"Come on Baby, just give me the how, where, when and why and I'll leave you alone."

"I was straddled over his leg in the pool at Michael's party because I wanted him to. *And,* Mr nosy, before he did me, I gave him one first. I think that satisfactorily answers all four of your points," I spat out at him, realising I now had the shits. There was no need for me to have had to divulge this information to him as it was none of his business. I hadn't received blow-by-blow encounters of his past life and felt cheated out of my own memories. I went to climb out of bed.

"Where are you going Baby?"

"The hell away from you!" I started crying and dragged my jeans on, not caring where I was going.

"Hey, what's wrong?" he asked, sidling up behind me, trying to draw me against him.

"You! You couldn't have embarrassed me more if you had deliberately tried Lorien," I said, swiping at my running nose. "You've just made me feel so horrible and none of it was even any of your damned business. You seem to think pushing my buttons for your constant amusement is... amusing! But I am *sick of it*. You push and push and reword and pose the questions differently until you get exactly what you're after and it's not only an invasion of my privacy, it's degrading." Now fully clothed, I went for the door. He captured my hand and dragged me back to him, wrapping himself around me. "Let me go Lorien!"

"No Baby, I want you to calm down."

"I don't want to calm down!" I wrenched free and took off up the hallway; he caught me again.

"Ash, please, talk to me." I turned to face him and let him have it.

"Why do you have to know everything? That is the only thing that was precious to me before you came along and now it's just a memory of crap! He was my first real boyfriend, and you have no idea of what that means to a girl. I can't make it go away and I don't want to."

"Have you ever thought that maybe I'm jealous of Eli?" That stopped me short.

"I can't apologise for every kiss, every hand holding encounter because you were second in line at the time."

"No, of course not, but you have to understand even though I approached it in a joking matter tonight, he's given something to you that I never can."

"And what exactly is that?"

"Your first one... your awakening..."

"And then I dreamt about you and it was all over, goodbye Elijah. Why is it that my past is always under discussion? I don't have any information on your Sydney girlfriend, but I don't want to know, I don't need to know... There's nothing I can do to change it so why beat myself up over it? It was before you even knew I existed."

"Exactly, however I knew you when you were going out with Eli."

"Lorien, I still don't know what this is all about. Elijah may have 'awoken' me, but you were given the greatest prize, my virginity."

"I know that, and I love that it was waiting for me."

"We can hear you!" I heard Michael call from the lounge room, and I blushed a deep crimson, knowing that Elijah would also have overheard. I led Lorien back to the bedroom and shut the door before continuing.

"Christ, can you imagine this conversation if I *had* slept with Elijah?" I added. I didn't even want to think about that. "I love you Lorien and that won't ever change. But please, don't take anything more from me. My past is my past and I treasure the moments I had with Elijah. I didn't love him as I do you, but they were so special, so sweet and loving. He cared for me in a way no one else had before him and that's always going to be a gift in my heart, regardless of how I now love you."

"I understand Baby, but I can only tell you how I feel..."

"Well, I don't think I can help you with this Lorien and I have nothing else to say."

"I've been pretty stupid, haven't I?" he asked quietly.

"Yes, all you've done is torment me into a crying jag and I hate it."

"Do you hate me?"

"Don't be silly, I love you, even when you drive me crazy." I didn't want to, but I found myself smiling at him. He smiled back. "You can be very selfish at times though..."

"Only when it comes to you." I knew that.

"Just love me Lorien and stop worrying about the things we can't change."

"That sounds like pretty good advice," he agreed. "Am I forgiven?"

"I suppose so, although I still feel like I want to hit and punch and scream."

"Right here Baby," he said, pointing to his chin. "Come on, I can take it." I drew my fist back and he closed his eyes, poised. I kissed him softly and his eyes opened slowly. "I don't deserve you."

"I know," I said and grinned at him. He sat on the bed and I climbed onto his lap.

"Feeling better now?"

"Kinda." We sat silent for a while.

"Do you want to go back to bed?"

"You never give up do you?" I laughed.

"Nope, and you should be happy now."

"I am, but why?"

"We've just had our first fight," he said and grinned at me.

Easter Sunday

"I had always been taught not to take the Lord's name in vain,
But I can't help but scream Oh God when you're taking me again."

L Standish, 'Ten New Commandments'

WHEN I WOKE, Lorien wasn't there again. Surely after last night he couldn't possibly be up and active already? I sat up and found him in the corner of the room, camcorder running. "What are you doing, I look horrible!"

"I think you're beautiful, even if you snore when you're drunk." I grabbed a pillow to throw at him and noticed the decoration on the bed.

"Oh Lorien!" He'd surrounded me in petals, chocolate bunnies and Easter eggs.

"Happy Easter Baby." He put the camera down and came over to sit on the edge of the bed.

"When did you get all this? When did you *do* all this?" I asked, running my fingers through the petals.

"It wasn't easy, but it was in the back of the car, carefully hidden from those lovely prying eyes."

"I didn't get you anything!" I complained.

"Oh yes you did, I had my fill of chocolate last night," he grinned at me devilishly. "Well, maybe not my fill..." he leant down and kissed me. "I'm sure there will always be room for more." He smiled and I started handing him the rabbits and eggs, making room for him to climb in with me.

"Not this morning Ash. The rest of them are waiting on you to get up. We're spending the day at the beach."

"Can't we follow them?" I whined. He shook his head, smiling. "Can we shower?" I asked brightening, raising my eyebrows at him, hopeful.

"Already had one." He seemed to have an answer for everything this morning. He turned around to get my swimmers out of the drawer and I saw his back.

"Lorien!"

"What?" He turned in surprise at the tone of my voice.

"Your back!" He tried to look over his shoulder. He couldn't see naturally, and there was no mirror in this room. "I'm *so* sorry!"

"What's wrong with it?" I beckoned him over and he sat with his back to me. I ran my fingers lightly over the deep scratches and he flinched. "Ouch, what are you doing back there woman?"

"What did I do to you last night is more the question." He laughed,

"I see! That explains the stinging sensation in the shower."

"Pull your boardies down," I said, leaning over further to see if I'd rendered his bum in the same way.

"I'm wise to you Ashlyn!"

"Seriously Lorien, let me look." It wasn't much better off. In fact, being paler than the rest of his body, it actually looked worse. "Oh Sweetheart, does it hurt?"

"Not really. Nothing a day at the beach won't clear up." I had serious doubts one day at the beach would be able to clear *that* up.

"You're going to have to wear a shirt all day."

"Why?"

"To cover it." He laughed, saying,

"You left your mark on me Baby; you'll have to live with the consequences."

"You love to stir me as much as Michael!"

"No, I just love you." He leant down and kissed me again, lowering me to the bed, his lips now at my throat. When the slow lapping became a hard sucking, I knew I was on the receiving end of a hickie.

"No Lorien, don't you dare!" I said, trying to push him off me, but I was locked down by his forearm and all I could do was struggle futilely.

He finally let go with a loud smack and laughed at his accomplishment. "What a beauty!"

"That's the sin-bin for you for the rest of the day!" I said, frowning at him.

"What's that mean?" he asked, moving in closer.

"No more touching!"

"Let's see if you can withstand your own punishment, little miss easily-aroused..."

"Fifty bucks!"

"You're on." I went to shake his hand and he said, "Uh, uh, uh! That's touching."

"I don't think I'm going to be very good at this," I laughed.

"I know it."

Bree, Michael and Simon had already left in Michael's car and Elijah was waiting on us. "Well check you out," he said. "Nice neck accessory."

"Lorien did it deliberately." I grimaced.

"Why?" Lorien turned around and presented his back to his twin and Elijah whistled between his teeth. "Christ, no more vodka for you two!"

When we arrived at the beach they'd already set up, all we had to do was join them. I stripped off to my tankini and decided on a swim first; I needed to freshen up, feeling a little hung-over. Although early autumn, the temperature was still at an acceptable level and the salt water purified me, body and soul. I could see Lorien talking to them as a group, assuming they'd seen his back. I chuckled a little to myself.

I waved him out and a few minutes later, he sprinted to the water, diving in and surfacing near me. I went to put my arms around his neck, and he backed away. "Sin-bin remember?" He smiled and hooked his arms over a rocky ledge, putting himself on display for me, trying to entice. I wanted that bait. I could feel him reeling me in, my mind fighting against my body like a fish on a line. I poked my tongue out and started to swim out, happy to say it was a victory for the fish in the end. He drew alongside me, matching my stroke.

When we'd swum about fifty metres, I turned to follow the breaker line and after a few hundred metres more, we stopped for a breather. Well I did, and Lorien stopped with me. "Everything OK?" he asked, swimming the few metres back to me.

"Just taking a break." I went to swim closer to him and caught myself. He smiled, then pointed behind me,

"Look." Elijah was out on his board and we watched him, drifting our way slowly towards shore.

On the walk back I asked him what they'd said about his back, reaching out to take his hand as he did mine, but stopped in time. We laughed, not knowing how difficult this was going to be at the onset. However, it was a game now and we would play until there was only one winner. "What do you think their reaction was?" he said.

"I can just imagine." I laughed loudly.

"Well enjoy it Ash, the best is yet to come..." I was confused for a second then remembered my neck.

"Lorien, I have to go home looking like this!" My fury with him was raw again.

"Your neck will heal before my back does," he laughed.

"You can wear a shirt."

"You can wear a scarf!"

"You're proud of it!"

"So are you!" Was I? "No comeback?" he said, thinking he'd won.

"I am *not* proud of it!"

"You love me!"

"I do not!" He tried to smack my bum and I jostled away from him. "No, no no!" He chased me back to our camp.

"Ash, you're getting burnt," he said after we'd caught our breath, lying on our backs under the umbrella. Bree and Simon were swimming near the breakers watching Elijah, and Michael was sleeping on his stomach. "You haven't got any sunscreen on have you?"

"No, I haven't, I got straight in without thinking about it." He reached into the communal bag and grabbed the sunblock, lathering up his hands. "You can't apply it to me," I reminded him.

"What am I going to do with it?"

"Rub it on yourself!" He pulled a face at me and rubbed it quickly into his chest and arms. It was better than TV. I rolled onto my stomach and he onto his side, smiling down at me. I sighed, sinking myself further into the towel, grinding slowly further into the sand, uttering a breathy groan. *You're a tease!* he mouthed.

"I'm going to win," I said and winked at him, slowly running my tongue over my bottom lip and drawing it into my mouth. My eyes languid, I ground myself into the sand again. He smiled and shook his head, so I tried a new tactic. I sat up, checking where everyone was before peeling my tank over my head. "Oh dear," I said in mock dismay, "what a lot of sand I have stuck to my body." I demurely ran my hands over myself. He screwed his face up and made dramatic clutching gestures at me.

"No... mustn't!" He jumped up and ran to the water. I laughed, replacing my top.

"Is this a little sex game?" Michael asked.

"I thought you were asleep!"

"Never assume I'm asleep," he said, pulling his glasses further down the bridge of his nose before peering at me over the top. "Do you still want that sunscreen on?" he asked, sitting up.

"You never were asleep." I said, rolling onto my front again. As he smeared it all over my arms, shoulders and legs he said,

"I'm really happy for you Ash. You two make a great couple."

"For your amusement?" He laughed and said,

"Yes Darling, *always* for my amusement, but you seem to keep stumbling into my traps!" We both laughed and he continued, "It's great to see you both so happy though. Roll over..." As I rolled over, I pulled all of my hair behind my head to get it out of the way and he burst out laughing. "Snap! I don't have to set a trap; you just walk into them!" I remembered my neck... "Jesus, you two *were* in the wars last night, weren't you?" he asked, moving his finger across the massive hickie. "It's like the size of my fist! Ash you are one lucky girl if he has a sucker on him like that!" I swiped out at him playfully.

"Isn't it *vodka* that's supposed to make your fanny sore?" I said and he laughed. We spent so little time alone lately; it was great to be having some friend time with him again.

He covered my front in sunscreen and then I did him, glad he was putting it on for a change. "What's the sex game about today?" he asked in all sincerity.

"If this comes back to bite me Michael..." I warned.

"I promise!" So I told him. "Do you reckon you'll be able to hold out?" he asked, checking out Lorien in the water.

"I've got more weapons," I laughed.

"So, you got your happily ever after, Ash," he said, laying back on the blanket. This was a statement, not a question. "To think your little heart was broken and then Prince Twin rides you off into the sunset after all."

"I have *you* to thank for that." I lay down next to him and hugged him. He draped his arm around me, squeezing my shoulders.

"Nah."

"Yeah!"

"OK then, yeah." He smiled down at me and kissed me on the cheek. "You know you're OK for a girl." I pulled a face at him,

"So are you." He laughed.

Lying on our stomachs we got a good game of noughts and crosses happening in the deeper wet sand. I was ahead by two games when Lorien wrung his wet hair out, down my back. I rolled over to abuse him, and he plonked a lump of seaweed on my stomach. As I got to my feet, he took off up the beach, knowing I was in hot pursuit. I pegged the weed at him as hard as I could and was surprised to see I'd actually managed to splatter it against his legs. A few metres down the beach he stopped dead and I screeched to a halt, not wanting to run into him. "What are you going to do about it?" he asked.

"Nothing," I said, and stood there smiling, my arms crossed in front of me. He took a tentative step, and then another, watching my face.

"I give up." He ran at me and this time it was me who took off.

"Find some control!" We laughed crazily as he chased me in a zigzag across the beach.

He thought he had me cornered against the rocks. I ran left and he dodged in that direction, closing the distance between us. I feigned right and he cut me off again. "Come here little one..." he crooned. "Come to Lorien!" I saw a wet, green mass sailing through the air, coming from the ocean. Simon had hurled a clump of weed at us and it was going to smack Lorien right in the back of the head. When he turned in surprise, I shot around to the other side of the rock. After a few seconds I peeked around the left side; Lorien wasn't there. I turned to try the other way and he was standing directly behind me. Grabbing me, I screamed.

"That scared me," I laughed then recollected our bet. "You owe me a cool fifty, loser."

"I don't have it on me," he patted himself down.

"I'll have to take it out of your hide," I said, sidling up to him. He raised his eyebrows at me, and I turned him around in renewed realisation, checking out his back. "Look what I've done to you..." The salt water had helped a little, but it was still angry looking, redder in fact than it had been this morning.

"It was through a touch of love," he said and turned back around, hugging me to him.

"I hope you never love *me* that much." He smiled and kissed me as another clump of weed hit the sides of our faces. Simon was a good shot.

We walked past the water's edge to get out of weed-range and Lorien sat down where the water was nearly waist deep. "Come and have a cuddle." I sat straddled across his lap and the waves moved us slowly in a gentle undulation. "It's been a great few days," he sighed and pulled me tightly against him. The first time we'd spent a substantial amount of 'away' time together I didn't want to go home, ever. Now we were together every night, going home was not the tragedy it had once seemed.

"We've had lots of dirty sex, you dirty boy." His smile became a leer.

"Not today…"

"And whose fault is that?"

"Theirs!" he motioned behind him to the rest of the clan.

"We didn't have to come with them."

"Aren't you glad we did though?" I nodded, it was yet another great day and I loved the beach. He was silent for some time, in his own thoughts. When I looked down at him, he was grinning at me.

"What's that about?" I asked, tucking his damp curls behind his ears.

"I was thinking back to our first day at Glassread." This made me smile.

"And?"

"And... there must be a cave or an abandoned rock ledge around here somewhere."

"As wonderful as that sounds you have Buckley's chance *mate*."

'Why?" he asked, unconvinced.

"Our friends weren't there for starters. Who knows when one of them would come looking for us, just on the off-chance of finding us fornicating."

"Fornicating," he laughed.

"Michael called us the fornicating duo the other night, it sort of stuck."

"We're eating!" Simon called out, interrupting our thoughts.

"That was *my* intention..." He stared at me, his head slightly lowered. My stomach rolled lazily, and I tingled, trying to suppress a shudder. "Second thoughts?" he asked. I smiled and ground my pelvis against him, lowering him back to float in the shallows, my arms on either side of him supporting me as I kissed him. "You are *such* a *tease*," he whispered, then continued the kiss. I could tell he loved it...

I could hear them on the beach, a crescendo of voices steadily rising, "Whoooaaaaaaaaa!" and then the sound was cut off completely as a wave crashed over us; we came up spluttering.

"Bullseye!" yelled Elijah, the rest of them still laughing loudly.

"They could have warned us it was coming," I said, getting to my feet.

"It wouldn't have been any fun for them though, would it?" He took my hand and we walked back to them, ignoring their high spirits as we flopped onto the blanket; Lorien giving them the finger, making them laugh harder.

"Watching you guys is better than going to the movies, I swear." Simon sighed, going back to his sandwich, shaking his head and chuckling.

I was happy to lie like this for a while. I felt tired, but warm and secure with Lorien lying on his stomach next to me, his arm draped over my back. I dozed, only partially aware of the proceedings going on around me. "Are you eating, Lori?" Elijah asked several minutes later. Lorien grunted at him, half asleep and staying there for the moment it seemed.

"Leave him alone, there's plenty left," Bree said. Lorien rolled onto his side and sidled in behind me, using one arm as a pillow, wrapping the other around me. We slept, our breathing falling into the rhythm of the wind and the waves.

I was awoken by a loud crunch, feeling a little disoriented as I opened my eyes. Lorien was still lying behind me, but was now eating an apple at my ear. I scooted onto my back, looking up at him, my eyebrows drawn. "You woke me deliberately," I accused.

"Nuh uh, that's why I didn't move, I thought *that* may have woken you," he answered around a mouthful of apple. He offered it to me and I took it, wanting to get rid of the salty taste in my mouth. He leant into the esky and grabbed a sandwich, shaking it at me. I shook my head and he put it back, coming out with another apple. He took a huge bite and grinned at me, apple juice running down his chin.

"Kiss me," I said. He immediately spat out the apple and launched himself at me, working his lips against mine in the most delectable of ways. I came up laughing. "I meant with the mouthful of apple." I turned to look down at him still lying there, smiling at me.

"Are you trying to choke me, woman?" I rolled to lay on top of him, my forehead pressed to his and he kissed me again, just as intimately. I tilted my head back as he ran his lips down my neck, nuzzling into me just above my collarbone.

"Lorien!" I pulled back. He'd tried to give me another hickie.

"You looked lopsided Baby!"

"How about I get your name tattooed around my neck?"

"I'd never forget who I was," he smiled at me. "I'm sorry Ash," he crooned, drawing me back down.

"You aren't!"

"No, I'm not," he laughed, pulling me to him regardless.

It was still only mid-afternoon when we packed up to go back to Michael's and there was going to be a line-up for the shower. "Is there a hose out the back?" I asked him, happy just to rinse the salt off me; I wasn't concerned about shampooing and so on.

"I think so," he said, and I went to have a look. Coiled on a hanger against the side of the house it was, fully in the shade. I turned it on lightly and the rest of them came out into the backyard as I ran the stream over my hair, letting it course down over my body taking all the salt and sand in its wake. It was really cold but rejuvenating, making me feel so much more refreshed and vibrant.

"Next," I said, and Bree took the hose from me. Lorien handed me a towel. I was happy to dry off in the heat of the backyard and lay it on the grass, sprawling over it face down. Bree handed the hose to Lorien when she was finished and I watched him, his hair wet and straight, his brown muscles flexing as he moved the spray across his chest and stomach. When he stuck the stream down the back and then front of his boardies, I laughed aloud and he flicked the hose at me.

"Having a good perve?" he asked.

"Yes, thank you."

When he'd finished, he passed the hose to Simon and came over to lie directly on top of me, soaking me again with cold water. I tried to buck him off with no success so reached behind to grab him. Instead, he grabbed me, holding my arms straight out in front, immobile for the second time this weekend. "Do I need to get the cuffs?" he asked, but not quietly enough.

"You're joking, aren't you?" Bree asked, sitting down next to us, drying her hair with a towel.

"What are they up to now?" Simon asked as he plonked down next to her. I looked at Bree with my eyebrows raised and a puppy dog look on my face, begging her not to say anything. *Thank you*, I mouthed to her a few minutes later when I caught her eye and she smiled at me. *I want to talk to you!* she mouthed back and I was unsure what about. Lorien and I? Her and Simon? Something altogether random? She certainly had my curiosity aroused and it was a nice change to just *being* aroused.

Michael bustled the twins and Simon off to get another few cartons of beer and I was thinking this a sham to get rid of them for a while. Usually when Bree wanted to talk to me it also included Michael. When we heard the car pull out, I asked them what was going on. "I just wanted to catch up with you Ash. It's been ages, and I really do want to know if you have a set of handcuffs in the bedroom." All three of us laughed.

"Two pairs actually."

"What?" they asked incredulously, laughing again.

"You two are into some pretty serious stuff then?" Bree asked, a little timidly. I thought about all the toys we actually had in the room with us and of what Elijah had walked in on Friday, and laughed. But how could I explain any of this to them properly without it sounding like we were becoming sexual perverts. I certainly didn't think of myself in this way, it was simply silly fun, albeit incredibly *erotic* silly fun.

"Well come on, out with it Ash." Michael prompted. I gave them a rundown on the shopping excursion, deciding not to mention the camcorder episode.

"Body paint! So, that's what Lorien had on his face last night. What's it taste like?" Bree asked.

"Want to try it?" I asked, standing to go and get it.

"Bring it all out," Michael said, "and grab some beers too please!"

I stuffed it all into the bag it came in and upended it onto a towel in the backyard. They had a good chuckle, picking up the blindfolds, playing with the cuffs, tasting the body paint. When Bree picked up the ring she did as I had, trying to open it like a bracelet. When I told her what it was, she dropped it immediately saying, "Ewww."

"He hasn't used it yet," I laughed.

"Chances are he's going to though hey?"

"Probably," I rolled my eyes, not that it would bother me if he wanted to, considering what it was for... Michael cuffed himself to Bree and then Bree to me and they looked at each other in recognition.

"Lorien's back!" They laughed in unison.

"Try to get the blindfold tied around her with your hand cuffed, Ash." Michael said shortly, always a game at the ready. It was a difficult thing to do, as I had to manoeuvre her cuffed hand at the same time I used my free one, but I was finally successful.

"Your go," I told Bree.

"And leave the blindfold on whilst you do it," Michael added to ensure a more difficult level.

Bree had it tougher than I, as both of her hands were cuffed. She reached for Michael who kept moving away, making it impossible. "Will you stay still Michael!" she laughed, realising he was avoiding her searching hands. We all laughed, not hearing the car doors close as the guys came home. As we heard their voices coming down the side path, I panicked.

"Crap!"

I started fumbling around on the towel looking for the keys to the cuffs, knowing I would be too late to get everything out of sight before they rounded the corner. Simon and Elijah broke into peals of laughter the second they saw us sitting there locked together, Bree blindfolded. I checked Lorien's face and he seemed OK with it, a small smile at his lips. I didn't think he'd care; this was my embarrassment and he was lapping it up. I'd been *so* busted. Elijah and Simon sat down with us, forming a circle. There was nowhere I could run and hide, not without dragging Bree and Michael with me and I doubted Michael would have allowed it. I was already blushing before they'd even opened their mouths, still looking frantically for the key to free me from Bree and Michael. "Christ Standish, what have you done to our little Ashlyn?" Simon laughed, picking up the body paint. "She was such a sweet little girl before you came along… it explains your back though mate, and her neck." He shot Lorien a grin.

"Shut up Simon!" I warned him, but knew it would do no good. He picked up the brush, still coated in dried chocolate and went to stick it in the bottle.

"I wouldn't use the brush Simon," Lorien said, taking it from his hand. He smiled at me, both of us knowing where it had last been. "We forgot to wash it out Ash," he said and winked, focussing the attention back to me.

"Was it on you or her?" Simon asked.

"Shut *up* Simon!" I told him again.

"That makes me think it was on you Ash." He was wrong.

"That brush has been dipped repeatedly in the body paint for those of you who tasted it…" Lorien said, taking special notice of Elijah, who currently had his finger dipping back into it for another try.

"Argh!" Bree and Michael screamed, rubbing their palms over their tongues. I hadn't thought about it when they wanted to try it. I suppose I should have realised, they should have realised, it *had* already been used.

"You don't look too worried Elijah," Bree said. He shrugged his shoulders,

"I went out with her and he has the same DNA as me. What difference does it make?" He dug his finger into it deeper and sucked a huge gob of it into his mouth. "It's good." He threw me a smile and I blushed even harder.

"We'll be throwing that out so hook in bro," Lorien said as he bent down and picked the keys up off the grass where I'd flicked them at some stage, whether during my panicked search for them or possibly, when I first upended the bag. I smiled at him in relief, wanting to end the manacled trio so I could put everything back out of sight. He smiled at me widely and dropped them into his pocket, turning and disappearing into the house.

"Lorien!" I screamed at him. "Get back out here!" A few minutes later he did, camcorder in hand. He sat a far enough distance from me so I couldn't reach him and started recording.

"This is too good to miss, Ash," he said laughing. I put my hands to my face groaning, and they all laughed again including Bree and Michael. I'd dragged Bree's arm with me, and it was sticking out at a weird angle, hanging from my cuff.

"Up girls," Michael said.

"Where are we going?" I asked.

"Michael has to pee," he said, smiling widely.

"Lorien," I whined. "Please, open the cuffs."

"You got yourself into this Baby, work with it," he advised. Michael dragged us over to the fence and Bree warned him,

"You'd better be a lefty when you hold that thing." Michael laughed and reached into his boardies, starting to pee into the bushes as Bree and I turned our backs on him.

He laughed through the entire flow, taking longer than it should have. The twins and Simon were enjoying our confinement too and I knew we'd be linked together for quite some time. "At least get us another beer," Bree said. Elijah got up and went into the house, bringing out six.

"Don't give any more to Michael, we'll be camping at the fence all afternoon," I said laughing, having now passed the initial embarrassment stage.

"What can we make them do?" Lorien mused, his finger tapping at his chin, thoughtful.

"Bree's ticklish," Simon told him, and started to make his way over to us.

"You'll be single in five minutes if you lay one finger on me Simon," she warned, trying to look stern but breaking into a laugh. "Please Si, don't..." I couldn't believe he sat back down, deciding to leave her alone, and I was glad. If she started bucking around, Michael and I would be dragged with her and it would probably hurt.

"Did you bring all this with you Standish?" Simon asked.

"No, we got it when we went to the supermarket the other morning."

"What supermarket do you go to?" Michael asked, knowing the story already. "I must say though, this is impressive," he added, picking up the ring and looking through it. Lorien laughed, the camera still recording.

Simon had been looking at Lorien pensively which didn't bode well. I prayed he wasn't going to put the pieces together, having taped our sexual liaisons before and after we'd bought the accessories. It was screaming at me so clearly, what was on that camera, and I assumed they could all hear it too. Simon obviously did, asking Lorien what else was on it. "Nothing else, not what you're thinking anyway," he laughed. "Care to have a look?" I stared at him, eyes wide and mouth agape. *It's OK*, he mouthed, understanding he must have transferred it to the laptop. I relaxed and saw Elijah's face contort from the corner of my eye, his hand to his mouth, trying to conceal a massive grin. He knew what *had* been on that camera. I realised uncomfortably I now had to pee.

"Lo-re-en..." I sing-songed.

"Yes Baby?"

"Unlock these cuffs."

"No Baby." They all laughed, having no idea how the two beers I'd consumed were filling out my bladder.

"Do you love me?" I asked, kittenishly.

"Yes Baby."

"Well take these damned cuffs off me!"

"No Baby." This was such an ever-amusing game to him; taking it all in his stride, making me suffer for bringing out the gear in the first place.

"Do you ever want to have sex again?"

"Most definitely Baby."

"Well take these damned cuffs off me!"

"No Baby." *I need to pee!* I mouthed. Elijah and Simon saw it too and broke into laughter again. Lorien just grinned at me.

"What?" asked Bree. The three of us were sitting in a line so neither her nor Michael noticed the interchange.

"She needs to pee," laughed Simon. Michael reached past Bree with his free hand and pressed it firmly against my abdomen, increasing the pressure.

"Michael, stop it," Bree laughed. "If she wets herself I might cop it too."

"Keep that camera rolling bro," Elijah said.

"Please Lorien," I whined as I tried to scoot away from Michael's hand.

"Say 'I love you Lorien'." I poked my tongue out at him. "Put that thing away if you aren't going to use it," he laughed, and prompted me again, "I'm waiting Baby..."

"I love you Lorien!"

"And you are the best boyfriend in the world..."

"And you are the best boyfriend in the *whole wide* world!"

"The best kisser..."

"The best kisser, the most erotic lover, the most handsome, smartest, incredibly talented, biggest dick in the world...! Does that cover it?"

"Pretty much," he said, grinning, "although I'm not sure whether you were *calling* me a dick or referring to it," he drawled out, eyebrows raised with his head tilted to the side. *I'm sorry*, I mouthed. There was nothing I could get past him, and my furtive attempt to lay insult had not gone unnoticed. He reached into his pocket for the keys, smiling back at me. When his face turned into a look of surprise I thought he'd lost them and said,

"You're *kidding* me, right?"

"Yes," he laughed, pulling out the keys he unlocked me from Bree. I bolted inside.

On the way back out, I flicked on the stereo and saw Bree still cuffed to Michael and I laughed at them, passing them a beer and one to each of the others. "You don't deserve this," I said, pouting at Lorien as I held the beer away from his outstretched hand. "The only thing I should give you is a punch in the nose."

"Ooh feisty…" Lorien said. I knew Elijah wouldn't remember saying those exact words to me when I was fighting him off on his birthday, so didn't even flinch. A sneaky look at Elijah confirmed this.

"Come on Baby, don't be mad." He knew I wasn't, but I was going to make him pay now. I held my hand out for the keys and he sighed and passed them to me, giving him his beer. I unlocked Michael from Bree and stowed them safely back in the bag. They also needed to go fairly desperately as Michael headed for the bushes again and Bree ran inside.

"Now put your hands out," I ordered, which he did, grinning.

"Are you going to cuff yourself to me?" he asked. I ignored him as I tried to cuff him at the ankle, but they were too small so instead I moved one of his arms under his leg and then cuffed both of his wrists. "Who knew how much more fun these would be?" he asked as he looped his leg over the chain, freeing it. I hadn't realised how easy it would be to escape from what I considered a body knot when I cuffed him. Not that it mattered, he was still bound and that's the way he would stay until I chose to free him. Remembering the keys were back in the bag, I put them down the front of my tank bottoms in case someone else thought they'd release him.

"Kiss me…"

"No!" I went to sit between Simon and Elijah.

"Kiss me," he said, standing.

"Kiss this!" I shot back quickly, pointing to my bum.

"Yeah! Go for it twin," Michael laughed as he finished up and came back to join the group.

Lorien was so damn quick at times and was nearly on me by the time I got to my feet, realising he was coming at me. As I turned to run, he slipped his cuffed arms over me, capturing me at the waist. "Gotcha!"

"No kiss for you!"

"But Baby…" he started to run his hands across my waist and wiggled against me from behind. What I thought was an attempt to turn me to face him I knew was a ploy when I felt his hand work into my bottoms, snatching out the keys. He had them off before I could blink and he grabbed me, kissing me unashamedly in front of the boys. Drawing back, he grinned. "I love you Ash," he said and kissed me again tenderly.

"Yes, yes, we all love her, but you come and sit with me. I want you to be *my* girl again for five more minutes."

Michael took me by the hand and pulled me down to sit with him, his arm around me. Accepting his defeat, Lorien lay back, resting on his elbows. I noticed Elijah had a wistful smile on his face, possibly wanting me to be his girl again for another five minutes. I was certainly less maintenance than Keren.

The toys became too much for Michael after a while and he said, "I have an idea." He got up and grabbed the blindfolds. "Everyone sit in a big circle with your backs to the centre." As we shuffled into position, he told us to cover our faces. "I'm going to blindfold two of you and you have to guess who each other are by touch."

"Michael…" I said in warning. This could be disastrous.

"Keep your mind above your navel for once please Ashlyn!" he admonished, and they laughed. "Now no making noises, people who aren't blindfolded, or you'll give away who hasn't got one on."

When he said OK, I was blindfold-free and turned around to see who had - he'd blindfolded the twins and it was hard not to laugh. He stood them up and led Lorien within a metre of his brother, telling them to go for it. I wondered briefly, what someone looking over the fence would make of this.

No sooner had one of them made contact they both said each other's names. "It's not easy to fool a twin," I told Michael.

"I guess not," he said, passing the blindfolds to Lorien, and Elijah returned to his space in the circle. I felt it at my eyes, knowing I'd be his target, unaware however, there was only one blindfold in play for this session.

"OK," he said, and when they all obviously turned around, I could hear a few muffled laughs, but didn't know to whom they belonged. "Go for it Ash, you're in position." I reached out in front of me and felt nothing so took a small, tentative step forward and felt a hand on my wrist, guiding me to what ended in a handful of crotch.

"This better be who I think it is, and God help you if I'm right." They were rolling on the ground clutching at their stomachs as I ripped the blindfold off. Lorien still had my hand against him and was smiling at me; unintentionally I hadn't drawn back either. His eyebrows raised.

I snatched my hand back, laughing, and got onto my tiptoes to kiss him briefly.

"OK, back into the circle," I said, picking Simon and Michael once they were settled.

We played until it got dark, and Michael switched on the lights, firing up the brick barbeque. We ate hamburgers and drank more beer, laughing and talking. It was great to be spending a fun night as a group, with Lorien and I managing to behave ourselves for the several hours we were outside.

Home Again, Home Again

"It's not hard to walk away, to leave when there are no options,
The hardest thing is always going home."

L Standish, 'Divided Road'

MONDAY FINALLY ROLLED AROUND, and we reluctantly dragged ourselves out of bed for the last time, hearing the others stirring. I stripped the sheets and pillowcases, putting them in the laundry bag Michael had left out for us all. I sat down on the now bare bed sighing, wondering if we would ever sleep in it again. Lorien sat next to me. "Sad thoughts Baby?" He drew my face to his, brushing his lips to my temple.

"Just wondering if we'll be here again, it's been such a great long weekend." I looked up at him, and knowing what thoughts were now racing through my head, I blushed. As always, he was straight onto it and chuckled, pulling me forward to kiss me.

"Are you coming back to my place?" he whispered, running his hands down my throat and across my shoulders.

"Uh huh," I breathed. The thought of him being in the spare room at home tonight was inconceivable.

We checked under the bed and in the drawers and wardrobe to ensure we had everything before closing the door behind us. Elijah was in the kitchen already dressed, his bags on the coffee table. "Morning guys," he greeted us, coffee cup to his lips.

"Got the keys Eli?" Elijah threw them and Lorien caught them in his left hand, going to unlock the boot.

"What time do you want to head back Ash?" he asked, getting up to make Lorien and I coffee.

"Whenever you like, it doesn't worry me," I said, sitting and taking the cup from him.

"What time do you want to get going Lori?" he asked his twin coming back through the front door for a load.

"No point putting off the inevitable."

"Just because your playground has been dismantled doesn't mean I can't surf," he threw at him, grinning.

"Whatever you want to do Eli, it doesn't faze me." Lorien looked to me and I shrugged my shoulders.

"Another day at the beach doesn't worry me either." Lorien grabbed more bags and I helped him, making it the final load.

When we came back, Elijah said he was happy to go straight home, realising our stuff would be in the hot car and we had electronics and chocolate, also mentioning the holiday traffic we'd no doubt encounter. It was just going on 9.00 am. If we left now, we'd be home by 10.30; both boys were happy to wait to have breakfast until then. This settled, we said our goodbyes to the others, thanking Michael for his hospitality. "Come over on Wednesday for a swim," he said. We'd be there.

Lorien drove so I could sit up front with him, leaving Elijah free to fill us in on the bits and pieces we'd missed over the weekend. There was surprisingly a lot. He gave us the reaction to the fortune cookies once discovered, what had happened to Frankie and Cyndi, the list of punishments we'd not been privy to... "What did Simon mean by 'planning something'?" I asked Elijah, referring to Simon's explanation as to why Cyndi and Frankie couldn't make it.

"He wasn't sure either, but we'll find out soon apparently. That's all Frankie told Simon." I wondered briefly if we were soon to become faux aunts and uncles... They hadn't been at the twin's birthday in February. The last time I'd seen Cyndi was December so she *could* be entering her second trimester by now, showing nicely. I went to ask the boys what they thought about my suspicions as they both broke into laughter.

"I'm glad I didn't get that one," Lorien said, still smiling. Elijah was filling him in on the punishment lists, making us guess who wrote each one. Other than mine, they consisted of give Ash a hickie, the electric chair, fondle the boobs on the girl of your choice, get Bree a beer and impregnate Ashlyn.

"Why is it always me?" I complained, rolling my eyes.

"You always were Michael's favourite target," Elijah confirmed.

"And his," I jostled Lorien's elbow, and he nudged me back, grinning. "How the hell would Bree have been able to impregnate me if she'd lost?" I asked, laughing at the thought.

"I think they might have been rigged Ash, that one definitely being Michael's." Ah, it tickled us all... "So, whose is who?" Elijah prompted.

"Lorien's was to give me a hickie," I glared at him for effect, "Bree was the beer, Simon was the boobs and yours therefore was the electric chair."

"Correct."

"Thanks for not sticking it to me." He didn't answer, instead barking out a quick laugh, possibly at my choice of words. Lorien reached over and took my hand, smiling at me when he noticed my blush. Quickly changing the subject, I asked Lorien, "Which one were you glad you didn't get?" assuming it to be the pregnancy issue.

"The electric chair, what else."

A rubber band snapped in my head taking my thoughts to the strength of our lovemaking, on one instance it being so full of love and power to create new life inside me. I knew right then I wanted to be a mother one day, and I could see a picture of myself holding a beautiful baby girl who looked just like her handsome daddy. My body felt flushed at the idea of the essence of impact we could have on each other, and I looked at Lorien who was already focussed on me. He tilted his head to one side and smiled lightly, silently questioning my thoughts. I shook my head and turned my attention back to the road, not wanting to express such intimate feelings in front of Elijah. I could hear Lorien chuckle, knowing I'd once again been visiting Daydreamville.

I then felt badly for Elijah. His whole weekend had been turned over when Keren decided to leave on Friday. "Have you heard from Keren since she left?" I asked him over my shoulder.

"No, she told me she wasn't going to ring until we got back."

"Are you OK?"

"Sure, and it'll be fine. I'm guessing Lori's told you everything?"

"Yes," Lorien squeezed my hand. "Is there anything I can do to help Elijah?"

"I think her knowing you know would possibly make it worse for the moment, but thanks anyway." I felt a little helpless, wanting to be able to do something to make him as happy as his brother and I were. Unfortunately, this one was well out of my hands.

We got home not long after 10.30 am, and Elijah was still regaling us with the notes in the fortune cookies. As we opened the door, he was in the process of telling us one of Simon's, "'For arsehole to be licked it must be perfumed well'." Cara and Nick were on the sofa as we entered; overhearing Elijah's words, their eyes stared at us widely. "It's OK Mum, it was a fortune cookie." We all laughed again as Cara and Nick passed a smile between them.

"Yours son?" Nick muttered with a grin, going back to his paper as Cara stood to greet us each with a hug.

"Looks like you had a good time kids…and it looks like you brought more home than you took!"

"We divvied the food up before we left," Lorien interjected, moving the brown paper bag away from the reusable shopping bags as his mother went to take them to the kitchen island. Deciding it was best out of the way entirely, Lorien took it and the laptop up to his room.

"I'm going to have a shower," I said, and grabbed my and Lorien's bags.

"Here, I'll take those," Elijah said, taking the bags and following me up the stairs. When we reached the hallway outside Lorien's room, I said,

"Thanks for not mentioning the laptop show to anyone," a little embarrassed. Not saying anything further to make my already pink face go red, he leant down and planted a kiss on my cheek, taking my chin in his hand to rub his thumb across it, smiling at me.

"No problem," he said finally and winked. He went to his own door, leaving Lorien's bag in the hallway.

"Good luck with Keren," I encouraged, and he flashed back a smile before closing the door behind him.

Lorien was fiddling with the camcorder when I opened the door. "Ready to watch it again Mr Eager?"

"I'm transferring it onto a USB so I can get it off the camera." I looked at him open-mouthed.

"You insinuated it was already *off* when Simon was starting to get nosy."

"I had to bluff Ash. If he thought he'd find something he would've made it his mission to watch it."

"Pretty high stakes there Maverick!" I said, dragging his bag through the door. He got up to take it from me and threw it onto the bed. "See the bag, feel the bag, be the bag," I chanted, wanting him to throw me onto the bed as well. He laughed loudly and took me in his arms.

"Let me get something to eat first," he said, kissing me on the tip of my nose.

"I'm going to have a quick shower, see you in a bit." I kissed him back and went to walk into the bathroom, but he didn't let go of my hand and my arm stretched out behind me.

"Oh no you're not," he grinned down at me, "you can wait for me." He wended his arms around me and kissed me deeply, making his intentions clear.

"OK," I whispered, my head spinning when we came up for air.

"Ten minutes, I promise." I smiled at him and he led me back downstairs to get some breakfast.

Even though every single member of this family was aware of Lorien's and my physical relationship, I still went up the stairs before him, alluding to *not* being in the shower together once he came upstairs. He thought it was cute that I kept up the charade. I did it for the sole purpose of being able to look his parents in the eye.

I locked Elijah's side and flicked on the shower radio as I lathered up my salty hair, singing and jigging along to the music. I didn't hear him come in and I didn't know how long he'd been standing there. It was only when I rinsed the soap out of my hair did I notice him, and I screamed. "God, that was like 'Psycho'," I laughed. Instead of a knife however, he had the camcorder in his hand.

"Sorry Baby, I didn't mean to scare you," he said and positioned the camcorder on the bench so its eye was angled into the shower. He quickly stripped off, joining me. There was a knock at Elijah's side of the door.

"Are you alright Ash?" I covered my mouth with my hand looking at Lorien, my eyes huge.

"It's OK Eli, I scared her," he answered for me.

"I should've known you're in there too." Then he was gone.

"Did you lock his side?" he asked, squirting shampoo into my hands.

"Of course!"

I washed his hair and then conditioned it, loving running a comb through, taking it to its full length. I caught my hand under some of the driblets running out from the tips, reaching around to rub it into his pubic hair. "Oh, soft," he said turning, pulling me under the water jet in a kiss, the conditioner running out of his hair coating both our faces.

He returned the favour, conditioning my hair for me and as he ran the comb down my back, he said, "It's getting so long, it's nearly to your bum." He ran his hand down my slick hair, not stopping once he found the rounded flesh beneath it, tickling between my legs from behind, teasingly. He ran his hand down again, forming a ponytail, milking conditioner from it before he brought his arms around me, working it into my pubes also. He slowly slid his fingers across my body in a silken caress, asking me about the daydream I'd been zoned out over in the car. My groin twitched thinking back to my imagined passion of making a baby and I knew he was assuming it would've been something a little more casual.

"Can we talk about it later?" I asked, turning to face him. His eyebrows drew in slightly, the nuance questioning if everything was OK. "What you're thinking I was thinking is unlikely to be what I was actually thinking…" I said and laughed at the riddle I'd created.

"Something new? You'll have to tell me now…" he implored, pulling me against him, the conditioner now draining from my hair, still coating us in a soft lustrous film.

"It's not really something to be discussed in the shower."

"Try me."

I told him, without editing my thoughts and the way they made me feel, not expecting it to be instant arousal, which it was for him too I noted as he hardened against me. "And you said it wasn't applicable shower talk…" he scoffed, pressing into my stomach. I laughed and he kissed me, and the camcorder played its role, capturing our practise of impregnation.

The bubble of pleasure broke with a snap when we got out of the shower. "Lorien, you didn't have a condom on."

"No." He straightened up to look at me, the towel frozen at his hair.

"We were just talking about the erotic coupling of making a baby and you don't put a condom on?" He knew when my period was due as well as I did.

"It shouldn't be a problem Ash," he said, drawing me into his arms. "A smidge dodgy maybe, but unlikely." I let his words soothe me, making me feel better.

"Me and my big mouth," I said, not revelling in the irony.

"Are you guys going to be in there all day?" Elijah called from his side of the door. I wrapped the towel around me as Lorien unlocked it and slid the door open.

"All yours bro." After he'd stepped back into his room, he cursed and slid the bathroom door back open.

"Hey!" Elijah called, yanking his boxers back up, knowing I could see him from where I stood.

"Zoink!" Lorien said, grabbing the camcorder off the bench. "Sorry Eli, but it's nothing she hasn't seen before." The pillow I had just thrown at him smacked him in the face as he turned back to me with a massive grin. "You'll keep!"

I got dressed and started to go through our bags, putting away his clean clothes, making a pile on the floor with the dirty. Lorien climbed into the pappadum and picked up his bass guitar not plugging it in, choosing to play it acoustic for the moment. He had a few notations on the manuscript on his desk at times, adding or alternating riffs, erasing some altogether. "Holiday's over, back to business?" I asked, as I folded my clean clothes. He smiled up at me in response, continuing his editing. I lay on the bed to watch him at work, eventually swapping the bass for the lead.

"Have you got your violin here Ash?" he asked.

"Which one?"

"Either, I just want the bow." I reached under his bed, pulled out my acoustic violin case, and took the bow out, handing it to him.

"Like I know what to do with it. Come here Baby..."

He scooted to the back of the chair and held the guitar in one hand by the neck to allow me to climb on in front of him. Laying the guitar horizontal over my lap, he encircled his left arm around me to work the frets. "Bow." It was an awkward position, so I shifted slightly, making me perpendicular to him and easier to draw the bow across the strings of the guitar. My eyes opened wide and I smiled when I heard the familiar melody to 'Ashlyn's Song', alternating my bowing to correspond to its flow.

"Oh Lorien, that was fantastic!" I cried, when we were done. There was a slight knock at the bathroom door. It was Elijah.

"That was great. I could hear it from my room." Elijah and Lorien had dually penned 'Ashlyn's Song' and his pride was warranted; it was his praise too.

"Grab the bass Eli." He perched on the bed and we played it through again, Lorien singing this time, and I was more impressed than I had been before.

"Thinking of adding it?" Elijah asked.

"Has a better sound doesn't it?" We both agreed with him. "I'm not sure how we can work it though; two of us are needed to play it this way." He looked thoughtful for a moment, his eyes brightening. "Can I teach you to play the lead Ash?" he asked. I mirrored his excited look with my eyes wide and a grin on my face, saying,

"No!" and let my grin slide into a smile. He pouted. "I'm not the maestro you are. Just leave me alone with my violin please."

"OK, it was just a thought." He kissed softly behind my ear, letting it go.

We ran through a few other songs, but it was definitely a style meant for 'Ashlyn's Song'. "Leave it with me and I'll have a think about it."

"When's the next rehearsal?" Elijah asked.

"Matty is away until next Monday, so tomorrow week." I still didn't like Matty and the fact we were now going to be rehearsing at his place was even worse. Fortunately, the three of us could practise without him and Lorien promised to keep the sessions at Matty's to no more than an hour and a half.

There was a knock at the door and Lorien called out to come in. "That sounds wonderful kids," said Cara as she and Nick came into the room. "Will you play it for us again?" When we'd finished they both clapped, Cara saying, "I'm assuming you're still both considering doing your Bachelor of Music?" We both nodded and I went to get up, to move away from their second-born to a more appropriate area of the room. Lorien's arm around my waist flexed, holding me in position as he leant down to put the guitar on the ground, taking my bow from me and sitting it on his desk. Both hands free, he dragged me back against him and started to kiss the back of my neck lightly. I jabbed him with my elbow and I heard him chuckle, thinking this was hilarious. "I'm glad to see you're both so happy," Cara said, an amused expression on her face having obviously caught our little interaction, and came to give us both a kiss on the forehead.

"Thanks Mummy," Lorien said, grinning up at her. She tousled his hair, smiling, and then turned back to me placing a hand to my forehead.

"My you're hot Ashlyn; you should put on a cooler top." I couldn't see Lorien's face, but I could sure see Elijah's. He was trying not to laugh, knowing what this shirt was concealing at my throat from his parents. Thankfully, Nick then turned the conversation to Elijah.

"Have you made up your mind yet?"

"Yep, I'm going to do medicine." Lorien whistled between his teeth,

"Wow, five years bro!"

"Six actually, including the internship after I graduate."

"Well good for you son," Nick said and clapped Elijah on the back.

"I hope you don't mind me being absent on your birthday Ash, but it's the same day I sit the UMAT exam." All four of us looked at him curiously, as none of us knew what the UMAT exam was. He laughed, realising this and said, "Undergraduate medicine and health sciences admissions test."

"That's a mouthful!" Nick laughed.

"It's not something I can study for either. This will make or break me though if I want to be a doctor."

"You'll do fine Eli," Cara said and planted a kiss on his forehead too.

"Thanks Mummy," he said, replicating Lorien's earlier cheeky response. She rolled her eyes at him and she and Nick left.

"Haven't you got something to do Eli?" Lorien mumbled, his lips still working against my nape.

"You two are always at it. Where do you find the energy?" he laughed.

"Don't blame me!" I cried, trying to wrestle out of Lorien's grasp.

"Goodbye Eli..."

"Sorry Ash," Elijah said. "Call if you need anything." He walked through the bathroom door, sliding it closed behind him, but not before he threw me a grin.

"That was so rude Lorien," I chastised.

"I want to be rude with *you*," he murmured, bringing his hands up to caress me, lowering them again to tuck under my shirt.

"You were, less than an hour ago."

"I just can't get enough of you Baby," he whispered.

"Splattered frogs, raw liver, dead bodies..."

"What are you doing?" he asked, finally drawing back from me. I scrambled out of the seat and turned to face him.

"Taking your mind off it." He rose slowly then sprung at me, tackling me onto the bed.

"Just a little kiss and cuddle then..." which turned into our next sexual session, naturally. I couldn't get enough of him either.

I did so love school holidays. We awoke at 10.00 am the next morning, stretching and just loving the cooler days, taking our time getting out of bed. We still managed to rise before Elijah.

The mail carrier had been and there were two letters, one addressed to each twin in fancy handwriting, in a fancy envelope. Lorien tore his open and two pieces of paper fluttered to the ground, which he picked up before I could reach them. "What is it?" I asked when he took me into his arms to hold me in place, reading the card behind my back.

"Well, well, well," he said, drawing it out for optimal frustration.

"Lorien, what is it?" He handed me the card and one of the slips of paper. It was a wedding invitation from Frankie and Cyndi including details of their registry. "Wow, good on them," I said, then started to laugh. I'd thought Cyndi was pregnant. Getting married hadn't even entered my mind when Elijah explained Simon's version of why that hadn't come last weekend. "What else came with it?"

"I can't remember, but you'll notice the invitation is only for Lorien, not Lorien and partner."

"I'll have one at home too, wise guy," I said and rang home immediately. I asked Mum to open the envelope for me and there was only one slip of paper, of which she assured me several times before I finally hung up. "Tell me..."

"No." He put it behind his back, making me reach for it. "Oooh Baby," he growled, squirming himself against me as I tried to grab behind him.

"Why won't you tell me?" I pouted, pulling out old reliable. When times were tough, go the pout.

"Because Cyndi and Frankie have asked me not to, that's why."

"What would they tell you that they wouldn't tell me?"

"This is going to kill you isn't it? When's the date...?" he looked at the invitation again and laughed, knowing it was over three months away. Elijah came down the stairs and Lorien passed his envelope to him. "Watch this one - she has hands like a piranha."

"O...K..." Elijah responded slowly, looking at his twin with a bemused expression.

"He gets one too?" I whined, "Lorien, tell me." Elijah opened the envelope and two pieces of paper fluttered to the ground, as they had done from Lorien's. I launched myself at them and Lorien swung me by the waist to bring me up and back to him.

"No, no, no, little one, mustn't touch." I hated not knowing what was going on and I knew he'd subtly drive me insane over the next three months. Elijah smiled with recognition at his twin once he'd finished reading all the inserts.

"Lori, I don't think they'd mind if you told her."

"You're making this worse Eli!" he warned him. "They asked us not to and I don't intend to, case closed."

"Fair enough, it's your funeral." A small smile broke out on my face. Elijah would tell me if I asked him to, he seemed to think it was OK I knew.

"No, there will be none of that either." Lorien guessed my facial expression. "Eli if you tell her..."

"I won't, I'm not getting into the middle of this." I flumped down on the sofa, my arms crossed in front of me and a look of scorn on my face. Lorien came and sat next to me, trying to take me in his arms but I moved away.

"I didn't mean to tease... I promise I won't mention it again and I won't rub your face in it, OK? Let it be a surprise, for Frankie and Cyndi."

"OK," I said, mostly play-acting before but still desperate to know what was inside that envelope! He knew me too well though, taking his and Elijah's paper, tearing them into confetti before throwing them in the bin.

"Now, may I please have a kiss?" he asked. I sighed deeply, forlornly,

"If I have to." I had to laugh as he rubbed his hands together briskly.

"Christ, let a person wake up will you," Elijah mumbled as he went through into the kitchen.

My mobile phone rang a few minutes later and it was Michael. He'd just spoken to Cyndi and they were going in to see her and Frankie for lunch. Did we want to go too? I did want to go. I chatted for a while, asking him specifically as to whether he had one or two slips of paper in his invite, and I was left with no more information than I had before he rang. The twins were keen to go as well and that took care of what we were going to do today. I was also secretly hoping I would bust them whispering behind closed doors... but knew neither of them was that stupid.

THE BAND

The Epitome of Matty

"When you give away to someone else who you once loved
It's second hand, no longer new,
Glass and sand."

L Standish, 'Village Row'

"NO!"

"Ashlyn, I'm losing my patience," Lorien warned.

"I don't care, I'm not going." Elijah had been sitting on the arm of the sofa watching this little interaction with great amusement. We were due at Matty's to do our first rehearsal at his place, and I did *not* want to go.

"Come on Ash, we talked about this... We're going to him so he doesn't have to be over here leering at you. I thought it made you uncomfortable?"

"Do you think it'll be any better in his personal environment? I still don't see why I have to come, the three of us can rehearse and you two can rehearse with him."

"It's called being professional."

"I am no pro then!"

"I *will* take you out of here kicking and screaming if I have to."

"Go for your life Lorien," I challenged him.

After I'd been unceremoniously carried to the car and dumped on the back seat, we were on our way to Matty's, me still silently fuming and

Elijah had been no help. "I didn't bring my violin." Lorien reached down to his feet and pulled out my electronic violin case. Elijah did likewise, pulling out my acoustic.

"We thought of that Ash and brought them both so there could be no more excuses," Elijah said, and grinned at me over the front seat.

When we pulled up, Lorien asked for a minute alone with me and drew me into his arms, holding me for a while. "Baby girl, do you think I'd let anything happen to you, let him say or do anything to upset you, make you uncomfortable?"

"No," I sighed, "but you don't always hear it."

"Can you ignore the smart-arse comments from him?"

"I suppose. But you can't leave me alone with him Lorien, not even for a second."

"I promise Ash."

"Well, OK then..."

"That's my girl, thank you Baby." He leant down and kissed me sweetly. I thought about acting up again next time, as I did like this method of thanks. Matty was at the door, watching us.

"Are you guys coming in or are you going to stand out there pashing all day?" I groaned at Lorien and he rubbed my back, smiling down at me. *It will be OK*, he mouthed.

"It had better be!" I warned.

Matty gave us a quick tour of the house before we started. It was a one-bedroom place with a tiny kitchen and bathroom, the living room being the only other room. He had a double foam mattress on the floor of the bedroom and several milk crates that were barely serving their purpose as shelves; most of his clothes seemed to be strewn around on the floor. The bathroom consisted of a shower stall, small vanity and toilet. I made a mental note to myself to make sure I *always* went to the bathroom before we came here in future, I didn't think it had ever been cleaned and the kitchen was not much better. A few fat, lazy flies alighted on the uncovered margarine on the bench, enough to make me nauseous.

Lorien held my hand through the quick sightseeing expedition, keeping his promise to me, possibly realising how much closer to the bone my reflections of Matty had been before we started to argue the point of my attendance today. His nose was wrinkled slightly. No joy was on his face either.

I was hit with a wave of relief when Matty led us into a garage through a doorway off the living room; his drums were set up on a square of carpet. I was glad we'd be rehearsing in here instead of the dingy little house. "Are you guys ready to set up?" Matty asked us but his eyes were solely on me.

"Sure, let's get the instruments," Lorien said, and I grabbed his elbow, my head tilted to the side, eyes wide. "Come on Baby, you need to pick which of your violins you want to use." All three of us went back to the car, Matty in tow.

"Are you plugging in with us Ashlyn?" Matty asked suggestively. I knew right then I would not be using my electronic violin when we were at his place and made a big show of taking my acoustic one from its case, ignoring him.

After nearly an hour and a half Lorien called it quits. We were sounding brilliant, and I was hoping he'd make this a weekly session instead of twice weekly. I was certainly going to push that point with him when we got home. "Are you guys ready for a gig?" Matty asked. Lorien turned quickly.

"Do you have something set up for us?" His eyes were bright, his excitement obvious.

"Yeah, Sommersett Golf Club, two dates, Friday week and the following Friday. Their entertainment pulled out and they're stuck trying to find someone else."

"How did you get wind of it?"

"The other band I play for was going to take it but the lead singer can't make it, so I grabbed it for us."

"Excellent, thanks Matty, I owe you one." Matty glanced at me and smirked. I did not intend to be 'the one' Lorien owed him.

I found myself sulking in the car on the way home, not clearly sure as to why. When we got home, Lorien held me back whilst Elijah took the guitars inside. "You're due for your monthly visitor aren't you Baby?" He was right, I hated when he was right, especially when concerning my body. "Just a little bit cranky today? A little PMS creeping in?"

"You are *so* pushing your luck Lorien!" He chuckled and drew me against him.

" I should get you stirred right up and drag you upstairs to my room so you can have your way with me. Smack me around a bit hey?" I had to laugh.

"Thanks Lorien, I would really like that."

"I might too…" he growled. He had lightened my mood however, and I was thankful; it's not fun feeling cranky.

"What a pig!" Elijah said as we sat at the dining room table whilst the twins had a snack, consisting of three toasted sandwiches each.

"I thought of him as a pig before I saw the sty he lives in." The twins laughed at this, but it was true.

"Are you sure you don't want one Ash?" Lorien asked as he pulled the last two sandwiches from the jaffle-maker, adding them to the stack.

"Positive." I sat and watched them make short work of the food, washing it down with copious amounts of juice.

"You two eat like geese, you're allowed to chew you know." I had to whack Elijah on the back after my statement; this gander had caught part of the sandwich in his throat as he laughed at my reference.

They finished at the same time and pushed their plates away, sitting back content. "I needed that," Elijah sighed.

"Hope our jeans will still fit," Lorien jibed him, referring to the yet unseen clothing they'd be wearing when we performed.

"You haven't mentioned *your* costumes yet, or shown me what they look like."

"They're certainly not costumes," Lorien laughed.

"Yet I'm expected to wear one?" I said, "That's unfair."

"You're the centrepiece Ash, the beautiful, crystal, eye-catching centrepiece that sets off the surroundings so elegantly."

"Nice try Lorien. I want to see you in your gear." He looked at his brother and Elijah shrugged. Lorien grinned at me and leant over to whisper something to him.

"That explains a lot, and that's one wave I don't want to be surfing!" They both laughed and I was ready to kill Lorien.

"You just told him, didn't you?" He was not overly successful in hiding his smile and I found myself bursting into tears. He pulled me to him, holding me tightly.

"Shh... Sweetheart, don't cry. I'm sorry, I should know better than to push your buttons today."

"It's just the stupid hormones," I sniffed, knowing I was being super-sensitive. Unfortunately, it was something a premenstrual woman could not always avoid.

"Better?" he asked, and I nodded, wiping my nose with the tissue he handed to me from a box on the bench. "You're not pregnant if your period is coming," he whispered.

"Oh yeah!" I brightened a little at this thought. "Crisis averted," I said, enacting wiping sweat from my brow.

"I wouldn't call it a crisis Baby."

"What would you call it then?"

"A surprise maybe, but not a crisis."

"Well, that's a nice synonym for 'holy crap'!" He smiled down at me tenderly, swinging me gently in his arms.

"Lorien..."

"Hmmm?"

"Go and put your gear on... and take Elijah with you!" I called out as he made his way up the stairs. Elijah rolled his eyes at me and followed, both humouring me, neither of them wanting me pissed at them today.

I gave them an appreciative wolf-whistle when they came downstairs. Although simply dressed compared to what I had to wear, they both looked scorching hot. A pair of plain black jeans and a vibrant blue singlet was their entire 'costume'; however, the singlets emphasised their chest and arm muscles, the colour making Elijah's blue eyes more pronounced and highlighting both of their hard, brown bodies. I circled them slowly, Elijah looking slightly uncomfortable. "Hey pretty boy, don't get all bent out of shape," I said, stealing Matty's line. "There will be more eyes than just mine on you next Friday night."

"Stop it Ash, you're making me feel so cheap!" he said in mock chagrin. Lorien just stood there, enjoying my reaction and as I passed behind him, I ran my hand over his curves, "Somebody hand me a spoon I'm ready to eat." My hands moulded to his chest, then spread out, trekking their way down his shoulders, finding his hands through their slow procession. I pulled his arms out wide and leant into him. "You look delicious," I growled.

"Might have your hands full there bro," Elijah laughed. "Looks like she's going to eat you alive." Lorien didn't laugh. In fact, he didn't take his eyes from mine, staring into them deeply as his flashed. *I'm really horny*, I mouthed.

"You usually are at this time of your cycle."

"Man, I'm getting changed," Elijah said, picking up on the partially unheard conversation. "And don't go shagging around down here either, Keren's coming over shortly." Lorien was still standing with his hands in mine, a slight smile on his face. Neither of us spoke, neither of us moved, we stood trance-like, enveloped in each other's eyes. And then I pounced...

He stumbled backwards a few steps by the force of my body impelling his, ending up backed up against a dining room chair. He caught my fire instantly, returning my kisses with equal passion. "Put me on the table Lorien," I gasped, and he yanked a chair out of the way and lifted me up, his hand instantly at my briefs, dragging them off in one movement. Neither of us considered Elijah only upstairs, nor Keren who would soon be knocking at the door. We were consumed only with each other and the rest of the world disappeared. There was no time for such pleasantries as foreplay, he laid me across the table and ripped open his jeans, inside me immediately. His force was urgent, hammering. He brought his thumb down to circle against me, not sweetly and softly but urging my passion into immediacy, my orgasm already upon me.

"Oh God... Lorien... Lorien!" I called out, not realising how loudly I was yelling his name, but I didn't care, I was flying. He pulled me over the edge of the table and sat on the chair, dragging me with him so as not to break our inflexible seal.

"Take me with you..." and I did, seconds later as his head reeled back, nearly toppling us both over the chair backwards. His hands grabbed my thighs as his mouth burnt against mine. Our breathing was that of a marathon runner, and it didn't seem it was going to slow any time soon.

He held me against him for several minutes after some of our control had been regained. I held his face in my hands, kissing him softly, over and over again. He caressed my thighs, still inside me and neither of us made a move to break our connection.

There was a knock at the door, and we waited for Elijah to come running down the stairs to open it. Lorien grabbed my briefs, shoving them playfully down my shirt as I adjusted my skirt, making sure I was covered. From the way we were sitting, it could have been innocent coupling, sharing a kiss on the dining room chair, only we knew better. At the thought of a public performance, I could feel him hardening inside me and I grinned down at him. *Naughty boy!* He responded with a quick flex and I frowned at him. This was taking it a bit far; actually having sex in front of his brother and Keren was a little different to being impaled on his previously spent force. I shook my head quickly at him, my eyes huge. He nodded back just as quickly and flexed again, harder this time, driving me slightly upwards. I suppressed a moan. Thank God they were kissing and paying no attention to us. "Please Lorien, don't, it's all I can do to not writhe against you as it is. I am *so* horny..." I whispered at his ear.

"Excellent," he grunted. Holding my hips against him, he pushed into me firmly, locking the two counterbalancing forces against each other for a mind-blowing few seconds before releasing his grip. I wanted to lean back, to rip my shirt open so his hands and mouth could explore my fevered body further. Instead, I smiled sweetly at Keren and Elijah, hoping they would get the hell out of here after a quick acknowledgement.

"Keren," I smiled.

"Ash," she replied, smiling back, unaware of what was happening before her very eyes. Elijah looked a little more suspicious as he eyed his twin, noting the tenseness of his body, the fervour in his eye.

"Lorien," she nodded to him and he nodded back, not speaking.

"Well, isn't this pleasant," I said, having no idea what to say, how to get them out of the room. Lorien pushed again and I laughed nervously to cover the groan that tried to escape. I was praying he could put the 'twin thing' to good use and send his brother the silent signals to get them out of here. Elijah's eyes narrowed as he took another look at his brother, sitting with me innocently on his lap.

"What?" Lorien asked. Elijah shook his head at us and took Keren by the hand. I had to admit she looked a lot happier lately, not completely back to normal, but obviously working on it.

The second his door closed, we gyrated against each other, the frenzy already building. Lorien stood, locking me to him at both hip and mouth, and then lowered me to the carpet. I looked up into his eyes as he propelled me to my peak, and we reached it together. It had taken less time than to count down to an official blast off. "Oh Baby, that was wild."

"You are the best Lorien, I mean that. Whew!"

"Compared to who Ash?" he laughed, refusing to take my praise.

"I don't need to, that was the ultimate, just like every time. And I feel a *lot* better now," I laughed. "Do you think they knew?"

"Didn't look like Keren had a clue, but I'm not sure about Eli." I got to my feet and went into the bathroom to readjust my modesty. Lorien had put some music on, and we spent the next hour cuddling on the sofa. I wasn't cranky anymore, but someone was...

Elijah brought Keren down to see her off and when he'd closed the door behind her, turned to his brother. "Can I see you outside for a sec?" Lorien looked at me with raised eyebrows and followed his brother onto the side verandah, sliding the door closed behind him. I tried to make out what was being said, but there were very few facial expressions or hand movements, although Lorien laughed at one stage and stopped almost immediately. Whatever had tickled his fancy had obviously not tickled Elijah's. When they came back in, Elijah walked straight past me, heading back up to his room.

"What's wrong?" I whispered to Lorien, although I had no idea why I was whispering.

"Oops." He smiled at me.

"He knew."

"Yes, and he's really pissed about it."

"I feel terrible Lorien."

"No you don't, you feel great." He pulled me on top of him and ran his hands slowly from my shoulders to thighs, tasting my flesh through his fingers.

"What did he say to you exactly?"

"I embarrassed him. I should have more respect for you, him and Keren…"

"Hang on," I cut him off. "Why are you getting all the heat for this?"

"He would never blame lovable, innocent Ashlyn for any of it," he said sarcastically, smiling at me.

"Sweetheart, he saw our little sex show on the laptop. I doubt he thinks of me that way anymore." I kissed him lightly.

"I think he's still carrying a little torch for you Ash - we hurt him."

"Oh piffle, he does not. It's been eighteen months since we broke up, well over."

"I call 'em as I see 'em…" he smiled up at me.

"Ooh, twin sandwich!" I laughed, using one of Michael's favourite lines.

"Don't you even think about it Ashlyn!" he frowned at me playfully and then his look changed to one of concern. "You don't still have feelings for him, do you?" I sat up.

"Of course not Lorien, I love *you*. I love Elijah too of course, but he feels more like a brother now than an ex-boyfriend."

"That's good to hear, not that you could survive without a regular dose of Lorien in your bloodstream, hey Baby?"

"Hmmm, you've got that right." I leant down to kiss him, feeling aroused all over again. I was certainly in a mood today! "Lorien, are you ready to go again?" I whispered.

"Whenever you want it Baby, I'll have it for you, but I think we should take this to my room." I jumped straight up, dancing up the stairs as he followed behind me, laughing and smacking me lightly on the bum.

1, 2, 3, 4

"In this politically correct world, I can't refer to you as my girl
I not allowed to tell you, that I love you,
As much as I do."

L Standish, 'PC Girl'

THE TWINS HAD LEFT fifteen minutes ago to get spare bass and lead guitar strings. Our first official gig was tonight, and we were all excited, however I was excited in a way they were unaware. I'd been considering this for a long time, knowing how much Lorien would love it, and I realised if I was ever going to get the opportunity to make this movie for him, now was my chance. If I couldn't go through with it, I would simply erase it and he would be none the wiser.

I set the camcorder on his dresser, climbing up behind it to check the angle and zoom before hitting record and sitting on the edge of the bed. "This one's for you Baby," I smiled and winked at the camera. I teased my hand inside my shirt, lying back on the bed so the view would be from underneath, allowing him to see what I was doing to myself. It wasn't as difficult as I thought it was going to be, finally stripping off and going with my own flow, doing all the things I knew would excite him, that were beginning to excite me.

It was a completely different sensation being the master of my own domain. My fingers knew exactly what my body wanted, and they were skilled psychics, pre-empting every desire. As the intrinsic waves started to crash, I looked into the camera and moaned loudly, whispering his name over and over as I came for him. When the waves eased into ripples, I continued to tease myself gently for effect as I approached the camera, "I love you," I said and hit the stop button.

I dressed quickly so I could watch it back. If I looked horrible in any way, it was being deleted regardless, although I was sure he'd want to be the judge of that. I watched it back twice just to make sure I could live with the look of myself, saving a copy of it through his laptop onto a USB and erasing it from the camera completely. What was I to do with it now? Keep it for a special occasion, show it to him the second we were alone, show it to him the second he got home so we could *be* alone? It didn't matter; he was going to *love* it. I marked the USB with an X, hiding it in his bookshelf for now. As I walked out of his room, I knew when I would give it to him, on my birthday...

When the twins got home, it was time to get changed and leave for Sommersett Golf Club. Matty had picked up the gear last night and was transporting it straight to the club. All we needed to do was get there, ready to go on. "Are you feeling OK?" Lorien asked, putting his palms to my cheeks, then one to my forehead. "You look a little flushed." I grinned at him and started to laugh. He had no idea.

"Must be nerves," I told him as he hugged me fiercely, lifting me from the ground.

"This is going to be so cool," he said and kissed me deeply, his passion for the night's event equalled to what he had for me. He pulled back, patting me lightly on the bum, "Go and get changed Gorgeous girl, we can pick this up when we get home."

Bree, Michael and Simon arrived soon after, wanting to come in with 'the band', to be seen with 'the band'. I realised with their enthusiasm that I was in 'a band'. What was I doing? How on Earth was I going to get up there in front of all those people and perform, including our parents? I knew all along that this was going to be the end result - performing. But, here it was upon me and I hadn't really seen it coming. A panic attack bloomed, and I sat on the sofa, breathing quickly. "Your twin under there?" Michael asked, then realising my distress, came and sat at my knee looking up at me, worried. "Are you OK Ash?" I shook my head, gripping onto the cushions of the sofa tightly.

"She's hyperventilating." I could hear Lorien in the distance, about two kilometres away it seemed. He came and sat beside me, holding a paper bag over my nose and mouth. In a few minutes, I was breathing regularly. He bobbed his head down to my face level, "Baby?" I looked at him, my eyes still wide. I didn't think I'd blinked in five minutes. Everyone evaporated onto the side verandah, leaving me alone with Lorien. "Ash Baby, talk to me..." He drew me into his arms, holding me tightly, rocking slightly.

"It *is* nerves..." I admitted. He didn't notice the stress I put on the 'is', my previous excuse now having come to fruition.

"Why so nervous? You sound great Sweetheart." He pulled my forehead to his chin, tightening his embrace.

"It just hit me that I'm in a *band* and we're about to go onstage to *perform* in front of people who are *paying!*" My breathing started to escalate again and he soothed me,

"Shh Baby, shhh," he said as he ran his hand slowly over my back. "You perform all the time in front of our Music class and the entire school. There's no need to be worried or scared about tonight. It'll be like always, it'll be fun..." I calmed a little and gave him a small smile. "I'll be right there beside you," this thought did make me feel a lot more secure, "and Eli too." I nodded and smiled up at him, shaking it off. "There it is, there's my smile..." He leant down and kissed me softly. "I love you Ash."

"I love you too Lorien, thanks."

"You OK now?"

"Yes, I don't know what came over me; it hit me like a train." He smiled and hugged me against him.

"Stage fright, jitters, cold feet, nerves..."

"OK Lorien, no need to reinforce them again."

"Sorry Baby," he laughed and took my hand, twirling me around as he inspected me in my outfit. "What a hottie!" I blushed, and he hugged me to him again. I pulled away feeling confident, ready to get my makeup done when he stopped me. "I'm not finished with you yet."

"I'm not going on stage without makeup." We had to leave in fifteen minutes and time was getting away.

"Can I watch?"

"No. Bree!" I called. "Whenever you're ready!" She came in through the door, Michael following, and we went upstairs to the bathroom to finish my look. "Make it as heavy as you like Bree, I don't mind being in camouflage tonight."

We searched for our parents when we got there. Keren was waiting at the door and Elijah gave her a big hug before moving in to kiss her softly. I could see Cara standing and waving from the table to the left of where our equipment was set up, sitting with Nick and my parents. I instantly relaxed. This was near where I would stand, and I loved my parents, or maybe Lorien's, for choosing their position so carefully.

They had held the table next to them for Keren, Bree, Michael and Simon and they staked their claim at it. When everyone was deep in excited conversations, I took a moment to survey the room, seeing how many people were here, who was here. I saw Matty sitting at the bar and he winked at me, pretending to scratch at his groin, the motion being a little less subtle than that. I noticed Mr O'Dowd sitting at a table near the back and I tapped Lorien on the arm, motioning to him as I went over to say hello. 'What are you doing here?" I asked as I sat down.

"I couldn't miss my favourite student's first live performance, could I?" he smiled at me. "Well done Ashlyn, you and Lorien will do wonderfully. I'm very proud of you."

"Hey Mr O," Lorien leant over the back of my chair and shook his hand.

"Hi Lorien. I'm looking forward to hearing some new pieces tonight."

"That you will Sir, quite a few you haven't heard yet. Baby," he smiled at me, "it's time." I looked up, seeing Matty sitting at the drums, twirling his sticks around his fingers, loosening up. My throat threatened to close up again and Mr O'Dowd noticed my expression, taking my hands in his.

"A little stage fright Ashlyn?"

"Her second bout tonight," Lorien explained.

"Take a deep breath and hold it, now take in more, hold it, one more deep breath... OK let it all out." I exhaled in a whoosh. "Feel better?" he asked. I did! I gave him a kiss on the cheek and thanked him, then scooted to the front of the room, Lorien behind me. He gave a quick intro of the band's name and then Matty was clicking his sticks, bringing us straight into 'Skulling Champagne'.

I was having a marvellous time. The knowledge of my friends and family cheering us on made my heart so light and I was proud, so very proud, of the way we played and Lorien's strong voice. We performed as a tight band and we sounded great. I felt actual disappointment when we stopped for a break after the first set, sitting at the tables with our family groupies. Everyone was keen to congratulate us, chattering again in excitement, bubbling with effervescence.

After ten minutes, I was tugging at Lorien, "Come on Baby, let's get going again..."

"Baby? You're in a good mood now aren't you, it's not often you call me Baby, Baby."

"Let's *go*," I stressed, eager to start again.

"Want to start with 'Merciful Mayhem'?" he asked grinning.

"I... I...," I wasn't sure I was quite that eager yet. "Second song?"

"No problem." He gave Elijah a nod and looked for Matty who was perched in his regular position, watching me, at the bar. He nodded back, understanding we were starting and Lorien took me in his arms, kissing me. A few members of the crowd who were not with our group whistled and he realised where we were. He pulled back, grinning at me. "Let's go."

We ripped through the second set as quickly as the first it seemed, and once again, I found myself back at the table, taking a break before our final set. Mum and Dad were so radiant. They hadn't heard us play before and although I'd told them of Lorien's talent and the band's ability, they were amazed at how well we were doing.

"Really professional Ashlyn, we're so impressed with you all."

"Lorien would like to hear that," I told them, and they approached him on his way back from the bar. He smiled at me over their shoulder, taking in their praise with the gentle humility he always did when people fussed over his natural talent. I truly believed he would achieve stardom one day…

I caught his eye and found a quieter area of the room and he followed me, handing me my drink. "Doesn't look like the olds are leaving for the final set, Mr O'Dowd either." I noticed him still sitting at the table where we'd spoken with him earlier.

"Then they'll get what they paid for hey?" Lorien had left the slightly raunchier songs like 'Ten New Commandments' and 'Once A Year' until the final set, assuming our parents may have left by then. We should've known better of course, but it didn't matter, it was his material, and it wasn't really that carnal. I was glad however that it was Lorien singing to them about crying out for God whilst having sex, and not me. I started to laugh, couldn't keep it in if I tried, and when Lorien questioned me on my sudden attack of the giggles I explained my thoughts to him. "Oh great Ash, very comforting, thanks!" He wasn't worried though. He never worried.

We started our final set and in no time, it was all over, Lorien finishing by calling, "You've been a great audience and we've been 'Listening at Keyholes'." The applause was hard to determine as so much of it was coming from right in front of us. I grabbed Lorien and hugged myself to him with one arm, my other outstretched, holding onto my violin and bow. I felt them being taken from my hand and then I really let him

have it full force. He held me tightly, "I love you Ashlyn, so very much..."
he leant and whispered in my ear, lifting me off the ground.

"My turn." Elijah was standing behind him and Lorien let me go,
allowing me to give his brother a big hug too. The twins then did that male
clinching, back-slap thing they do in lieu of an actual hug.

We re-joined our friends. I was a little concerned what Keren's
reaction was to Elijah's and my embrace, but her face was glowing and
her hands were waiting for his waist. Mum had my violin and bow in her
hands and I blushed a little, knowing it was she who had taken them from
me. None of our parents were in a rush to leave, in fact everyone seemed
settled in for the night, not that there was a great deal of the night left. Mr
O'Dowd came to speak to Lorien and I again as he was leaving,
congratulating us on a splendid performance and to let us know he'd been
grading us. We laughed and Lorien shook his hand. He waved to our
parents, stopping to chat with them briefly on his way out.

Michael and Bree, having patiently waited their turn, were on me.
"You looked so hot Ash, even I want to have sex with you," Michael said
as he hugged me, I laughed.

"Me too!" squeaked Bree and I laughed even harder. I had to go
to the bathroom desperately and Bree came with me. It was the only
place Michael didn't join us. *In time that could possibly change,
depending on the venue*, I mused, standing at the vanity checking my face,
waiting on Bree.

When we came back out, I saw Lorien handing some cash to
Matty who counted through it and smiled, whacking him on the shoulder.
He then leant into him and mumbled something in his ear, looking at me
over Lorien's shoulder. Lorien pulled back abruptly and spun in my

direction, quickly turning back to Matty and more words were spoken. I slowly circled around them, making sure there wasn't trouble brewing; I wished I could read lips. Matty went back to dismantling his kit and Lorien crossed the room to me, putting on a smile as he neared, removing the thunder that had previously been there. "What was that all about?"

"Just giving him his share of the money." He pulled me to him, kissing me deeply, his hands crawling over my rear. I was sure this was for Matty's benefit as my back was facing him, but that was not my concern. Matty could eat his heart out.

"Give me some well-earned cash, man," Elijah said beside us and Lorien broke the kiss, smiling at me jubilantly.

"Here you go bro. Now don't come asking for more when that runs out."

"Thanks Dad!" He pulled a face at Lorien and took off to find Keren again.

"You'll get your share the second we get home," he growled, rubbing himself against me lightly, not wanting to put on too good of a preview show in front of our olds. We left twenty minutes later...

"Leave it on Ash," Lorien said as I went into the bathroom to remove my makeup.

"I didn't know you liked a lot of makeup," I said kittenishly.

"I'd never thought about it before, even though I couldn't take my eyes off you the *last* time you had makeup on..." My bemused expression leading him to continue, "At the Year 10 formal..." he hinted.

"You Philistine, you had a date, and I was with your brother." I smiled at him and he shrugged his shoulders,

"What can I say Ash, I was in love with you." It made me so happy to hear how much he loved me, have him always confirming and reminding me of it in so many wonderful ways. As he seductively ran his hands the length of my body, exploring my crevasses and plains, the heat in his eyes told me he was just about to confirm it again. "God you are so *sexy* Baby," he said softly, leaning down to kiss me long and deeply, the heat now a raging inferno and we burned together in its wake.

Thrice times a lady? Yeah, I don't think so. As we lay there catching our breath after the third bout of lovemaking, he grinned and hooked his jeans off the floor, reaching into them to count out my share of the money. "God Lorien, I feel like a hooker," I laughed, then stopped, sitting up. "Wow..." I exhaled, counting the one hundred and twenty dollars I was holding in my hand. "We made four hundred and eighty bucks tonight?"

"Five hundred, I gave Matty the extra twenty for using the van." His brow furrowed slightly at the mention of his name.

"Wow!"

"Is that the only superlative you can find?" he asked, smiling again, pulling me back down to the bed. He worked his lips sensuously around my throat, ready to slate up number four, as we welcomed the approaching dawn.

5, 6, 7, 8

"And if you ever fear you've done it wrong, chances are you have."

L Standish, 'Empty Guarantees'

I HAD TO ADMIT, our second gig was as successful as our first. We had the crowd in the palm of our hands from the moment the first note played. The only thing that didn't impress me was the groupie chain, which formed in front of us on the floor, and the barmaid who kept giving all three boys free beer.

On one such break, Lorien came back and handed one to Elijah and Matty as we walked outside onto the verandah to cool down.

"As the barmaid obviously doesn't want to sleep with me, I'll just go and get my own, shall I?" I asked Lorien, trying to keep the resentment out of my voice.

"Ash, I'm sorry, I'm not thinking straight. Here," he said, passing me his glass. "I'll go get another." He leant down and kissed me, smiling as he drew back. *I'm sorry*, he mouthed, and I instantly forgave him. Matty followed him inside, his glass already drained.

Elijah and I chatted with excitement, also watching the girls eyeing him off through the window. "You could have any of them you know," I suggested and smiled at him over the rim of my glass.

"But I don't want any of them." He laughed when they started checking me out, obviously confused as to which band member I possibly 'belonged'. "Let me put my arm around you." He slid up against me, making it seem we were together. "This will spin them out when Lori comes back," he laughed.

"I don't want them thinking I get passed around, thank you very much!" He was right though, it was funny, and the girls at the window turned their backs on us. "Where's Keren anyway?"

"She couldn't come tonight, had other plans..."

"Are you two doing OK?" I asked.

"So-so, we'll get there. You're a hard woman to be compared to," he smiled down at me.

"Are you sure there's nothing I can say or do, Elijah? I feel like it's my fault."

"It's sorting itself out Ash, don't worry about it."

It was at least ten minutes later when Lorien came back out onto the verandah, no beer in his hand. "Woo!!!" he shouted; he was wild. Matty followed closely behind him with a smirk on his face. What had they been up to? He took Elijah's hand from my waist and grabbed me, swinging me around. "Baby, Baby, Baby, what a night!"

"Put me down, my skirt is halfway up my back!"

"OK!" He put me down and shoved me backwards against the railing. "I want to fuck you right now!" he yelled at the top of his lungs. What the hell was going on? He grabbed my breasts in both hands, forcing his tongue down my throat. When I'd finally managed to break the seal, I said,

"What's going on Lorien?" as calmly as I could under the circumstances. I was now getting *very* strange looks from the girls at the window, and I didn't blame them. He grappled with me and I kept slapping his hands away. "Stop it!" He wasn't listening and I looked over his shoulder for Elijah. "Elijah, help me!" He swooped in and eased his brother's hands off me.

"Easy tiger, you don't want to hurt her…"

"I'd never hurt her, I love her!" he yelled as Elijah moved him away from me.

I sought out Matty through the sparse crowd on the verandah. He had managed to find a spot, which afforded an uninterrupted view of the antics. When he realised I was looking at him he winked at me and blew a kiss. Lorien broke free from his brother, coming back to me, and I found myself cringing a little. Elijah stayed right behind him as he crossed the deck.

"I'm sorry Ash. I didn't mean to frighten you." He held me to him; his entire body was a mass of heat, twitching ghoulishly under my hands.

"Are you OK?" I whispered, the first feeling of real unease passing through my mind.

"OK? I am *so* OK! Let's get the final set done and we can par-tay!" He bolted back inside and we followed, Elijah shooting me a concerned glance as he held the door for me.

Whatever was wrong with him didn't affect his voice or playing. If anything, it made him stronger. When I performed 'Merciful Mayhem', he whooped it up in the background, whistling me and cheering. "That's *my* girl!" he screamed at one stage. It was not the kind of performance owed to this wonderful song.

When we finally finished, I was glad it was over. Maybe now I could make some sense of this bewildering turn of events. I was certain Matty had given Lorien some form of drug. It wasn't like him to be acting this strangely. After our final bows, Elijah was at my side. "I don't like the look of this, I'm going to put our gear in my car. Give me your violin Ash."

"I'll carry it." He unplugged their two guitars from Matty's amps and put them into their cases and I followed him to the carpark.

"At least I know these are safe. Matty can look after his own stuff."

When we re-entered the function room, Matty and Lorien were dismantling the drums, nearly running to the van with the various pieces of the kit. "I think we'll leave them to it. Want a drink?" I nodded and followed him to the bar, watching Lorien over my shoulder. I was beginning to feel afraid of him, which was ridiculous.

As I watched, a girl came over with a marker and lifted her shirt, getting him to sign her chest, which he did with a massive grin on his face. She leant into him and whispered something in his ear, placing her hand on his pec lightly. When he drew back from her, his eyebrows were raised, a smile on his lips. I was reaching the end of being a polite girlfriend. Something was about to give if he kept this up. "Come on, ignore him, let's go outside," Elijah said, and I followed him out onto the verandah again, wondering if I should be leaving Lorien alone.

We sat out there for some time, Elijah getting a pitcher so we didn't have to keep getting up for drinks. Lorien made his way through every now and then, whooping it up. On the occasions he remembered I was there, he managed to slobber all over me on the way past to the next exciting place he needed to be.

We ignored him standing with Matty at the end of the verandah, and he flicked a coaster at me to get my attention. Once he had my gaze, he stuck his tongue out and circled the tip of it with two fingers, sucking them into his mouth. This pantomimed stimulation was obvious, which Matty thought was hilarious. On the last instance he shot past, he took the beer from my hand and skulled it before racing back inside the club. "You realise he's out of it," Elijah said, refilling my glass.

"I suspected as much. Is there anything we can do?"

"Not until tomorrow when his feet hit the ground, and I imagine it will be with an almighty crash." I laughed with him, praying the worst was over, knowing it wasn't.

I had to use the bathroom, so Elijah came with me, saying he needed to go too. "Wait here if you beat me out," he told me, and I thought he may have been playing the protective big brother with me. I was glad.

Regardless of the fact that the love of my life was acting like a complete moron, I was so happy about the success we had tonight and I all-but bounced out of the bathroom; I was on such a bittersweet high. I looked around for Lorien, unable to see him anywhere. I searched through the crowd taking compliments and avoiding pinching fingers and came to a dead stop. He had *the* barmaid up against the wall near the emergency exit door. Her head was thrown back as he dragged his mouth around her neck, his hands groping under her shirt. I was unable to move, not fully comprehending what I was seeing. She spotted me over his shoulder and tipped me a wink and I wanted to launch myself at her and scratch her eyes out, but I just stood there, stunned. "Ash," it was Elijah, "what..." He followed my gaze and realised what had me so transfixed. "Oh my God, you bloody dickhead Lorien. Come with me Babe, come on..." He pulled at my arm, forcing me to follow him from the room out onto the verandah. "Ash, Honey? Babe, can you speak to me?"

My face crumpled into tears and he took me in his arms. "Shh Babe, it'll be OK." He rubbed my back slowly, trying to soothe me as best he could whilst my heart splintered into a million tiny pieces, turning indeed into ash. I clung to him, crying loudly on his shoulder and he pulled me to him even tighter. "It'll be OK, Shh."

"Can you get him off her?" I cried out, the vision of the two of them together was all I could see, whether my eyes were open or squeezed shut.

"Will you be OK for a second?" I nodded and stood in the corner of the verandah, out of everyone's way.

Several minutes later, I felt hands gliding around my waist from behind and I turned, expecting to see a repentant Lorien. It was Matty. "So, everyone gets a turn tonight hey?" he drawled before leaning in to kiss me.

"Get off me!" I yelled, pushing at him. Even though skinny, he was surprisingly strong, and I struggled to keep him away.

"Matty," I heard Elijah say. As he turned around, Elijah drew his arm back, his bunched knuckles near white and I watched in slow motion as he punched him in the face. Matty went down and stayed there, unconscious.

"Could this night get any worse?" I cried as he took me back in his arms, trying to soothe again. "Where's Lorien?"

"He's not very happy with me at the moment, didn't care much for the way I removed him from the situation." I didn't ask. I didn't want to know. "But it's OK Ash, everything will be OK..."

I pulled him to me, looking up into his eyes. "Oh Ash," he sighed against me, his hands caressing now instead of soothing, working their way down my back. I wanted him to kiss me, to have a kiss from a pair of familiar lips that could possibly erase the whole situation in one romantic gesture, making me feel here again, real.

"Kiss me Elijah," I whispered, "please."

"How I would love to Ash, but I can't. You're angry and upset and it would be unfair of me to take advantage, knowing you'd regret it later."

"I wouldn't."

"You would," he smiled down at me and lightly kissed the tip of my nose, "as tempting as it is..." He drew me against him and held me tenderly, his arms and hands still betraying the thoughts of that elusive kiss, a kiss we both wanted to happen. Lorien burst through the door.

"What the fuck have you done!" he screamed at Elijah. His pupils were huge, and he paced frantically, running his hands over his wet hair; in fact, his whole upper body was wet. "And you, you slut, I turn my back for five minutes and you're in the arms of my brother!" Elijah was watching him carefully, knowing his reactions were impromptu and erratic; not knowing what he would say or do next. Elijah moved me in behind him to keep me out of the line of fire. "Don't protect her! She's not yours to protect, she's mine!"

"Lorien, if you don't calm down I will knock you out too."

"I'd like to see you try *big brother*," he said. The look on his face was ugly, a look I'd never seen before.

"Elijah..." I whispered.

"What? What do you need from him?" he hissed at me and then knelt down to Matty who was starting to come around. "You've punched out our drummer you fuckwit! Do you realise what this means?"

"Yes, it means I'm taking Ash home. You can get there the best way you can mate!" He went to lead me to the carpark, Lorien interjecting once more.

"If you take her, I will kill you!" Elijah moved me away and then opened his arms wide at his brother.

"Well give it your best shot Lorien!" He ran at Elijah and Elijah grabbed him, walking Lorien backwards until his back was against the brick wall of the club. "Don't make me do it little bro, but I will if you force me to. You've done enough damage tonight and you are *not* doing any more!" Elijah shoved him against the wall once more to punctuate his intention and then let him go. Coming back to me, he put his arm around my waist and led me to the car. "Come on Babe, I'll take you home."

I cried all the way to Warden, Elijah didn't interrupt me, didn't say a word until we were in my driveway. All the lights were out; Mum and Dad had gone to bed. "Are you going to come in for a while?"

"I don't think that's a good idea, do you?"

"Please Elijah. I won't attack you I promise; I don't want to be alone right now." He got out of the car and followed me into the house. I made some tea and we drank it at the breakfast bar, neither of us had spoken since we entered the house.

"What are you thinking?" Elijah said eventually.

"It's conflicting," I smiled weakly. "One minute I want to cry and cry, knowing I'll never love anyone like I did him, sorry Elijah," I smiled in apology.

"Think nothing of it," he smiled back. "And the second emotion?"

"I want to tear his balls off and feed them to him!"

"Good, that's it, be angry not sad!"

"I'm not enjoying either option," I said, looking down into my tea, hoping to find the answer in its murky depths. It wasn't there of course.

"I wish there was something I could do Ash. What a wanker."

"You did enough Elijah, thanks for your support tonight. I don't know what I would've done without you." He stood and came around to my side of the bench and held his arms open. "You're not asking me to take my best shot, are you?" I laughed.

"No, I want a hug please." I gave him the biggest hug I had in me. "Is that supposed to hurt?" he teased. I laughed and hugged him again, gently. "It'll be OK Ash," he whispered. I didn't see how it could be. He'd been with another woman.

"Elijah?"

"Hmmm?"

"Why was he all wet?" He drew back, grinning.

"I flushed him." I couldn't help but laugh at this image.

"It didn't cool him down any."

"No..."

When he left, I went upstairs and sat on my bed, feeling numb. I fingered the small diamond at my earlobe, the twin of which was in Lorien's, and I took it out, laying it on my bedside table. I slipped into an uncomfortable slumber, my conscious thoughts colliding with my sleep dreams. I was hidden in the forest; someone had secreted me here and I was too afraid to move. I could hear Lorien stumbling around in the dark, looking for me.

"Ashlyn..." he cried, "Ashlyn!" I couldn't answer him, so great was my fear, but of what... something was lurking I couldn't see, and it had me paralysed in terror...

Burning Down the House

"She said life's a bitch the second time around
and then I knew,
The scars across her back were where
she'd had her wings removed."

L Standish, 'Tears of an Angel'

"ASHLYN... ASHLYN... wake up..." When I opened my eyes, I found Mum sitting on my bed, shaking me gently.

"What time is it?" I grumbled, wanting to roll over and go back to sleep.

"Time to get up, we have a trip to make."

"Where are we going at this time of the morning?"

"It's nearly 11.00 am and the Standish's are expecting us. We have some things to discuss that concerns us all."

"What *things*?" There was no way both sets of parents could already know about last night, not that it was really any of their business.

"Up young lady, we'll discuss it when we get there." I got out of bed and went into the bathroom to shower and change. I felt morbid and the stone that was my heart cracked a little further, forcing the tiny pieces of it through my bloodstream, making it even more concrete. *Lorien was with another girl...*

The hot water didn't help, nothing was going to help; I was so alone, and I didn't want to be. I missed him already but couldn't allow myself to. Lorien was completely and solely at fault here, I was only in this place because of the decisions he'd made. Was this how Elijah felt when we broke up? Giving him no alternative but to break up with me as I drew myself away from him, wanting him to make the decision, as I was too much of a coward to do it myself? I felt a weight of dread settle in my stomach and realised this meeting with the Standish's did not bode well. I wasn't even sure what was going on.

Cara and Nick met us at the door,, and they directed Mum and Dad to the sofa, asking them to take a seat. Lorien came bounding down the stairs and took me in his arms, leaning down to kiss me. I pulled away from him. Did he really think his actions brought no consequences with them? Was he even there last night? He looked edgy and still seemed to be having a hard time focussing. "Ash?" he questioned as I reefed myself free from his grasp and went to sit at the dining room table. My head felt heavy and everything was so surreal I wasn't sure *I* was even here. "Will you come outside with me Baby? We obviously need to talk."

"In all seriousness Lorien, you do *not* want to hear what I have to say to you." He looked confused and turned when he heard his brother coming down the stairs. Elijah came over to me, rubbing my back lightly.

"How are you doing today Babe?" he asked and sat down next to me.

"Babe?" he questioned, looking at Elijah narrowly. "Can someone let me in on this secret?" Lorien lashed out at us.

"I need to fill you in on some of the details from last night Romeo," Elijah shot at him sarcastically, which did nothing to change the look of confusion on Lorien's face.

"Between you and her?" he asked quietly, nearly thinking out loud it seemed.

"Don't be a smart-arse on top of everything else Lorien," I spat. Elijah chose to ignore him.

"Come on Ash, we'll go outside whilst the olds coffee it up first." I stood and walked out behind him, Lorien followed.

"Eli, please, can I have just a few minutes with her?" Elijah looked at me and I shrugged. The way I was feeling I didn't care what Lorien did. My emotions were that of a stark beach, nothing but dry grains of sand blowing directionless in the wind. Elijah went inside letting me know he'd be back in a few minutes.

"Can you tell me what's going on Ash, you're scaring me," Lorien whispered as he tried to take my hands.

"Don't touch me!"

"But why Baby, what's wrong?"

"You really have no idea?" I could tell by the expression on his face this was the case, but it didn't excuse him for his behaviour last night. How could it ever excuse his behaviour? If I were to forgive him, it would make me an idiot. I didn't trust him anymore, and there was more than a little grain of hate mixed in amongst all that dry sand. He'd broken my heart in the most savage of ways. "In short," I counted off on my fingers, "1. Lorien takes drugs from Matty, 2. Ashlyn finds slutty Lorien with slutty barmaid, 3. Elijah comes in to break you apart and Matty decides to have his turn with me, 4. Elijah knocks Matty out, 5. Lorien goes off his head at both his brother and me. 6. Ashlyn's heart is broken," I finished with a sob, tears welling at my eyes. "Why Lorien, why did you have to do it? Don't you know what you've done? I loved you with all of my heart. I thought we'd always be together but just like that," I snapped my fingers, "it's over and I never even saw it coming. I'm not ready for the onslaught of the emotion of wanting to hate you when I still love you so much." I started to cry harder. "But, I *can't* love you anymore."

"What have I *done*?" he mumbled, his face lowered into his hands.

"You've ruined my life!" I got up to walk around to the back verandah and Elijah came through the door. He took me in his arms to console me as he did last night, but no hint of the past was contained in his comfort or in my head. He was my brother again.

"Get your hands off my girlfriend!" Lorien raged at Elijah as he stood, coming over to break us apart.

"I'm *not* your girlfriend Lorien, just keep away from me!" I said through gritted teeth. Dad was at the door.

"This looks like it's going to be a more difficult conversation than we first realised. Are you OK Ashlyn?" I had no idea of what was going on anymore. Did our parents know? How could they? What other reason would we be over here all together if not for *this* reason? I felt hot and cold, my head was swimming and the next thing I knew I was looking up into the face of Elijah as he laid me on the sofa.

"What happened?" I mumbled, sitting up, seeing Elijah walk back out to his brother, slamming the sliding door shut behind him.

"You fainted Honey. How are you feeling?" Dad sat next to me, his arm around my waist.

"Lorien, get in here!" Nick yelled out and both twins came inside. "There's no need for you to be here Elijah."

"If this has something even remotely to do with me or the band then I have every right to be here."

"Fine, stay, you may think you're entitled to be here, but you are *not* entitled to your opinion."

He turned his attention to me and Lorien, who sat on the floor near my feet. He wasn't game to touch me but wanting to be as close as he could for the moment - until he had a chance to make something of the tumult. He was wasting his time... "We received a letter from the school yesterday, us and the Mercy's." Lorien looked at me, eyebrows drawn, not understanding and I found myself looking back at him with the same expression, unintentionally. "It appears our little prodigies have been skipping classes, quite a few classes so far." Mum handed me their letter whilst Nick passed his to Lorien, now understanding why this meeting had been called.

"Twenty! Twenty Ashlyn! What on earth have you been doing?" Dad said. I went to look at Lorien again and caught myself in time. This was going to be my problem with my parents. I didn't care what he thought or how it was going to affect him anymore, I lied to myself.

"I have a fair idea of what they were doing," Nick said. "I think it's time we set a few ground rules regardless, and first and foremost is there will be no more band until school is finished. Since you obviously can't handle the extra workload, that privilege is now revoked."

"Dad!" Elijah complained and his father silenced him with a glare.

"You can leave any time you like Elijah, this matter does not concern you!" Elijah shut up. That rule didn't worry me. The band was finished anyway as far as I was concerned, it didn't bring out the best in Lorien and I didn't want anything to do with Matty ever again, or Lorien for that matter.

"I think the kids should cool it too," my father added. "I'm not saying you can't see each other, that would be impossible with you being in the same classes anyway, but the every night stay-overs and unsupervised liaisons are to stop this instant." Dad didn't realise he was shutting the stable door way too late, that illusive horse had already bolted. Lorien and I were no longer an item, whether he accepted it or not.

"Is that it?" I asked, ready to go home.

"You have nothing to say? I thought we'd get a fight out of you both over the second condition if not the first," Mum said, concerned. She was getting a first grasp of the bigger picture. When I knew what I was about to say to her I wanted to shove my hand into my mouth to prevent the ugliness of the statement, but it spewed out, nevertheless.

"To be quite honest with you Mum, Dad, I'm nearly nineteen and I will do whatever the hell I want and if you don't like it under your roof then I'll do it elsewhere." I walked out the front door, heading for Sommersett station. Warden had its own train station, and it was only a fifteen-minute walk from home, so I took off under my own steam.

Mum and Dad weren't there when I got home about an hour later; not all the trains stopped at Warden as they did at Sommersett. I supposed they were out looking for me, but I didn't care. I went straight to my room and collapsed on my bed, howling with the tears and anguish I feared were never going to abate. I had never felt so alone and wretched in my whole life.

Sometime later my door opened, both Mum and Dad were standing there looking at me with strained faces. "Are you OK Honey?" Mum asked softly. I rolled over to look at them through my swollen, tear-stained eyes, confused why their wrath had suddenly become concern. "After you left, we managed to get the story from Elijah about what happened last night." I started to sob again, and Mum wrapped me in her arms, rocking me against her in an attempt to calm me. It helped, about as much as chipping an ice-cube from the mammoth berg that sunk Titanic... My mobile chirped and Dad picked it up.

"It's Lorien."

"Ignore it." A few minutes later, my 'Mission Impossible' ring tone burbled out, he was now trying to call. Once again, I wouldn't let Dad answer it. Finally, the landline buzzed, and Dad went to pick it up from the extension in their bedroom. I couldn't hear the conversation, only muted mumblings.

"You don't think you're being too hard on him Ashlyn?" Mum asked, pulling my face back so she could look at me properly.

"How about I ask you that question if Dad ever does it to you Mum. He was with another girl! How can I ever forgive him?" Dad returned in time to hear the end of our conversation. My parents passed a glance between them, and Dad came to sit down next to Mum on my bed. They looked at each other for a short time and Mum finally nodded. What was going on?

"Trust me Ashlyn, if this conversation didn't need to be discussed then it wouldn't be..." I waited for him to go on. He looked at my mother and she continued.

"Not long after you were born, I had an affair."

"What?" I didn't believe what was coming out of her mouth. I looked at my father and he nodded. "Why? How could you Mum?" She cut me off.

"As *you* said, you're nearly nineteen and I expect you to listen with maturity. Can you do that?" I understood she was telling me this for a reason and waited for her to continue. "The whys and wherefores aren't important; the fact your father and I loved each other is what helped us get through it. Your father," she paused. "Do you want to answer this Dom?"

"We had a tiny little baby Ashlyn, you, and we not only loved you with all of our hearts, we loved each other as much. It took some time but we both agreed we wanted to mend the bridges. We worked at it and it was *that* effort which has made our love so special and enduring." They looked at each other warmly, and for once, my first reaction wasn't 'ewww'. I understood what he was saying to me.

"Can I ask you some questions?" They nodded, Mum saying,

"We can only do our best to answer you Ashlyn, but some things may not be your business." I took that under advisement.

"Was it only once Mum?"

"Yes."

"Did you want to do it again?" She smiled at my father before answering,

"No."

"Did you ever want to get back at her Dad?"

"Is that how you feel about Lorien, Ashlyn?" he asked with concern.

"Not really… No, I don't." I knew it wouldn't make the pain go away or repair the damage to the small piece of coal that was now my cindered heart; it was also the last thing on my mind.

"I didn't want to either, and I can tell from the conflict on your face that you aren't thinking of it as an option. It's not in my girl's make-up anyway." I smiled at him. "Perhaps you can understand where we're coming from a little better now, what makes our marriage so special." I nodded.

"Do you love Lorien?" asked Mum.

"I did, with all of my heart and soul. That's what makes this so unbearable. I just want it to be OK again, for the pain to go away... I feel so empty, but I can't trust him now, can I?" I finished lamely.

"Trust is something that has to be earned. You gave it to him once, a long time ago and he did something stupid, which has broken that trust. I want you to remember Ashlyn, and I'm not in any way taking his side, but Lorien was not acting rationally was he?" I shook my head. "Do you know him to be that kind of person as a rule?" I shook my head again. "So, it's possible, just remotely, but possible that he made a mistake?" I had nothing to say to that, but it gave me something to consider.

"How can I pretend nothing happened, Mum? How can I give him back something that he tore apart in front of me with his bare hands?" I started to cry again. I felt very sorry for myself now, caught in a web of conflicting emotions, and I didn't know which ones to heed.

"It's called growing up Honey, and accepting that none of us are immortal and faultless," Dad said.

"And if he does it again?"

"Do you think he will, in all honesty Ashlyn?" he asked.

"No."

"Then what's the point of making yourself and Lorien miserable? That boy loves you a great deal and he comes from a loving and caring family. He wasn't thinking at the time, wasn't Lorien, he was someone else entirely."

"Why are you sticking up for him?" I said, crying harder.

"Even though you're not capable of believing this at the moment, he makes you so incredibly happy Honey." Dad smiled at me and I knew he was right. "Perhaps the whole vetoing the private relationship is actually a Godsend for you. It will give you the time you need to evaluate your relationship and make sure it's exactly what you're looking for. Who knows what you'll decide a few months or years later on down the track. He's either right for you or he's not and you'll know one way or the other when it feels right. You know we love you and would never do anything to harm you. Don't you think we'd want you to stay away from Lorien if we didn't think he was good for you?"

"I know he's right for me, I wanted to spend the rest of my life with him," I said, a little embarrassed. This was not the usual thing I would say to my parents, but we were talking frankly and now was the time to be open and honest with them.

"Why don't you get cleaned up and go see him?" my father suggested.

"What about your new rules?"

"We want you two to cool it for a little while, not forever. There's nothing stopping you from still having a relationship, but we want to make sure you're both focussed on Year 12 and not only on each other." I blushed, remembering the letter they'd received from school, which had started this whole conversation in the first place.

"I guess you're right." Mum hugged me to her tightly and I stood and gave Dad a big hug too. They'd made me feel a lot better and I started to believe it didn't have to be the end, only the end of movement two. In a symphony the movements flowed from one to the next, bearing force to become richer and faster paced after the second movement's lull. Possibly this was the way for Lorien and me also, working to the maximum crescendo of our happy lives together.

"You can't make an omelette without cracking a few eggs?" I joked, sniffing and rubbing a tissue to my nose.

"You can't make lemonade without lemons," Dad smiled at me. I gave them both a kiss and went to have a shower.

I then checked my messages from Lorien. There were several of them now, including two missed calls. Their tone and intent were similar, begging me to forgive him, expressing his love for me and how deeply sorry he was. I felt a little guilty and then stopped myself. This was his fault; he should be thankful I was prepared to discuss it and see what could be amended. Still, I didn't want to go into this with a bitter heart and make him pay for it either. I felt better already, unsure of the words we would speak and the outcomes we would reach, but my heart felt a lot lighter than it had in over twenty-four hours. Or so I innocently believed.

Instead of going to his house, I took the rear entrance to the school and parked my car where he wouldn't be able to see it. I walked slowly down to the oval and sat myself behind a giant tree to wait for him to arrive, not that he knew he was coming here yet. I sent him a text: *Go to school oval and text me when you're there.* My phone chirped almost instantly, *On my way.*

I could see him as he ran across the basketball courts nearing the oval, obviously pressing send; my phone chirped again. *I'm here.* I waited for him to sit, but he looked around. Was he expecting me to be here? If he had, his hopes diminished and he finally sat with his right-hand side facing me, about fifty metres away. I considered the drug that had him edgy when we got to his place earlier was still playing havoc with his body, making his ability to *need* to sit down difficult. My heart went out to him. I texted again, *Are you thinking about what you've done?* I could see his fingers moving and then my phone rang, wrongly assuming he'd been replying to the text.

His head angled around when he heard my ringtone, looking in the direction where I was sitting, but not able to see me. I let him come and find me, not silencing the ring. I was sitting cross-legged with my back against the jacaranda, my eyes downcast. "Ash..." he said tentatively, unsure as to what this meeting was about, and he just stood there, not knowing what to do.

"Sit down Lorien," I told him, still not meeting his eyes. He sat facing me, our knees almost completing a circle, however there was still a minute space between us; he didn't want to push it.

When I opened my mouth to speak, I burst into uncontrolled tears, not being able to get any words out, not sure what they were meant to be. His hands hovered to mine, wanting to take them and finally he did, pressing my palms against his hot cheeks, leaning his forehead down to rest against mine. He let me cry.

It was several minutes before I could stop the torrent and he sat there with me in that frozen position until I was done, moving my hands to hold between his in front of us, as my breath slowly calmed again to a regular tempo. A fat tear dropped onto his wrist. It didn't come from my eyes and I realised he was crying too. "I'm the lowest form of life," he said, barely above a whisper. He started to gently rock forward and backwards, our foreheads still joined, moving me with him. I wanted to soothe him, to let him know when he was in pain it made my pain even more unbearable, but I stayed quiet, letting him speak. "To think what I have done... to the most precious gift I'll ever have. I've hurt so severely my most beautiful Baby girl... I said I'd never do that and look where I am right now; sitting here hoping and praying, *begging* for the forgiveness that I have no right to ask for. I'm so sorry Ashlyn, I don't deserve the wonderfulness that is your love..." he trailed off in a whisper as he drew his face back from mine.

I finally looked up to meet his eyes. The sorrow and pain he saw in them made him grimace, knowing how deep was my grief and that he was solely responsible. "Do you have any idea how I felt when I saw your hands and lips on another woman?" I sniffed. This simple question brought fresh tears, not out of control this time, but to slowly leak down my face. He shook his head, his eyes shining with the tears about to fall from his own.

"No, I don't, and I can't even bear to think about you with someone else," he said softly.

"You have an inkling of an idea then don't you? Not totally, not completely, I haven't broken *your* heart." He dropped his face, but not against mine this time and I knew he was crying when his shoulders started to shudder.

"Lorien," I said and waited until he looked up at me, "don't ever do it again." His wet eyes were now full of hope, unconceived hope he was not expecting to find on this day or in the future.

"You can forgive me?" he asked as I wiped the tears from his lashes.

"If you ever make me feel this miserable again for whatever reason, there will be no second chance, whether in five hours or twenty-five years. Do you understand that?" He nodded and smiled fleetingly at me.

"I can make you that promise Ash, I'll never do anything to hurt you again."

"You *can't* make that promise Lorien, look at what we've just been through, but I don't ever want to be in this situation again with you. Is that too much to ask?"

"Of course not. I love you Ashlyn and I promise," he corrected himself, "I will *always* do my best to make sure you're happy and *want* to be beside me, *need* to be."

"We have to go back a few steps. You have to re-earn the trust I gave to you without question the first time."

"I'm just so glad that you're letting me try. You will let me try, won't you?" he asked, his face a grimace again.

"Yes, my Sweetheart, I'll always *want* you to try." He moved around to sit beside me, to take me in his arms. Instead, as he neared, I put mine around him and he nestled his face against my chest, drawing his arms around my waist tightly.

"Baby girl, you've made me so happy, so complete again. I thought this would be the end and I feel so blessed to be able to still have you; a second gift you've given to me."

I didn't agree with him, my heart still felt heavy and torn. The image of the two of them wanted to flash in front of my face, unstoppable. When I left the house to come here I had no idea how hard this would continue to be, regardless of the spring that was back in my step as I walked to the car. I explained this to him, letting him know there was a lot of damage to be repaired, not only to our relationship, but to my heart as well.

We sat there for hours comforting each other, letting our bodies become one again but not in a sexual way, we hadn't even kissed yet. It was more like allowing the balm from each other to heal ourselves in an almost spiritual aura. I ran my hands over his hair, his back, holding him for a long time before he reversed the position and wrapped me against him, hugging me tightly, rocking again and making me at peace.

The late afternoon sun eventually reminded us that it was nearing dark. Considering the hours we had sat there, it felt like barely one. "I love you Lorien," I whispered, my voice cracking due to not only the many shed tears but the fact I hadn't spoken for many of those hours.

"No Baby girl, I love you." He put a finger to my chin and raised my face to look at him. "This time it will be forever..." He kissed me, firmly and sweetly, not building with the passion our sweet kisses usually worked into. It was a true lover's kiss, full of the spring and summer it brought back to me with the strength of its vow.

I surprised Lorien by getting out of the car when I pulled into the Standish's driveway. He smiled and took my hand, "I didn't think you'd want to come in. I'm glad you do; Mum and Dad will want to see you." I wasn't ready for my own reaction however when I got inside the door. Elijah came up to me,

"How are you doing old girl?" he asked, a cheeky smile on his face. I grabbed him and burst into tears again. What was wrong with me? He let me cry for some time and then Cara took me from his arms, holding me tightly to her.

"It's OK Sweetheart, let it out..." She rubbed her hand across my back slowly, "You've been through a very difficult time and tears are the way the body allows the soul to heal you know?" She drew back slightly to look at me and I smiled at her through my tears, nodding. Nick handed me a wad of tissues and I wiped my face, but the tears still flowed.

"Dear sweet child, to think one of my own has done this to you, come here." I went to him and allowed him to comfort me. I loved the Standish's like my own family, and felt so at ease with them. They *were* my family and I was their only daughter. Being in his fatherly arms made me feel a lot better and I eventually regained a little composure.

"Your shirt's all wet," I laughed as I drew back, looking where my cheek had been lying against him.

"Have you eaten, are you hungry?" he asked, his arm still around my shoulders.

"Not if you're making kippers," I laughed, and he joined me.

"How about something simple?" I nodded and sat down. My legs felt weak, and I didn't trust them to hold me.

Nick went into the kitchen and I looked around for Lorien. He was standing at the island bench, watching from the sidelines. His father patted him on the shoulder as he went past to get to the fridge, and I noticed the same tearful shimmer back in his eyes. He was hurting through my pain and I knew he was truly sorry. We were certainly a family in torment. "I think I'll give your mother a call and let her know you're here. You shouldn't be driving," Cara said.

"She knows where I am. It was actually Mum and Dad who got me to come over and speak to Lorien." His face was one of shock, not expecting my parents to be on his side in any way and I went into brief details of the conversation I had with them before deciding to forgive him, leaving out the details of my mother's tryst.

"Let me make the call Mum. I need to thank them for giving me their baby girl back." He came to me with the phone in his hand and leant down to press his lips against my fevered forehead before sitting next to me. I wrapped myself around him and he raised his arm to let me against him, pressing my face into his side.

He held me to him tightly throughout the duration of the call and I found myself nodding off, the stress of the day finally taking its toll. "She's exhausted." I heard Cara say as Nick brought two bowls of hot soup and some rolls to the table for us; unaware of how hungry I was until the first spoonful hit my stomach. I emptied the bowl quickly.

"Some more?" asked Nick and I handed him my bowl as I reached for a roll. I looked at Lorien and smiled, feeling more energized.

"I love that smile," he whispered, smiling back at me. His father took his bowl and refilled it again and we made our way through another full bowl of soup.

"Anna told me she loved me," Lorien said to his mother and father.

"You're very lucky son," Nick said.

"I know that Dad. Do you think I could possibly feel any worse?"

"A lesson has been learnt here I think," Cara said, and she came around to hug us both briefly. "Now who would like cocoa?" It was unanimous.

Lorien took ours onto the verandah to drink in privacy and his family respected our wishes. With the mugs on the table, he looked at me sadly and opened his arms. I went to him and curled onto his lap. "I'm so scared Ash," he whispered. "What if you can't find it in your heart to forgive me? What if I've broken what we had, beyond repair? I don't think I can live without you in my life." He lightly fingered my vacant right lobe, having noticed I'd removed the diamond stud.

"I know I can't live without you in mine, Lorien." I lifted my face to kiss him softly.

"Eli felt this way about you too and look what happened there."

"You know that's different, it's not like what we've just been through."

"I know, but I'm still so scared Ash. I love you so much, you're everything to me." He wrapped his arms around me so tightly, his cheek to my forehead. I nearly couldn't breathe. When his embrace relaxed, I said,

"Maybe you just don't know any better. Maybe there's another girl out there waiting for you and you for her." He drew back, searching my face for sincerity.

"Don't say that, there'll never be anyone else for me. No one has ever loved as fiercely and so totally encompassing as I love you, Ashlyn." He softened a little and drew me back against him. "If there was a woman out there I could possibly love more than you it would kill me in the process. My heart explodes now with my every thought of you."

"I know it's not currently our favourite subject and a little close to home, but don't you think after last night you may *want* to kiss or sleep with someone else one day?"

"Ashlyn Mercy, you need to understand now that when we're a little older I'm going to ask you to marry me, and I would die if your answer wasn't yes." His words thrilled me, and I laughed.

"Yes."

"Yes what?" he asked in true confusion.

"I'll say yes, when we're a little older, when you ask me to marry you."

"You're just saying that to make me feel better."

"Why would I do that? You're the one who cheated on *me* remember."

"Don't Ash," his words were filled with pain. "I can't stand it - what I did to you, to our families, to my brother."

"To your body…" I reminded him.

"Yes, to my body…"

"Are you feeling better?"

"The soup helped a lot."

"So, what was it like, how did it make you feel?"

"The speed?" I nodded. "It was the second biggest rush of my life." He smiled at me knowingly, brushing his lips over mine.

"Keep going…" He kissed me again, briefly but so warmly.

"I meant to keep going about how it made you feel, not keep going as in kissing me," I laughed. "Not that it wasn't wonderful of course."

He looked into my eyes, picking up one of the mugs and holding it to my mouth for me to drink. We shared that mug and then the next over the course of his reflections. "Well, it sounded like a blast." I told him finally.

"That's a good word for it, and it was like something raging inside me, not anger, but a storm bursting to get free. I had all the power in the world and felt I was capable of anything. I only feel normal now and coming down the other side wasn't fun at all. And today, knowing the damage I'd caused in my wake… I know one thing - I'll never touch it again."

"How can you remember all that and not remember the other girl?"

"I don't know. Until Eli told me, I was oblivious to what I'd done. When you got here this morning, I had no idea why you were upset with me."

"I was more than upset Lorien." He smiled weakly at me; he was aware of that. "Who knows what it was anyway, being Matty's."

"Matty," Lorien growled. "I'd forgotten about him."

"Elijah took care of it."

"And then I abused you and Eli," he said, shaking his head in shame. "I don't remember that either. Hey, did you see today's paper?"

"I haven't really done much else than this today Lorien."

"Well check this out." The Sommersett Mail was sitting folded on the table. He leant over and grabbed it, opening it to page three. I was surprised to see a pixelated photo of who was obviously Matty under a caption reading '*Youth Charged for Selling Drugs to Local Teens*'.

"What the hell?" I said and leant forward to read the article. "He could be facing 10 years?"

"Not his first offence apparently, and Mum said the three students caught buying it off him on the school grounds have been expelled."

"Do we know them?"

"No, they were Year 8s."

"So young."

"Not really, we just never got into that stuff as a group," he reminded me.

"Until last night anyway," I reminded him right back.

"Yes," he said sheepishly. "After the outfall with my parents today, Mum showed me the newspaper and my eyes nearly fell out of my head. It could have been worse though I suppose, we may have been dragged into it some way if he had been selling and busted last night." I considered the consequences and felt a little ill. "It's not something I am proud of Ash." There was something I was also not proud of.

"I need to tell you something Lorien," I started. He looked at me, waiting for me to find my words. "I asked Elijah to kiss me after I'd found you with the barmaid."

"And?"

"He wouldn't. He said I'd regret it, but I didn't care at the time."

"Do you wish he had kissed you?"

"No, I'm glad he had some control. Regardless of the situation with you and me, I would have regretted it. It would have also been so unfair on Elijah. I'm sorry Lorien..." He snorted softly, saying,

"I have no right to judge you Ash. I imagine it was a reasonable request at the time, considering what you'd witnessed. Even if he had kissed you, at best I would be disappointed. It was a response to my actions, and consequences aren't always a pleasant reminder." I pressed my lips to his, softly. I was glad I had told him.

"How did you get home?"

"I walked. It isn't far from the golf club, not when you're fully loaded. Sleep didn't come easily either and when I got up this morning, I was wide awake, still dealing with the after-effects."

"This is all that matters now Lorien," I said as I tightened myself against him, stifling a yawn.

"I think we'd better get you to bed, you're about to drop," he smiled at me warmly, lifting me into his arms before standing.

"Where am I sleeping?"

"In my bed of course."

"Where will you be sleeping?"

"With you."

"I don't think we're supposed to," I recounted for him. He stooped so I could turn off the lounge room lamp. The rest of the family had already gone to bed it appeared, and when I looked at my watch, I was surprised to find it was nearly midnight. How long had we been sitting out there? The whole day was like a daze now, fuzzy and surreal; my head felt the same.

"Our parents want the every day to become a few times a week. They never wanted us to stop seeing each other altogether and I think they realise it's impossible to go back to holding hands now. Well, that was the gist I got of it once you left this morning. We're not going to do anything tonight anyway." We'd arrived at his door and I reached out to open it for him.

"I'm not ready to have sex again Lorien. It may be longer than just tonight."

"Ashlyn, my beautiful Baby girl, I know what I've torn out of you and I know it will take some time to mend properly. When you're ready to continue our relationship on a physical level, you let me know OK?"

"OK." I was feeling safe and secure again. The pain that was still in my heart this afternoon, sitting on the school oval, was starting to wane. I knew it would be all right in time and I looked forward to being able to put this finally behind us.

Without question, we both stripped off before climbing into bed. The caress of our skin against each other was for once not arousing, but innocent in its pleasure. As he drew me to him from behind to spoon, I was nearly asleep.

"I love you so much Ash, thank you."

"For what?"

"For taking me back, making me a better person, realising all the wonderful things I have in my life, appreciating what true love means," I cut him off, rolling over to kiss him.

"I love you too Lorien, with all of my heart." I rolled back onto my side and was asleep almost instantly.

THE BIGGER PICTURE

The Bitter Pill to Swallow

"You're crying yes then screaming no,
you tell me fast but want it slow
I ask you, what the hell does that mean?"

L Standish, 'Merciful Mayhem'

THERE WAS A KNOCK AT MY DOOR, and I looked up from my studying, welcoming the break. It was Mum, "Lorien's downstairs." We'd only said our goodbyes this morning and he was already here for a visit. I followed her downstairs, finding him in the kitchen talking to Dad. He didn't rise to greet me, which I found strange. Normally he would come to me and hug me, if not kiss me, regardless of whether Mum and Dad were in the room. I went to him instead and kissed him lightly before taking the seat next to him. He leant over and whispered in my ear,

"I know something you don't know." *What now*? I thought. He was grinning. It couldn't be that bad then, surely? Dad excused himself and Mum came over and sat opposite us at the breakfast bar.

"I asked Lorien to come over this afternoon." So, this wasn't a social call. "I wanted to talk to you both about birth control," she said bluntly. I put my hands to my face, saying,

"Do we have to talk about this *now*?" Mum worked at the Doctor's surgery as a receptionist. As I'd been their little 'surprise' when in their early 20s, she was all over this like a rash.

"Yes, we do. I made an appointment for you with Dr Wood at 4.00 pm tomorrow afternoon and I wanted to speak to you both first."

"Mum! I'm old enough and more than capable of dealing with this myself."

"Are you currently *on* the pill Ashlyn?" she asked smugly. I wasn't.

"Do we have to talk about this in front of Lorien?" I complained.

"It concerns him too as he is the one you're having... intercourse with." I shot Lorien a glance; *intercourse*, I mouthed. He laughed and apologised immediately to Mum, not wanting to appear flippant about her serious addressing of this situation.

"I don't know... Lorien, are we having intercourse?" I asked him, smiling.

"Certainly not at the moment," he retorted. Even Mum tried to hide her smile. She continued,

"Are you currently using some form of birth control?" I buried my face in my hands again. This was going to be invasive and one of the most *horrible* conversations I'd ever had with my mother.

"We've been going out for over eighteen months and I haven't come home pregnant. What do you think?" I answered, my hands still at my face.

"We've been using condoms Anna," Lorien told her, easing my burden the merest smidge.

"Do your parents know about this?" I asked him through my fingers. He shrugged.

"Yes, they do. I spoke about this with Cara a few nights ago and we thought it best to get it out of the way, me being the one to speak to you about it as you're my daughter. It's not that we think you're being irresponsible, we just wanted to ensure you were taking some form of preventative action."

"Great, how am I ever going to look her in the eye again?"

"I believe you sleep in Lorien's bed with him when you stay there. Is that correct?"

"Yes," I drawled.

"Your father and I have spoken about this and we think since you are... having... intercourse, it's ridiculous Lorien sleeps in the spare room when he's here." I looked at her in amazement. "So, if you will allow me to finish this conversation Ashlyn, it may work to your mutual benefits." I shut up and let her speak. Not that we were currently having 'intercourse', and while it may be a bit longer before we started again, I would always want to sleep beside him.

"Now, have you both been tested for HIV and other STIs?" Mum asked.

"Yes Anna, *I* have," Lorien said and looked at me grinning, knowing I was about to inadvertently inform my mother that Lorien had been the receiver of my virginity.

"Ashlyn?"

"There was no need before Lorien came along," I mumbled.

"Fine, fine..." she said, "I wouldn't know, would I?" No, she would not. "I think it would still be a good idea for the doctor to run some tests while you're there, just to make sure everything is in check before you... stop using condoms..." This was difficult for her to discuss too I realised. Knowing someone was ploughing the fields of your one and only daughter was a hard pill to swallow, all pun intended. "Is there anything you'd like to ask me?" I was hoping this was nearing the end. I was done talking to her about my most private life, something that was only to share between Lorien and me. He put his arm around me and I hid my face against his chest, wishing the floor would open and swallow Mum whole. "Well then, would you like some coffee? There's something else I wanted to talk to you about."

"Thanks Anna," Lorien said. When I didn't move he added, "Better make that two." I was pretty sure they exchanged a smile.

Dad came back into the kitchen when he heard the kettle boil. "Are you finished?" Mum nodded. "OK, now it's my turn," he said, taking a cup from Mum and joining us at the breakfast bar.

"You two are determined to make this as uncomfortable as possible for me, aren't you?" I asked, pained. Dad ignored me.

"Your mother no doubt told you about the new sleeping arrangements?"

"She did Dom," Lorien answered for me. I was glad he was here now; I wasn't sure I would have made it through on my own.

"I don't want this getting rubbed in our faces. I don't want to hear it, I don't want to see it and I especially don't want to know about it. I'm not asking for a little tact and consideration from you, I'm expecting it. No moans or rattling of headboards, OK?" I burst out laughing at his analogy. Surely he must have guessed on at least one occasion Lorien slept here, something untoward would have happened? "Ashlyn, I'm not kidding. I'm not quite as acceptant about this as Lorien's parents and your mother. You're still my little girl and I would like to keep thinking of you in that way for at least a while longer."

"I'll be good, Daddy," I said and dropped a kiss on his cheek. He smiled and shook his head.

"Just to think Anna, we were one or two years older than them when we *had* Ashlyn."

"Well don't go putting any ideas in their heads Dom!" Mum said.

"So, is that it?" I asked, taking Lorien's hand and standing. "I thought we might go upstairs and have some 'intercourse' now." Lorien and I both laughed and when Mum joined us, Dad looked at her as if she'd lost it.

"It's OK Dom, an inside joke," she sighed and laughed a little longer. "Ashlyn, you are a worry." As we went to walk off Mum stopped us. "Hang on, there was something else we needed to discuss with you," reminding herself of what she was about to say when Dad came back in. "Sit back down please." We did. "Your parents and I, we," she looked at Dad and smiled, "have talked more about what the conditions are regarding the new rules about you seeing each other." I looked at Lorien and he put his arm around me, waiting for the worst. Mum smiled at me, "It's not that bad kids, I think you'll be able to live with it. You can see each other four nights a week, what four nights and where you choose to spend them are up to you. However, before any frivolity takes place you will first do all homework assigned for the day, and on the nights you aren't together we expect you to be putting in extra study effort towards your HSC." She waited on an answer.

"I can live with that," I said.

"Me too," agreed Lorien. We were both happy they weren't attempting to rip us apart as it would have been too much to bear; we'd nearly managed to do that without their help anyway. He drew me to him, planting a kiss to my forehead then smiled at me widely.

"If you're able to do these things well enough to restore your grades *and* you don't skip any more classes," she looked at us sternly, "then you'll be allowed to continue on as normal, as long as the grades stay up."

"I appreciate it Anna, Dom, and I'll tell my parents that tomorrow too. Let's go and decide on a schedule Ash, we'll get back to you."

"It's up to you, there doesn't have to be a roster," Dad said. The phone rang and we left Mum to answer it, going up to *our* room.

Once inside I went to him, kissing him slowly, letting it work into a more potent level. His hands slid down my back in a soothing caress; all was right with the world again. "So, what nights do you think Baby?" he asked softly, still holding me.

"Saturday and Sunday definitely, there's no homework so we get maximum staying power." He considered this.

"Sounds good, that way we'll only have a night apart every second day. It'll be hard, but not as hard as they could have made it for us." He grinned down at me, drawing in to kiss me again. It was impossible to believe that only yesterday morning it felt like the world was ending. The knock at the door was about to change it all again.

"Lorien," Mum said as she walked quietly into the room, taking him by the hands, "that was your mother."

"What's wrong?" he asked, the concern on my mother's face now mirrored on his own.

"It's your Nanna, Honey; she passed away."

"What happened?" he asked through a tight throat, working to hold his emotions together. I went to him and tentatively put my hand on his back, not knowing how to comfort him.

"She had a stroke but went quickly and with no pain. Your father was with her when it happened." Mum pulled him down to her shoulder and held him as only a mother can.

"What can we do Lorien, can we take you home?" Dad asked gently. He shook his head, staying in the comfort of my mother's arms for the moment. He eventually drew back, his face wet.

"Poor Dad, he'll be taking it so hard." He then came to me and my parents closed the door behind them quietly, leaving us alone.

Sitting on my bed, he drew me onto his knee, leaning his face against my chest. I held him tightly, trying to squeeze the pain from his very pores. "Ashlyn," he whispered against me finally, his choking sobs hitching in his throat. "I... I don't know what to do..."

"Shh Lorien," I rubbed my hand slowly over his back. "Do you want me to take you home?" He nodded but made no move to get up. I went to get off his lap and he pulled me back to him.

"Not yet..." And I held him again, and would hold him until he no longer needed to be held.

Sometime later, he looked up at me, a slight smile on his lips. "What would I do without you Ash?" I reached over to my bedside table and grabbed a tissue to wipe his face. He spotted the diamond earring I'd removed two nights ago and smiled at me sadly as he threaded it into my lobe. I kissed him lightly, drawing my forehead down to his.

"What can I do for you?" I asked.

"Just this, this is enough. Having you here with me is all I need." My heart ached for him, so deep was his sorrow. I wrapped my arms around him again and asked if he was ready to go home now. He nodded and I climbed off his lap and stood with him. Holding his face gently, I looked into his eyes. "I'm OK," he said. "I'll just go and clean up a bit and we can go." He kissed me softly before he left the room.

I grabbed a uniform from my wardrobe and went to talk to Mum and Dad. "How is he going Honey?" Mum asked when I came down the stairs.

"He's alright for now. He's washing his face and then I'm going to take him home." Mum saw the uniform in my hands.

"It's OK Ashlyn. All rules are off for now. You take as much time as you need to be there for him and the Standish's; you'll be able to make up the work when you get back to school. Lorien needs you." I was glad she felt that way, I wouldn't have been able to concentrate at school knowing what the Standish's were about to go through.

"I'll take it with me anyway. I don't have a clean one at their place." Mum smiled at me and nodded. "I have a big favour to ask you both."

"What is it Honey?" Dad asked.

"Can one of you drive Lorien's car and follow in yours? I'll take him with me. We may need both of our cars at their place... I know it's a lot to ask..."

"It's not a problem," Dad said and hugged me as Lorien came down the stairs.

"Ready?" I asked and he nodded.

"Thanks Dom and Anna." Dad hugged him as did Mum, planting a soft kiss on his cheek.

"Let us know if you need anything, any help with the arrangements, anything..." she trailed off. He smiled at her,

"I will." I walked him to the door, his arm around me.

"Ashlyn," Mum stopped me. "Are your spare keys on the hook in the kitchen?"

"Unless you've moved them. Why?"

"Don't worry about it now. Please give Nick and Cara our love and tell them to ring us if they need *anything*. We won't come in when we drop the car off." I understood.

The mood at the Standish home was what I expected. Lorien went straight to his father and taking him in his embrace, they held each other tightly. I went to Cara and hugged her, "I'm so sorry," I whispered. Tears were starting to run down my face for the pain and loss this family was feeling. Death was a lonely place, and no amount of comfort could reach the centre of the heart at times. Grieving was a sole thing, a private thing which everyone did differently.

"It's all part of life Ashlyn," she said when she drew back from me, rubbing my arm and smiling through her tears. I went to Nick and hugged him too.

"Mum and Dad send their love. If there's anything they can do you only need ask." He nodded against me,

"Thank you, Ashlyn," he said, giving me one last squeeze before sitting back down at the dining room table, head heavy, back bent.

Cara went to make coffee when Lorien finally released her. Their embrace had been as soulful as the one he'd shared with his father. Although Betty was Nick's mother, Cara had known her as part of the family for many, many years. His loss was also hers.

"Where's Eli?" asked Lorien.

"In his room, he's been waiting for you to come home." We took to the stairs in search of him and found him lying on the bed with his headset on. Lorien sat next to him and when Elijah felt his weight, pulled the earphones out and stood, hugging his twin to him fiercely. I'd never seen them share a moment like this and the tears freshened on my face. It was such a mournful time.

For several minutes they stood like that before Elijah realised I was in the room with them. "Come here Ash," he sniffed, and I took him in my arms, running my hands over his back, trying to relay my sympathy as best I could. Lorien came in behind me and wrapped his arms around both of us and we all cried together, for Nanna.

Monday went by in a blur and none of us went to school. Flowers started to arrive around 11.00 am with one arrangement being from Mum and Dad; they'd included my name on the card. People came and went, dropping off food or paying their condolences - no one was hungry, but the fridge was now straining to hold it all. It was strange people reacted this way to someone else's loss, but I supposed no one in the family would be thinking straight enough to consider meal preparation.

With each ring of the doorbell, the day seemed to slow by yet another clock-tick and eventually Lorien had had enough for the moment, taking me upstairs to get away from it for a while.

"How are you doing Baby?" I asked, sitting next to him on the bed.

"Since when do you call me Baby?" he smiled.

"Since right now when I want to wrap you up and hold you safe and secure like a baby," I said, smiling back at him.

"*My* Baby girl, how you keep my heart beating..." He sighed and ran his hands over his face. "I just don't know what to do with myself..."

"Want to play something?" He looked at me grinning,

"I thought that was off limits for the moment." He gently traced a finger down my cheek, looking into my eyes. The sadness in his was not as deep as it had been when Mum told him the news. He now looked very tired.

"Do you want to have a sleep Lorien?"

"What happened to Baby?" he asked, drawing me onto his lap. His lips rested at my neck and he began rubbing my back slowly. I smiled down at him, waiting on his reply. "No, I want to play something. It'll take our minds off it." Opening the wardrobe door, he rummaged through boxes of games I hadn't realised were there until this moment. "Want to go and see what Eli is up to?"

I knocked softly on the door at Elijah's side of their connecting bathroom. Elijah slid the door open, knowing it would have been either Lorien or me. "Hey Ash, what's happening." He stepped back to let me into his room and I followed him to the bed, sitting next to him. I took his hand, asking,

"How are you Elijah? How are you coping with it all?"

"You know, good and bad, ups and downs..." he smiled at me wanly. I looked around and noticed not one thing had changed since I used to hang out in this room before Lorien's became my permanent haunt.

"Running through fond memories?" he asked, smiling at me cheekily.

"Something like that..."

"How are you and Lori doing?" he asked, referring back to the other night.

"I owe you so much Elijah. I don't know what I would've done without you that night. It all seems like a nightmare now, looking back."

"It was a nightmare, my hand still hurts," he laughed, looking down at it, and drawing it into a fist several times. I put my hand over his, looking at him.

"Thank you, Elijah."

"Think nothing of it kid." He winked at me. "So, what do I owe the pleasure of having you secluded in my room alone after all these months?"

"Lorien and I are going to play a game and we thought you might want to join us, take your mind off things..."

"I can't imagine any game you two would be playing Lorien would want me joining in on," he laughed.

"You both have dirty minds!" I chastised, and he laughed again.

"Can I have a hug please Ash?" He stood and I went to him, holding him tightly. "I do love you, you know, I don't mean it in any raunchy way, I love you're in my life and it appears you always will be if Lorien is smart." The bathroom door slid open behind me.

"Looks like there's a whole new game going on in here hey?" Lorien said with a smile and came into the room. He had 80s Trivial Pursuit under his arm, which was much loved by him and his brother, keeping score with each game they played. I was not looking forward to taking them on as an individual, but it would be fun. He put it on the bed and sat, starting to set it up.

"Boys!" Cara called up the stairs. "You have guests!"

"I'll go," Elijah said, getting up. Lorien sighed and looked at me.

"How are you doing Ash? This is as hard on you as it is for us, especially considering the last few days on top of it all."

"I'm made of steel Lorien, I'm here to deflect your pain and Elijah's. It's currently my sole purpose in life." My words reached him in a way I didn't expect. He stood and drew me up to him, crying softly in my ear.

"I love you so much Ash."

The door opened a few minutes later and Bree and Michael followed Elijah. "Get a room," Michael said light-heartedly, seeing Lorien was upset. I stepped away from him to allow Michael and Bree to hug him.

"What are you guys doing here?" he asked.

"It's lunchtime. We thought we'd come over and create some havoc. For once Bree and I will skip the last classes," he said, his intent obvious. "Not that we intend on having sex in your house or anything." Bree laughed, as did we all.

"So, every man for himself?" asked Elijah.

"Or every woman..." I added.

We sat and played. It did the twins the world of good to get their minds off the situation for a couple of hours. At times our laughter was true, and foolishness replaced misery.

All good things come to an end however, and it was time for Bree and Michael to leave so they could get their bus home.

"Let us know when the funeral is," Michael said at the front door as we stood there bidding them farewell, the twins on either side of me, their arms overlapping around my waist.

"It's Thursday," Lorien said, "Northern chapel at Sommersett crematorium, 10.30 am." Michael nodded.

"We'll be there. Enjoy the twin sandwich," he said with a mischievous grin as they walked off.

"Michael!" I said, and the boys both laughed and hugged me. We watched them cross the road, running into Keren on the way across. They chatted for a few seconds before Keren continued over to us.

"How are you guys going?" she asked, looking at Elijah.

"Fine," Elijah said and smiled at her, removing his arm from my waist to take her in his arms. She looked at me over his shoulder and her face betrayed the jealousy she was feeling. *Too bad*, I thought. *At a time like this she needs to be thinking about Elijah's needs, not her own.* She could deal with it any way she chose for all I cared; she was not a priority.

Lorien and I went over to the dining room table where his parents were sitting, going through paperwork. Lorien put his hands on his father's shoulders, squeezing them, portraying all the words that didn't need to be spoken between a father and his son. Nick raised his hand to pat Lorien's; it was a sweet and loving gesture, and it tore at my heart.

Glancing at his watch, Lorien came over to me, taking my hand and leading me to the door. "We have an appointment." I had no idea what he was talking about and finally realised it was 3.45 pm on Monday. I was due at the doctor's in fifteen minutes.

"We don't have to go Lorien, so much has happened since we last spoke to Mum about this yesterday."

"Nanna would want our lives to go on and I need to get out of the house for a while." I grabbed my car keys.

I noticed a bag sitting on the back seat and opened it in curiosity. My mother had packed it for me knowing I wouldn't be home to get clothes before the funeral and I understood her asking where my spare car keys were. She'd obviously dropped this in here when they brought the twin's car home last night, knowing I would eventually find it. Inside were my black dress and a pair of heels, a few changes of underwear and some other bits and pieces she thought I'd need. I loved her so much right now and was glad I would be seeing her in a few minutes.

Mum was at reception when we walked in and she came around the desk to briefly hug us both, not wanting to impact too much on Lorien in public. "Hi Anna, thanks for the beautiful flowers. Mum and Dad really appreciated it." He leant down and kissed her cheek. We chatted, waiting for the doctor, giving Mum the funeral details among other things. Doctor Wood stuck his head around the door a few minutes later.

"Ashlyn, it's lovely to see you, come through."

"Do you want me to come in with you?" Lorien asked. Mum nodded to me so in with me he came.

It was all relatively painless with exception to the embarrassment of the gynaecological examination. He asked us a few questions and then wrote me out a script for the pill, warning me it would take a little time for it to become active and to keep using condoms for another couple of weeks to be completely sure. He went out to speak to Mum as the receptionist, not my mother, and Lorien leant over, whispering, "I see why they call it playing doctors and nurses. Shall we have a go when we get home?" I slapped his thigh lightly, smiling at him. We were then free to go; I was surprised it had all been so simple.

We said goodbye to Mum, and I thanked her again for her thoughtful actions and went into the Chemist next door to the surgery to get the script filled. "No time like the present," Lorien said and did some quick math, grinning at me lewdly.

"You just be calm, party boy." He took my hand as we walked back to the car.

"Can I drive?" he asked, and I handed him the keys. I pulled out the pamphlet the Chemist had given me with the pill and started to digest the information.

"Wow, are you in for some massive changes," I laughed.

"Such as?"

"And I quote 'the side effects of the birth control pill can cause mood swings, vaginal dryness, loss of desire, breakthrough bleeding, nausea and vomiting, weight gain, and breast tenderness'." He reached over and cupped my right breast gently,

"Feels pretty tender now." I smiled at him and took his hand, looking around at the passing scenery.

"Where are we going?"

"Glassread."

We walked slowly down to the baths and sat at the far end, our feet dangling in the water – it was freezing. "You're not having any impetuous thoughts today Baby?" he asked, putting his arm around me.

"Is that why you brought me here?" I asked, knowing full well what had transpired the first time we were here. He put his hand to my chin and tilted my face toward him, leaning down to kiss me. It was a truly wonderful kiss, sitting in the afternoon winter-waning sunshine and listening to the sounds of the small waves lapping at the shore. Glassread always held an aura of solitude and peace. It was one of our favourite spots to come when we wanted to be alone. Its calming effect refreshed us by simply being here, with each other. Lorien started to laugh quietly. I looked at him questioningly.

"I was just thinking about how difficult 'intercourse' would be, teamed with vaginal dryness." He chuckled again and drew me back against him, his lips brushing over mine, still smiling. "I suppose we should get back," he sighed, and we ambled our way to the car.

No one had eaten much over the day and whilst Lorien was in the shower, I decided to put one of the casseroles on to warm. "I can do that Ashlyn," Cara said, coming into the kitchen a few minutes later.

"Please let me Cara, I need something to do and there's so little I *can* do for any of you at the moment." She smiled and hugged me.

"Thank you, Ashlyn, we're very fortunate to have you here." She left me to it.

I went through the cabinets and drawers, pulling out crockery and cutlery where I thought it would be needed. I'd just finished setting the table when Lorien trounced down the stairs. Although it was only 6.00 pm, he had his silk boxers on, dressed ready for bed.

"How's my little housewife doing?" he asked, taking me into his arms in a bear hug. I ran my hands over his broad, warm back, wrenching my wandering mind back to the polite thoughts it had been having before he came downstairs half naked. It was one thing when we were in bed together without a stitch of clothing on, but when in full view and out of the bedroom scenario, he knew his bare chest and back taunted me so. In fact, every time since we'd been together, within ten minutes of him appearing anywhere dressed like this we would be racing for privacy - his room, my room, wherever we happened to be.

"What are you doing?" I complained.

"What?" he asked in all innocence.

"Why haven't you got a shirt on?"

"I'm home, what's the difference?" He knew damn well what the difference was, and he was going to make me talk about this, playing the innocent until I could get the words out myself. If that was the way he wanted to do it, fine, I could ignore it... However, my body was not listening and had its own agenda. I found myself pulling him to me, scratching my nails lightly down his back as I kissed him deeply.

"Hmmm Lorien," I breathed. I was ready to have sex with him again, right now in fact. I could imagine myself wiping everything to the floor in a crash with one sweep of my arm, Lorien draping me across the bench and ripping at my briefs, driving himself into me.

"Ashlyn Mercy, you should be ashamed of yourself." He pulled back, smiling at me. "You *have* been having more delicious daydreams, haven't you?" He sat on one of the stools and drew me to him, whispering, "I hope they're about me again?" I nodded, lowering my face a little. "What happened to waiting?" he asked quietly, plucking an eyelash from my cheek. He held it in front of my lips for me to blow on and make a wish. I smiled at him as I blew and then squeezed my eyes shut to show how important this wish was.

I sighed, going back to his last point and he was right. It was only forty-eight hours ago I'd told him that, and here I was already reneging on it. "I thought around your birthday would be a good time to get the lava flowing again..." That was still a few weeks away, a truly acceptable timeframe for what I'd discussed with him on Saturday night. I wasn't expecting myself to have dealt with his infidelity so quickly and thought Nanna's passing had helped me come to terms with the bigger picture. It was no longer about my suffering, or his, we were meant to be together, and I was ready to pick up where we left off.

"I don't want to wait anymore. I love you Lorien and want to love you emotionally and physically."

"I agree with your initial point. I thought about it after you left on Sunday morning and you were right."

"But I...," I interrupted him. He put a finger to my lips, silencing me.

"I think we should wait. It will build character," he said, smiling.

"Why do you want to wait?" I was confused about his side of the picture.

"I want you to know that most importantly I respect you. Our relationship is not about jumping into bed at every conceivable chance we get. I love you here," he placed his palm flat against my heart, "as well as here," he pressed his hands to either side of my head, "and of course here." He slid his palm between my legs, but only fleetingly. "Do you understand Baby - understand where I'm coming from?" I nodded and thought again what a wonderful man I'd managed to find, regardless of the mistakes he'd made over the last few days. I could smell the casserole and darted to the oven, pulling it out before it could burn.

"Whew, that was close. Want to call your family. Where are they anyway?"

"Dad was sleeping and Eli's in his room with Keren no doubt." I'll go and see who's available." I put a cork placemat in the middle of the table so the dish wouldn't scorch the tabletop, sitting a serving spoon next to it. I'd also thrown together a salad and buttered some rolls; it would do for a slap-up meal. Lorien came back down the stairs, his family falling in behind him.

"Thanks Ashlyn, this was very considerate of you," Nick said and dropped a kiss on top of my head as he went into the kitchen and pulled a bottle of wine from the fridge, pouring us each a glass. There was no skulling of drinks tonight.

The Debt We All Pay

"If I close my eyes I see can you as a little girl of five,
Dancing in the sun with a white dress on
I can keep this memory alive."

L Standish, 'Afterlife'

I WAS SITTING IN THE FRONT PEW with Cara, holding her hand. When Nick, the twins and their Uncle Howard carried the coffin into the chapel, we all stood and faced them. They walked in slowly to Nat King Cole's 'Unforgettable' playing softly in the background. The sight of them brought tears immediately to my face, breaking my personal vow I'd be strong today for Lorien and his family. The Minister approached them and offered words of comfort, shaking each of their hands in turn. Cara and I moved over to let Nick and Lorien sit between us whilst Keren moved to the end, to allow Elijah to sit next to his mother. Lorien took my hand and smiled at me with wet eyes as the Minister started the service.

The Minister delivered the eulogy as Nick didn't think he'd be able to. They also scrapped the song they were going to sing as a family during the reflection time, none of them thinking they'd be able to hold it together. The Minister did a wonderful job outlining her growing-up years, through her courtship with Nick's father, Thomas, and into their early life together.

It was after several years of marriage they finally gave up hope of ever having a family before they were blessed with their little boy. And, what a mischievous little boy Nick had been. The Minister regaled us with many a merry anecdote of his youth and the trouble he had found himself in - laughter through tears was the oddest sensation.

When he reached the part of her life when she lost Thomas I started crying again. Telling us how deep her grief was and her decision to move from the city to Sommersett where she lived out the rest of her life in a peaceful and loving existence; her family moving to be near her within six months of his death. He spoke of the love Betty had for Cara and the twins, Keren and I even getting a mention as to how happy it made her knowing how happy we made her grandsons. I squeezed Lorien's hand and he smiled at me, drawing his arm around me. "And now we'll have a few moments of reflection, during which we will hear Betty's favourite song," the Minister said and 'Always on my mind' started to play and a slideshow of photos commenced on the TV bracketed to the wall. It was a beautiful presentation, showing her over the many years of her life, including members of the family and surprisingly me and Keren again. It was the photo taken before we left for the Year 10 formal and I was with Elijah, Keren with Lorien. I kissed Lorien on the cheek and turned to find Elijah. I smiled at him and he winked, his eyes full of sorrow and tears. Lorien stood with his mother, father and Elijah, and each lay a white rose on her coffin, the music ending.

The Minister asked for anyone who wanted to share his or her memories of Betty. Howard stood and addressed us, talking about the union of the two families and the times they'd shared in laughter and in tears. The twins' Uncle Steve also spoke briefly, turning to the Standish's and addressing them, speaking of his sorrow over their loss and that he and Marie would always be there for them. It was very touching, as he was obviously not someone who took to public speaking well.

Finally, 'Amazing Grace' played on the bagpipes and we all stood to file from the chapel. Lorien hugged me to him when we got outside. We held each other, supported each other, cried against each other... By the time the majority of the congregation had joined us, we were pretty much drained of all bodily fluids. "I love you Ash," Lorien whispered, and I kissed him, looking into his saddened eyes.

"I'm yours Baby," I smiled up at him and he laughed, squeezing me against him. I felt a hand on my shoulder and turned to see Simon, Michael and Bree standing behind me. Michael hugged Lorien fiercely as did Simon and Bree in turn.

"We're so sorry Lorien," Bree said, a tissue still at her eyes. "It was a beautiful service..."

"Nanna would have loved it," he said simply. "Are you coming back to our place for the wake?"

"Yes, we're going to make a move now as we have to make a stop. We'll see you there," Simon said, lightly slapping him on the back.

"No worries, catch you at home."

It was over half an hour before we climbed into the car; the family speaking with all of Betty's friends and neighbours, introductions made and promises to stay in touch.

Mum opened the door when we returned to the house; they'd come straight back after the service to let people in as they arrived. "How are you doing Lorien?" She took him in her arms. With her standing on the step, she was the perfect height to administer cuddles.

"OK Anna, I'm... OK." He kissed her on the cheek and smiled at her. "Thank you so much for all of your help over the past week, we all appreciate it."

"There's no need to thank me Lorien. Your family would have done the same for ours. We're all-but one family now, aren't we?" He nodded and hugged her again before leading me inside.

The wonderful thing about a wake is the flood of every emotion: tears, laughter, frivolity and even good times. Nick had arranged a keg and that is where we found Dad, in the process of tapping it. He passed Lorien the first drawn beer. "Get that into you Lorien, it'll put hair on your chest!"

"No, it won't," I laughed. "He hasn't got one now."

"I believe your father was talking to *me* Miss Smarty!" He handed me the next beer and the three of us toasted Nanna. When Dad took a tray of poured beers around the newcomers, Lorien leant in and whispered,

"I thought you loved my hairless chest?"

"I do," I purred. "Feel like getting it out for me?"

"Only if you go first." I smiled at him, shaking my head. He knew that was *not* going to happen.

His mood became melancholy, raising his hand to my lobe with the diamond stud in it. "Don't ever take it out again."

"Don't give me a reason to," I shot back and wished I could eat my words. I hadn't meant to sound so aggressive, and it was especially not something I wanted to say to him on this day, of all days. He smiled sadly at me, knowing it was part of our past now but still something that would come back to haunt him on occasion. Such was the life of an apologetic sinner. However, he didn't need to be reminded of this from me and I vowed I'd never bring up the issue with him again; he was more than capable of instilling his own penitence.

When our friends arrived, we moved to the northern verandah, the twins not really wanting to play a big part in the receiving line, wanting to stay out of everyone's way where possible. It'd been a hard week for them and socialising with slightly inebriated guests was not what they wanted to do this afternoon.

We were all happy to take their lead, joined eventually by Peter, Julie and Casey who I hadn't seen at the service. I was sitting on Lorien's lap when Julie approached me. "Do you still kiss Lorien?" she asked, climbing onto my knee, making us a triple-decker.

"Yes Julie," I smiled at her and shifted slightly to make it more comfortable for Lorien. Casey had been sitting with Peter up until this point and now went to wriggle onto Elijah's vacant lap. I'd learnt early when young twins were involved things usually happened in pairs. Elijah hugged Casey to him and applied a few raspberries to her cheek, making her squirm and giggle.

"Are you kissing him now?" Julie asked, which I found strange as she could see our mouths were nowhere near each other. Lorien and Elijah burst into braying laughter, being some time before either of them could compose themselves enough to explain her question. Julie was looking cross; she'd not liked being laughed at by her older cousins. Elijah came around first.

"Have you girls been asking Aunty Marie about sex?" he asked, trying not to laugh as Casey nodded.

"Mum said it was nicer to call it kissing than the word we used."

"Is that what you think Lori and Ash are doing now Julie, kissing?"

"Maybe." She answered elusively. Good for her.

"Even though their mouths aren't touching?"

"Well, they could be fucking."

"Julie!" Elijah exclaimed. But there was no point in chastising her. Everyone was now almost in tears, including Peter, but the girls were still unsure why. For once Michael and Simon kept their mouths shut and were sitting back enjoying the show.

"That's a rude word Julie," Lorien said to her when he'd calmed down enough to be able to speak in full sentences again.

"That's what Mum said."

"So why did you say it again?"

"None of you knew what I was talking about, but you do *now* though!" She was right, what a clever little nine year old. She sat there, still on my knee looking at me. "Well?"

"Well what?"

"God Ash, don't make her ask again," Elijah chuckled.

"Oh, right...no Julie, Lorien and I aren't 'kissing'. I'm just sitting on his lap as you are on mine."

"*Do* you kiss him?"

"In the way you mean or like this?" I asked and leant forward to give him a quick peck on the cheek.

"I've never seen you kiss him like *that* before." She wasn't going to let me get away with anything today, so I kissed Lorien again, a little longer, a little more tenderly and on the lips.

"No, in the way I mean."

"In that case, yes I suppose we do."

"But you're not doing it now?"

"With a kid on their knee it would be illegal in most States wouldn't it?" Simon guffawed to Michael, their enjoyment obvious.

"No Honey, not at the moment."

"Will you tell me when you do?"

"No Honey..." I looked at Lorien, wanting him to put an end to the constant questions that didn't seem to follow any specific path. He smiled at me and shrugged his shoulders. He was going to let me suffer.

"Why not?" Another burst of laughter emanated throughout our small crowd. Julie jumped off my lap and stood facing them, hands on hips, scowl deep-set. "I'm not talking to any of you!" But how I wished she would. She came and leant against my thigh, repeating her question again in all seriousness, not caring that the crowd still laughed. I shot Lorien a scathing glare and stood up, taking Julie by the hand.

"Come on Casey, you'd better come too," and I led them down the stairs into the far corner of the garden.

We sat on the grass and I explained to them a little less clinically about the privacy and love of what their 'kissing' meant and it wasn't something that usually went on in front of other people. I asked what Marie had told them and I had to admit, their explanation was fairly solid, just a little remiss in the romance department. When they had no further questions they ran back to their parents, poking their tongues out at Lorien and Elijah on the way past. Lorien had been watching me the whole time our little trio was in the garden, a smirk on his face. I also went to walk past him, intending on speaking to Marie so she knew I'd been talking 'sex' with her girls. Lorien shot his hand out and grabbed me by the wrist. I poked my tongue out at him too and laughed, explaining where I was going. He came with me.

We milled around for a while once up, conversing briefly with the guests, chatting with my Mum and Dad, yakking to his family. Dad poured eight beers for us from the keg, and we took them back to the group, handing one to Peter also. "Thanks cuz!" he said to Lorien and proceeded to feel like a grown up as he sipped it cautiously; quite possibly having heard the stories on how the twins were feeling, post eighteenth birthday bash. The girls eventually forgave their older cousins, whom they obviously adored, and came back a few minutes later, begging them to get the guitars out and play some of their favourite songs. Neither was keen and Elijah suggested playing a game instead. They were happy with this idea and Lorien disappeared inside.

Keren was sitting next to Elijah on the wicker lounge and moved over when both girls insisted on reclaiming his lap. Keren wasn't overjoyed at this, possibly now jealous of two little girls who had known him all of their lives. "Are you going to be a Doctor Elijah?" Casey asked.

"Sure am. Will you let me do your check-ups when I'm qualified?" Both girls nodded. It was so cute, and I secretly grabbed my mobile, turning it into a Kodak moment. "Thanks Ash," he grimaced at me.

"Dad said you're becoming a doctor so you can look at women's hoo-ha's all day," Julie continued for her twin.

"What?" Elijah choked, looking at Peter who nodded, laughing. "Well, your Dad is wrong, that's what a gynaecologist does Honey. I'll be a regular doctor. The kind *you* go to see when you have a sore throat or a tummy ache."

"What a giroconolist?" Casey asked, her little face screwing up as she tried to pronounce the term.

"I guess it's someone who's paid to look at women's hoo-ha's all day," Elijah said, smiling at the rest of us.

"This is like good cop, bad cop," Simon grinned, bringing the laughter that everyone had been trying to keep bottled up, to the surface; the girl's faces taking on a look of thunder again. Lorien came back through the door, lead guitar in one hand and our two blindfolds in the other.

"Yay!" they chorused and clapped their hands together.

"One song!" he warned them. "What do you want to hear?"

"Something with hoo-ha's in it!" Casey exclaimed. Lorien laughed loudly, suggesting something by The Radiators might be appropriate. The girls looked around in true confusion and I could see what was coming. Sure enough, Casey didn't disappoint,

"What's a hoo-ha?" I shot Michael a warning glance, knowing he'd want to answer they were sitting on it. He just grinned at me and mouthed, *this is so cool!* He was enjoying the moment immensely.

"Ask your father in the car, he seems to be the expert," Elijah told her, putting Steve on the spot for the drive home. I could just imagine what Marie's take would be on the conversation.

"Will you play 'Afterlife' for us?" Casey asked. I was impressed she knew this song; it had been one from our play-list when we were still 'Listening at Keyholes'.

"I think that's a great idea, Nanna would love it."

He sang it to them, keeping it light for their sake, but after his comment, it was hard not to relate all the emotions of it back to Nanna. There were a few damp eyes when he'd finished, including his own. The girls didn't notice though, they watched him intently as he sang it to them, knowing it was all for them. My heart melted for him like gooey chocolate... "Now play..." Julie started.

"No, one song, that's it." He got up and moved the guitar into the rumpus room - out of sight, out of mind. Lorien took the blindfolds off the edge of the lounge he'd draped them over, causing Michael to ask,

"You're going to 'kiss' Ash in front of them after all hey?" The girls, now being a little more aware of this term, rolled their eyes, tsking him – he was so immature apparently. It had surprised me Michael had been so well behaved.

We got another game of blindfold going as we'd played at the Bay and the girls loved it. To slow it down and to remove us from the gameplay as much as possible, Lorien and Elijah blindfolded the girls and spun them around needing to then find each other, us calling out the occasional direction. "I hope they've had a wash," Bree said.

"They've only been around *all* of our heads Bree!" I reminded her.
"Still…" she smiled.

The afternoon sped by so quickly and soon Michael, Bree and Simon were bidding us farewell. The last to leave for the day was Keren. I assumed she'd be staying but they were still working some things out it seemed. It had been a long day…

Lying in bed, nearly asleep, I remembered to ask Lorien how the girls knew 'Afterlife' and told him of my surprise when they requested it. "It's their song. I wrote it for them when they were five."

"You would've only been fourteen?"

"It's been modified a bit from the original version, but it's still basically the same song, the same tune." His revelation stunned me a little. I knew he was talented when I met him at sixteen, why would I not think he'd been writing well before I came along. "Ash?" he asked tentatively when I hadn't made any form of comment. "Baby?" I smiled up at him and the crease in his brow softened.

"I'm in awe of you." He laughed and shook his head,

"Silly girl," he crooned, looking so deeply into my eyes full of love for him. "You've heard my songs before, why the groupie attitude all of a sudden?" he teased.

"I keep forgetting just how wonderful you are Lorien. I love you with all of my heart."

"You've had mine for the longest time," he whispered, taking me in his full embrace to kiss me slowly, deeply. My leg wended its way between his and I found myself unconsciously writhing myself against him, wanting to climb aboard the love train. I felt him smile through the kiss and I sat up to look at him. "I know what 'kiss' you're after Baby." I laughed.

"You have no idea of the effect you have on me Lorien." My passion had abated as quickly as it originally pulled into 'love station', population two, everyone off.

"Yes, I do, it's all over my leg." I smacked him lightly.

"They're gorgeous Lorien. I love it when we see the girls, not that it was a great occasion for it today."

"No," he sighed, looking up at the ceiling.

"Were they at the service? I didn't see them."

"Their neighbour was with them in the back pew, and she took them for lunch when it finished, worried it may have been too much seeing us all outside crying."

"A good friend of your Aunt and Uncle's I imagine." He smiled and nodded,

"They were neighbours before the girls were born." His expression had changed, now sad and morose as he ran his fingers gently through my hair.

"Nanna knew how much you loved her…"

"I'm not thinking about Nanna Ash, I'm thinking about you… if something ever happened to you…"

"Lorien, don't. It would be the worst tragedy for me too if something were to happen to you, but it won't. And we can't sit sullen waiting for the day when it does arrive, can we? Let's face it - one of us will go first someday." He smiled at me, "Can I have a kiss?"

"Always…" he sighed. I murmured to him several minutes later,

"This is not the kind I was referring to…" I felt him smile again, which warmed my body by a few degrees.

"Good morning Baby!" I was greeted as I woke, rolling over to nestle into Lorien's warm side. I'd been sleeping on my stomach, which was unusual for me, but explained the crick I felt in my neck as I moved against him. He was leaning on one elbow, looking down at me with a dirty-big grin on his face.

"Have you been watching me sleep?" I asked as he leant down to administer my good morning kiss.

"I didn't have a choice, you woke me."

"How could I wake you, *I* only just woke up." It was too early to be solving his riddles.

"You were calling my name," he said, smiling down at me, a knowing look on his face. I realised he was going to play this out for as long as he could, weaning me onto the information as he seemed fit to deliver it.

"Was I telling you to get off me?" I laughed.

"No, quite the opposite." His ever-wandering hand found the edging of my PJ top, working its way underneath to torment me into arousal, arousal that would not be allowed to erupt until my damned birthday next week.

"Leave me alone, you tease," I told him, moving his hand from my breast.

"Our abstinence has taken its toll on you Ash." He tussled briefly with my hand holding down my top, giving up the fight to move further south.

"I'm *not* playing these games this morning Lorien. Tell me what you're on about or let it be!" I softened my harsh words with a soft kiss to his pouting lips. He laughed and said,

"Well, here I am, fast asleep and I hear my name being called..." He worked his fingers slowly into the elastic at the top of my flannelette pyjama bottoms and I held his hand firmly, keeping it immobile.

"I'm listening..."

"And I wake to find you face down, grinding yourself into the mattress, at a furious pace mind you. Your little hands were all aflutter, grabbing at the sheets..." My traitorous mind and body had forgotten we hadn't made love for some time and what I'd taken to be last night's erotic encounter was actually my subliminal conscious, taking me to where I wanted to be.

"I don't believe you!"

"You don't have to, but look at what you've done to me." He whipped the covers back to reveal his anything but flaccid self.

"You always look like that," I laughed.

"Were you dreaming again Baby?" He shifted down to take me in his arms, his hand now safely teasing down my back.

"Are you going to let me use that?" I whispered and engulfed him in my 'little hand', caressing him slowly.

"Not in the way you want." He kissed me on the forehead and smiled at me, knowing where I would want to put it, signalling the end of our abstinence.

"But Mr Winky is *very* cranky this morning!"

"So will Lorien be if you don't leave him alone Baby. Surely you can wait eight more days?"

"Want some fellatio?" I asked in my best clinical terminology.

"Yes, I mean nope."

"A bit of hand relief?"

"Yes, I mean nope," he laughed.

"A smack in the head?"

"Which one? Actually, it doesn't matter, that's a definite nope to both," he laughed again. I sighed, deeply. Talking about it, regardless of the comical delivery, didn't make it any easier to cope with and I was *really* looking forward to my birthday. So was he, I assumed. "It's nearly over Sweetheart," he said, drawing me to him as he moved my hand up to his chest, playing his fingers lightly through mine.

"Lying like this and talking about it doesn't help at all."

"Ah excuse me. I'm Mr hard-on here."

"And I'm Mrs wide-on." He threw back his head and laughed loudly.

"You turn a wonderful phrase Ash."

"Your mother has said that to me before," I grinned at him, watching him deflate.

"You certainly know how to get rid of a guy's erection." I shouldn't have mentioned his mother - Mr Winky was asleep immediately.

"You're the most stubborn person I know Lorien."

"As you are to me..." I knew this was the case; when my mind was set on something, it became concrete. What a pity we'd never put our two forces together for good instead of evil.

I sighed again and started to climb out of bed, over this conversation. I'd be just dancing around the maypole all morning, for want of a better analogy, not getting anywhere except back to the spot where I started with him. He could be *infuriating* sometimes, especially when in one of these painfully playful moods, but he grabbed me, pulling me back to him with a growl. "You can always play with yourself," he suggested breathily into my ear.

"And you would just hate every second of that wouldn't you?" He grinned at me and took my hand, placing it over my pubic mound. "No way Lorien, you don't deserve anything that special."

"What if I soften the deal?" he purred, easing the front of my PJ bottoms, and himself, down my body.

"I won't need to play with myself then, will I?"

"How very honest of you Baby, and very true." He let go of my bottoms and they snapped back into place at the waist. I scowled at him, which he returned as a wide grin.

"I'm going to shower."

"I'll join you."

"Wait until you're asked." He pouted at me and I laughed. "Would you care to join me in the shower?" He answered in a quick pant,

"Yeah, yeah, yeah," pulling me back to the bed for another deep kiss before we hit the bathroom, starting with cold water only…

Happy Birthday to Me

"You don't need to be wrapped in ermine or dripping in gaudy jewels,
I am happiest most of all when you are in your birthday suit."

L Standish, 'Once a Year'

WE WERE SITTING AT MY BREAKFAST BAR doing our homework
when Lorien raised the subject of my birthday this coming Friday. "Do you
mind if I give you something that isn't tangible for your birthday?" he asked.

"Your presence is enough of a present Lorien," I said. He laughed,

"Thank you, that *is* lovely to hear, but seriously is that OK?"

"What did you have in mind?"

"An experience instead of a gift..." I looked at him dubiously and
he laughed again,

"Nothing weird or kinky, it's just somewhere I want to take you to
spend the weekend."

"I'm at your mercy," I told him, smiling.

"You *are* my Mercy, Baby."

We left straight after school on Friday and headed south down the
M1 towards Sydney. "Are we going to Sydney?"

"Are you going to ask me where we're going for the entire trip?"
he asked cheekily.

"Yes."

"Well in that case, yes, we're going to Sydney."

"To where you used to live?"

"I never thought about it, but we can visit my old haunts whilst we're down here if you like."

"I'd like to see where you grew up; get a little more insight into the depths of Lorien Thomas Standish."

"Well Ashlyn Diane Mercy, I shall grant your wish."

We were currently driving on Park Street and Lorien turned right onto Pitt, pulling up outside the Hilton Hotel. He handed the keys to the parking valet as they started to remove our bags from the boot. "Lorien wow! How can you afford this?"

"I got an advance on my allowance," he smiled at me. "Come on, we don't have much time."

"Where are we going?"

"You'll find out."

We checked in, our bags already in our suite when we arrived, and we both changed into something more formal, I into my black dress and Lorien into a suit. He looked so handsome waiting on the balcony for me and he turned as I walked out of the bathroom. "Gorgeous..." he sighed as I went to him, kissing him, and then he rushed us from the room, grabbing his wallet and the door swipe card on the way out.

The door attendant hailed a cab for us and within a few minutes, we were pulling up out the front of the Sydney Opera House. My eyes were greedy for all that was contained outside the taxi as Lorien ran around the back of it to open my door, holding out his arm. I saw the marquee; the Australian Ballet was performing Swan Lake in the Opera Theatre.

He escorted me up the stairs in the same courteous way that he'd escorted Keren, and Elijah had escorted me, to the Year 10 formal nearly two years ago. I marvelled again at how well the twins had been raised by their loving parents, taking into consideration all the little nuances that would ensure their sons were above reproach when it came to matters of the heart.

A lot of people were already milling around as we made our way into the waiting area outside the Opera Theatre, still having twenty minutes before the ballet was due to commence.

"Would you like some champagne Darling?" he asked.

"What happened to Baby?"

"We're at the Opera House my love, no common slang terms allowed here."

"Champagne would be ever so delightful Mr Standish, thank you."

"Would Madam care to take a seat? I shall be right with thee." I laughed and sat on the chaise sofa, holding the other space for Lorien on his return.

Our glasses clinked and our smiles were mirrored; I was going to enjoy this immensely as I'd never been into the Opera House for a show before. A few Music excursions had brought me here over the years when in the lower forms, but I'd not seen anything performed, just the same annual tour which ended up in viewing all the costumes held in its basement from previous operas and plays. When the bells started to chime, signalling for us to take our seats, I stood in anticipation. I couldn't wait to see the ballet unfold before me.

They called intermission after Act 2 and I followed Lorien to the bar, afraid I would lose him in the crowd if he went alone. We found a corner on the deck outside, and he toasted me on my birthday. "I love Tchaikovsky, no one has written a more difficult ballet to perform in history.

You already knew the storyline of Swan Lake, didn't you Odette?" he asked, smiling, naming me the female protagonist.

"Yes, Prince Siegfried, but I'm not sure why all the classics have to have such a miserable ending."

"It depends on how you look at it. It's a happy ending of sorts."

"Maybe, but it's a bittersweet happy ending. They both have to die to have their eternity together and that is totally symbolic in reality; we don't know there is an afterlife."

"Name another classic miserable ending through love's misfortunes?"

"How about Shakespeare's 'Romeo and Juliet'?" I offered.

"Point taken," he smiled and drained his glass.

My mind drifted a little, looking out over the harbour. The wind was slapping me with its winter fingers, tormenting at my hair and hemline. I drew my wrap to me tighter and Lorien put his arm around me. "Too cold Ash? Do you want to go back inside?"

"I'm fine," I smiled up at him and he leant down to kiss me. We were both fully aware tonight was the trigger to kick-start the end of our abstinence, although neither of us had mentioned it for a few days. I shuddered a little, thinking about getting back to the suite, thinking about the present I had for him. After we had packed the bags last night, I slipped the USB into the front pocket, knowing he wouldn't go rifling through it, and it was with great anticipation I looked forward to giving it to him. I shuddered again.

"Let's go back inside, you're shivering." He put his arm around my waist to direct me through the crowd and I stopped him.

"It wasn't that kind of shiver," I said and lowered my eyes. He put a finger to my chin, raising my eyes to look into them as a slow smile widened across his face. Standing there staring at each other was enough to make our breathing become slightly hurried, knowing what was going to transpire later.

"I love you Ash," he whispered, drawing me into his arms.

"I have something for you when we get back to the hotel which will make you love me even more," I whispered back.

"And I have something for you too...although nothing could make me love you more than I already do."

"Mine's *tangible*," I said, using his word.

"Oh Sweetheart trust me, so is mine." He moved in closer, and I could feel that indeed it was. The bells chimed again, signalling Act 3 was about to start, and we walked slowly back into the theatre to watch the tragic sweetness of Prince Siegfried and his Odette drown in the lake to then rise into Heaven together.

"So," he said as we walked down the steps from the Opera House, "do you want to have a drink somewhere or..."

"I'll take the 'or' option." I smiled up at him. "Besides, we have all day tomorrow and Sunday to do anything we like. I want to spend some time with you."

"We never do that, do we?" he teased.

"Not alone, someone's usually around."

"True."

"Can we get some more champagne and sit out on our balcony for a while?"

"I would like that very much. And, since it's your birthday Ash, we can do whatever you like."

"I'm going to hold you to that."

"I hope you'll hold me to something." He grinned and took me by the hand.

We decided to walk, as it wasn't very far. On the way, we stopped at a bottle-shop and he bought two bottles of Cristal. When I saw the price on the cash register, I couldn't believe two bottles of 'grog' could possibly cost that much, assuming it was a mistake. Lorien entered his pin number so I then assumed it wasn't.

Lorien rang room service when we got back to the hotel and asked for an ice bucket, some aperitifs, and other assorted finger-foods as he stumbled across them whilst scanning through the menu. Knowing there would possibly be an ill-timed knock at the door, I went into the bathroom to change. I'd brought the maroon babydoll with me, but I wasn't sure whether to put it on now or later. It didn't matter I supposed, we were in an expensive hotel and to hell with the staff and neighbours. I took off my clothes and hesitated, finally dressing in jeans and a warm jumper, leaving off the bottom layer. That could be another surprise for him later; I would save the babydoll for tomorrow night.

As I went to walk out of the bathroom, there was a knock. "Room Service." I opened my eyes wide at Lorien and scooted back in there, closing the door behind me. I could hear him speaking to the attendant and stopped to wonder what the hell I was doing. I started to laugh, keeping it as low as possible... what a dag. I knew what we were doing tonight, as did Lorien, but there was no sign stapled to the outer door informing the rest of the world of our intentions. My modest conscience had led me astray, but in a truly comical way. I sighed out the last laugh as Lorien opened the door.

"What are you doing in here?" he asked, leaning against the doorframe, his head cocked to the side. I started to laugh again, *what a dag*.

He took me by the hand and led me outside, shaking his head. He'd set out the food and the champagne was in the ice bucket, two glasses ready for action. Low, padded deck chairs stood on either side of the table. They looked inviting and I sat down, bubbling out the last few giggles and was calm again. He draped a blanket over me as I settled in and asked, "Are you going to share?" He tilted a glass and filled it slowly, passing it to me.

"I don't know if I'll be able to get it out right." I laughed out another sigh. "Funny," I said, nodding my head. He pulled a chair over to sit right next to me, climbing in under the blanket and draping his elbow over my bent leg, holding my knee lightly in his hand. He shifted slightly to better face me and raised his glass,

"Happy Birthday Ash." I clinked my glass against his for the second time tonight and as we drank our eyes locked; nothing was funny anymore. Our faces slowly descended toward each other's, our lips meeting in the middle.

I felt him take the glass from me and put it on the table, leaning in closer as a shot of fire seared through me. "Come and sit with me," he said quickly, and I scurried over to him, impatient to kiss him again. The downward motion of my settling into his lap carried my body forward to him under its own force, ending the movement with my lips hard against his. My arms locked around his neck as he pulled the blanket around us.

This wasn't a tender kiss, a sweet kiss; it was a kiss reserved for lovers, like the war bride waiting for her man to come home after months at sea. I couldn't get enough of my mouth against his, couldn't hold him tightly enough, all I could hear was our rocketing breathing and finally I gasped, throwing my head back for breath whilst holding his face against my throat.

"Oh God Lorien…" He continued to kiss around my neck, his lips to my ear, his hot exhalations paced with my own as I dragged my fingers through his hair. I'd been sporadically pressing my thighs together during the kiss, so worked up by him I was, and having caught my breath, I dragged his head from my neck, sealing his mouth back to mine.

"Someone's horny!" he mumbled through the kiss, reaching his hands up my back in slow drawing caresses, soothing not harrying, bringing my tempo back to a more refined level for a ritzy, public-viewed balcony.

His kisses were now lazier, deeper and longer. My breathing slowed and became more controlled, less hectic. When I finally drew back from this kiss, I held his face in my hands, looking at him.

"Wow, you're good." He smiled at me, breaking into a laugh.

"At what?"

"Bringing me back down. I was ready to rip your clothes off, but you brought me back to the ground."

"Not such a good thing really, I *should* have let you have your way with me… and I understand *now* why you were hiding in the bathroom before."

"You think so?" I asked cheekily and handed him his glass, drinking deeply from my own. It tasted wonderful. "This is really lovely," I told him and drained the last thimbleful from it. He finished his and moved forward to grab the ice bucket, sitting it next to him on the deck.

"It's the good stuff but watch it, it kicks like a mule," he said, refilling my glass and then his own, all perfected with his arms circled around me.

"I'm having a wonderful time," I sighed as I lay my cheek against his hair, so soft and appeasing. "It's my best birthday ever… tonight's going to be exceptional Lorien."

"I know." He moved his face up and kissed me lightly, a canapé in his hand, which he put to my mouth. It was nearly as good as the champagne.

"What was your best bit?" I asked, opening my mouth for him to feed me another. He laughed and spluttered crumbs,

"About what?" he laughed again, coughing. I gave him a few whacks on the back, and he drank from his glass, still chuckling when he'd cleared his throat.

"Swan Lake, silly." He was not aware I had changed the subject. "I liked the final Act when the spell was broken by Siegfried and Odette's deaths, and the swans came to life and trounced the crap out of Von Rothbart and Odile." He was looking at me with amusement. "What was your favourite bit?"

"It's always about the music Baby, and I think you're a little bit drunk." He kissed me on the nose, smiling up at me.

"That how is … what?" I stopped, laughing, knowing I'd made no sense; he was right. I tried it again, "How is *that* possible, I've only had one and a bit glasses."

"I told you, it has a kick." He fed me another canapé.

"Ewww, fishy," I said, pulling a face. He smiled widely, saying,
"It's caviar. Try this one."

"Much better," I nodded. "I have to pee, be right back..."

"My Ashlyn," he laughed as I climbed off his lap and trotted into
the room. On the way through, I remembered the USB and snuck it out of
my bag, putting it under the pillow that was usually my side of the bed.

I came and sat back with him, facing the other way to give his leg
a rest, grinning down at him. "You still haven't told me what you were
doing in the bathroom."

"Having a pee." I looked at him quizzically.

"When the room service arrived," he laughed, brushing his hands
over my forehead, moving my hair away from my face.

"You were pretty close before. When I realised I'd scurried off into
the bathroom to hide I knew how ridiculous it was."

"Ridiculous is a little harsh, Baby."

"Funny then."

"Yes, funny." He smiled at me and leant my forehead down to his.

"Lorien," I whispered.

"Yes?"

"Can I have another of the green ones please?" He sat up and
laughed loudly, pulling me against him tightly.

"You can have as many of the green ones as you want
Sweetheart."

He fed them to me, four or five in all, and I felt more stable. He
ate too, not that he seemed in any way tipsy, but he always ate. "Fuelling
up the fires?" I teased, taking the tiniest sip from my glass.

"They're already stoked."

"It's been a long time…"

"Tell me about it," he smiled.

"Lorien…"

"Do you want another green one?"

"No, I want to go to bed."

"Let me have a pee first." I climbed off his lap and he seemed to trot inside also…

I was standing by the bed waiting for him with the USB behind my back when he came and sat on its edge, looking at me. You could slice the air with a feather the room was so heady with sexual tension. "I have a present for you," I smiled at him coyly. He dragged me onto his lap, reaching behind to grab at what I held in my hands.

"Gimme, gimme!" he said playfully, having no idea what was coming, finally grappling it from me. "It's a USB… and marked with an X! When did you catch us at it without me knowing?"

"Just plug it in," I told him and knelt behind him on the bed to watch over his shoulder, allowing me to hide my face for now.

I ran a finger slowly across the back of his neck as the action began, watching his reactions to the show. I teased my lips to his nape, coursing them around the side of his throat to exhale in his ear, "Do you love it Baby?" He nodded. I ran my hands under his arms to reach around and caress his chest, invoking my enjoyment possibly moreso than his own, and gently scratched my nails over him. I glanced down to see his 501s fully tented out, not solely from my erotic explorations to his body no doubt, he hadn't blinked let alone moved a muscle since the show started.

I was coming for him on screen by now, and when I heard myself say I loved him, I knew it was nearly over. "Oh God, I love you too Ash," he said breathlessly as he whipped me down and pressed me onto the bed, his lips engaging mine in such a deep, open-mouthed kiss. "Oh no... Ash, Oh God." He shuddered against me and buried his face into the bed, laughing. "I can't believe that just happened!"

"What just happened?" I knew, but wanted him to tell me.

"What just happened, she asks? I unloaded in my pants Ash, that's what just happened." He laughed again and rolled onto his back, gesturing to the large wet spot on the front of his jeans.

"Mr Winky has left the building?"

"Only for a minute." He leant up and drew my face down to his, kissing me long and deeply again. After less than two minutes he mumbled, "OK, it's all good again." I drew back laughing and he quickly pulled me back to him. "What can I do for *you* Baby, I so owe you one... or two at least," he purred, rolling me over, still kissing me. I didn't answer; he could do what he wanted!

"Come on, tell Lorien what you like him doing to you *best*," he murmured through our soft lips.

"Whatever you want, my body is your playground ..." I sighed. He broke the kiss and leant up on an elbow, overlooking me as he ran a tress of hair from my forehead with his fingertips.

"Ashlyn," he whispered softly, looking deeply into my eyes, "are you never going to get past this veil of embarrassment with me Sweetheart? I want to give you what *you* want. You should be able to tell me... especially after what you just did for me." I blushed and he ran his finger over my cheek, "My sweet, embarrassed Angel..." He smiled at me tenderly and then changed the mood. "Let's get these pesky clothes off for starters…" He snaked his hand to the bottom of my jumper, raising it slowly and I sat up, allowing him to pull it easily over my head. "Hello twins," he said, lowering himself to me, moaning softly. He teased and bit me gently as his hand flitted across my other breast. "Hmmm," he sighed as he worked his mouth up to my throat. "Is *that* good Baby?" he exhaled to my ear. I nodded. His hand feathered down my stomach, sliding into the waistband of my jeans as he whispered, "You naughty girl, you forgot your panties." I felt a flash of heat run from my toes to my temples at his words. "Do you like it best when I *lick* you?" he asked, working his fingers through my pubic hair. "Or when I fuck you…?" he breathed into my ear. "Hard and fast or maybe *slow* and deep? Hmmm?" he moved his fingers to circle directly against me, my breathing already working into a pant.

"I want you to lick me first…" I whispered, flushing slightly.

"Hmmm!" He moved his lips back to mine, instigating another long kiss, making me burn for him.

He trekked his searing lips down my body, stopping to tease at 'the twins' again on the way as he flicked the button open on my jeans, dragging them down. He sat up briefly, pulling them off over my feet and reaching up to grab a pillow. "Lift your hips up Ash," he said softly and as I did, he slid it under them and moved down between my legs, lowering each of my knees outwards. "Comfortable?"

"Agitated would be a better word," I laughed breathlessly. He brushed his fingers over me lightly as he took in the topography. After a few minutes, I told him to stop looking at me, throwing an arm over my face.

"Oh Baby, you don't understand... not that it isn't *always* an exceptional sight," he leant forward to kiss me softly on the thigh. "There are two times it looks especially fine, when it's just about to be desecrated and after it has been. I'm just getting a good close-up of the 'before' shot..." he looked up at me, smiling lazily. When he brushed his finger against me again, I gasped and his smile widened, watching me watching him. He sighed deeply, saying, "The jealous mouth is starting to complain..."

He ran his hands down my thighs, spreading me completely open to him, lowering his mouth to me. I wasn't going to be able to stand much of this, and sensing my growing urgency, he dipped a searching finger into me as he brought me to an unparalleled orgasm, shoving my hand to my mouth to stifle the cries as my other hand clutched at the covers. My shins ran the length of his body needing a stabilising force, then gripped them against his sides. He didn't stop, bringing me on for another blast and I sat forward, moaning, "Ohhhhhh," as quietly as I could. My feet were now on his shoulders, lightly repelling him, using them moreso as support. The force of it collapsed me back onto the bed and I ran my hands over my breasts lightly, solely for my own benefit this time. He looked up at me and smiled, his face covered in my pleasure. He stood and quickly pulled off his jeans, which he wiped his face on before throwing them to the floor.

"I could hang a towel off this," he laughed quietly, motioning down to his erection.

"A whole set," I agreed and beckoned to him with my finger.

He came back to me at his own pace, slowly tonguing his way up to my breasts as he pivoted to enter to me, starting with a slow deep connection, grinding his pubic area against mine with each short stoke. "Lorien…" My breathing started to hitch again as I tried to fight off another wave, however I was jubilant with my ineffective wishing. As I writhed again, he stayed motionless, allowing me to use his body as my own personal tool and as I waned, he started to drive slowly, kissing me softly.

After several minutes of punctuating each stroke with a breathy groan, he settled back on his haunches, dragging my lower body up onto his thighs, showing no signs of nearing. "Aren't you ready…?"

"Whenever you want me to," he said and I smiled at him, letting him know now *was* OK. He changed his angle slightly and quickened his pace and after the final three massive thrusts, a smile broke out on his face, replacing the strained bottom-lip biting one that had been there a few seconds before. "That was incredible," he moaned, still slowly sliding himself in and out. He lay down over me, his lips nuzzling at my neck. "I love you so much Ash," he exhaled. When he had his breath back, he crawled down my body again.

"Where are you going?" I asked primly.

"There's one last thing I need to do… get a good look at the 'after' shot." He grinned up at me before starting his inspection. "Oh, poor Baby, all swollen…" He glided his finger against me before moving in to kiss it better. I didn't think it was possible to squeeze another one out, but within minutes he had me flying over the edge again, my head reeling with my own internal forces as he urged silently to keep going.

He came to lie next to me eventually, drawing me to him in another sensuous kiss, this time sharing the taste of our passion with me.

Lying there in the afterglow, I checked him out, as he had done to me before and after our lovemaking. "You're big, aren't you?" I asked a little timidly, holding him lightly in my hand, a harmless extension of his body at present.

"You only have my brother's to compare it to, maybe we're small." He chuckled lowly as he ran the length of my hair out between his fingers.

"I'd hate to see a big one then!" I said, making him laugh loudly. I circled my palm around him, noting my fingers only barely touched. "You swapped the ring we bought from the sex shop for a bigger one..." I answered finally.

"Do you know how you compare to other girls?" he asked smiling, and I knew this conversation was going places I hadn't meant it to.

"It's different for girls. We don't stand next to each other to pee for starters and even if we did, you can't see anything."

"It's not like guys go checking each other out at the trough you know."

"Not even Michael?"

"Especially not Michael. He would be so busted if he was caught," he said, laughing.

"Have you ever measured it?"

"Michael's?" he asked, amused. I jabbed him in the ribs with my elbow, turning his smile into a fake grimace. "I'd say all guys do at some stage. Curiosity... and before you ask it's about eight and a half."

"Centimetres? No way, it's got to be more than that." He was longer than that now and he wasn't even tumescent.

"Inches Baby, inches."

"Oh," I smiled at him shyly. "Why do you still use imperial measurements when everything else is in metric?"

"I have no idea. Maybe because it's more universal and men want each other to know where they stand in the pecking order." He laughed at his joke; I wasn't sure I got it. "You know what's going to happen if you keep fondling it like that..."

"Already?" I was used to his quick recoveries, but this was faster than I expected.

"It's been a long time Ash and I've kept my hands to myself except for once or twice. It's probably a good thing the first load escaped, I don't think I would have lasted more than a few seconds," he laughed.

"Am I making you uncomfortable?" It would be a first.

"Why would talking about this make me uncomfortable? You're the one with the verbal issues, Gorgeous girl." He snuggled into me, his face against my neck.

"I love Mr Winky," I said softly. I brushed my hand over his entire length one last time before I let him go, watching it twitch under its own force. "Are you making it do that or is he doing it on his own?" I felt his smile against me, not answering.

"You're his only thought, morning, noon and night... He only has 'eye' for you." He chuckled and we both fell silent for a while.

"Ashlyn..."

"Yes Lorien..."

"When did you make that?" I laughed, having wondered how long it was going to be before this subject came up.

"When you and Elijah went to get the guitar strings before our first gig. No one else was home and I knew it was my only chance to do it."

"Did you enjoy it?"

"I don't have to answer that!"

"You just did and it's the best present I've ever been given..."

"You'd better take care of it then." His eyes were closed, a smile played on his lips as he lay there serenely.

"I will," he said, lowering his hand over my stomach, playing his fingers lightly through my pubic hair.

"I mean the USB, not that!" He laughed,

"Had enough?" There was no such thing, but I was ready for sleep, my eyelids heavy, my body relaxed.

"I'm sleepy."

"I can fix that," he hinted, eyes still closed, nearly asleep himself. He rolled onto his stomach and draped his arm across me, pulling us both down into sleep.

My eyes flashed open, instantly awake as an unexpected orgasm burst through me, horny as all hell. Lorien had his hand between my legs, which is what had invoked me into such a delicious mood. "Morning Baby," he crooned.

"Good morning!" I rolled over and shared our first kiss for the day. He drew back smiling and hitched up onto his elbow.

"You asked me last night what my favourite bit was and here it is." I sat up slightly and realised he'd been watching my show again. "Just look at that, brings a tear to your eye..."

"Which one?" I asked cheekily and he smiled down at me, leaning in to kiss me again.

"Can we have sex now please?" he whispered. "I've been waiting for you to wake up."

"So formal this morning?"

"I thought I *should* ask first." He smiled, cupping his hand to my breast, running his thumb lightly across my already hard nipple. "I know you want it..." he grinned, "and I know I want it. Makes it kind of unanimous doesn't it?"

"I can't argue with that reasoning," I breathed. He entered me.

"Oh Baby girl," he sighed, "I love you so much..." His rhythm was already building to the urgency that shortly took him over the edge, capturing my eyes with his intense gaze as he filled me so completely.

"That was our first quickie," I said as he lay over me and I trailed my fingers lightly over his back, causing him to shudder a little.

"Who said we're finished? Hmmm, that feels good Baby...don't stop..." He was still inside me and I could feel him flexing, thickening, with every stroke I made across his back.

"My, you are excited this morning."

"You excite me all the time scrumptious... you've cast a spell on me you wicked witch and all I want to do is what we're doing now." He leant up on his elbows, looking down into my eyes, his fingers caressing at my breasts as he kissed me long and deep, slowly starting to grind.

He waited for me and as he felt me building, he quickened his pace, bringing his own force to fruition and we flew together, high up in the sky. "Man, that was intense," he exhaled, coming to lie next to me, drawing me into his arms.

"I can expect 24/7 service from now on?" I asked playfully, running my fingers through his hair.

"You may find this hard to believe but I could go again right now," he laughed and flicked back the covers to expose his already growing erection. "I'll save this one for the shower," he growled, running his lips across my throat.

"You'll have to take care of it yourself then," I said. He drew his eyebrows in, unsure as to my meaning. "You called me a wicked witch. If I get in there with you, I'll melt." He laughed,

"You make *me* melt."

"You only have to *look* at me and I melt."

"You only have to be in the room, and I melt."

"I only have to hear a word starting with L and I melt." He laughed at this, knowing I had him stumped in the melting department.

"Come on Baby, let's go and melt together," he said, chasing me to the bathroom.

We decided to eat breakfast in our room instead of going to the restaurant, having finished melting for the time being. He was unusually quiet and when I questioned as to why, he was reluctant to talk, instead flashing me a brilliant smile saying there was nothing on his mind. I knew he was lying but it didn't appear I was going to be able to coax it out of him just yet. I also found this strange. Lorien was always ready and willing to discuss anything. I couldn't get past the feeling he was keeping something from me.

He took me to the Eastern Suburbs for a drive when we'd finished breakfast, pointing out his old school, his home and where he and his friends used to hang out. I was hoping we'd run into someone he knew, his last girlfriend for example, but we didn't. It was a beautiful area and it must have been difficult to move from the beach to a lake, from a large city to a town. His answer of course was that he was happier than he'd ever been because we were together; the location was irrelevant.

Regardless of his sweet words and excellent tour guide attitude, there was still something troubling him that he would not admit to as I tried again to prise from him what the problem was. "You're imagining things Baby," he said, lying to me again. I knew if I was patient it would come to the surface eventually. I needed him to relax and unwind, allow his mouth to free itself from the chains that shackled his mind. There was no better place for this to occur than back at our room, focussing his attention on nothing else. "Where to now my love? The zoo, aquarium, Darling Harbour? Where would you like to go?"

"I'd like to do one of those tomorrow before we go home if that's OK."

"Of course it is but where do you want to go now?"

"Back to our room."

"You're a randy little minx. Have I ever told you that?" he asked, assuming I wanted to hit the sheets again.

"It cost enough, I think we should make the most of it Lorien; and that's *not* what I was referring to. You're the randy little minx my friend." He laughed and took my hand, putting it onto his knee.

"I see your point, and the view from the balcony is one of the best we'll get of the city. So, you're happy to hole ourselves up until checkout tomorrow?"

"Yes."

"Well then, we'll need some supplies..."

He pulled into a small village of shops and jumped out of the car, telling me to stay put and he'd be right back. He was gone less than five minutes and returned to the car carrying two paper bags. One obviously held bottles of some description and the other was much smaller with a chemist's logo on it. "What have you got there?"

"You'll find out soon enough," he grinned at me. I could only assume what was in that bag and in fact, had no inkling. We didn't use condoms anymore and I was confused what else he may need to get from a chemist that would be a surprise for me. Maybe it wasn't for me. Only time would tell.

When we got back to the room one surprise announced itself as he pulled two more bottles of Cristal from the bag and put them in the fridge, taking the already cold one we hadn't drunk last night and opening it. "Are you hungry Ash? Do you want me to order some lunch?"

"Not yet, I'm still digesting breakfast," I said and followed him to the balcony, waiting on room service to bring more ice for the bucket.

"You're not like anyone I've ever known Ash," he said, smiling at me tenderly.

"How so?"

"Most girls would want to be down there," he pointed to the city street so far below us, "painting the town red, wanting to go everywhere, see everything, spend, spend, spend. But not my girl, you're happy to just spend time with me, regardless of what we're doing."

"You've spent enough!"

"That's another thing. You appreciate so much, all that I do for you, all that I give you. It touches me here so sweetly..." he took my hand and pressed it against his heart.

"I love you Lorien, whether a hand-written note or a diamond earring," I touched my right lobe briefly, smiling at him. "Anything that's an extension of you means something to me." There was a knock at the door.

"Hold that thought," he said, going to meet the attendant. Was this conversation possibly something to do with what he'd been stewing over? Did he think I didn't love him enough because I wasn't expecting or wanting him to spend copious amounts of money on me? It seemed ludicrous, but you never knew what could be conceived in the head of a Standish.

He seemed reluctant to continue the conversation when he rejoined me on the deck, filling our glasses before sitting down. After a few moments of silence, I prompted him, "I held that thought..." He looked at me and smiled, not answering any further. "Lorien," I started gently, "Sweetheart, please tell me what's wrong. I can read you like a book mister, and I know there's something rattling around in that little head of yours..." I knocked lightly on his forehead, stressing my point.

"It's only ever about you Ash," he said, leaning over to kiss me. I let the subject rest again, for now.

"I'm sooo relaxed!" I sighed and shifted further slightly into the deeply padded chair.

"Totally relaxed?" he asked, sitting up.

"Yes... why?"

"Come with me." He took me by the hand and led me inside, disappearing into the bathroom and coming back with two fresh towels that he laid across the bed.

"What's going on Lorien?" I asked suspiciously.

"Strip Baby," he ordered.

"I'm already relaxed. You think you can do better?"

"I know I can, now strip."

Once I was standing before him naked, he instructed me to lie face down on the towels. I watched him reach for the chemist bag as I crawled over the bed, waiting to see what he pulled from inside it. I was ready to run if need be... He noticed my apprehensive expression and threw his head back, laughing loudly. "Do you think I'd ever do anything to physically hurt you, let alone sexually?"

"No, but I still want to know what's coming out of that bag!" He chuckled again and pulled out a small bottle of massage oil, showing me the front. "Oh, OK."

"OK?" I smiled and nodded. "What did you think was in here?" he started laughing again.

"To be quite honest Lorien I didn't know. That was what concerned me. It could have been anything."

"Baby girl, you do make my world turn..." he sighed and squirted some oil onto his palms, rubbing them together to warm it. I settled into a more comfortable position as he straddled over my thighs.

"Ohhh Lorien, that is *so* great..." I mumbled as he worked his hands and fingers into every muscle of my upper body, from palms to neck to waist he slowly rubbed and kneaded. He moved himself down my body to complete the massage, finally ending at my feet.

When he was done, I couldn't move; no muscle in my body was ready to be sent back into action.

"I just need a minute..."

"Lie there as long as you want Baby."

"Don't you want the same treatment?" I asked, looking up at him.

"Maybe later."

What felt like an hour later, but in all actuality was more like five minutes, I climbed off the bed. He held a Hilton robe open for me to wrap in, needing to shower before I could put regular clothes on. "Thank you Honey." I stood on tiptoe and kissed him. "That was wonderful, you masterful fingerer you."

"Meaning the piano fingers, the massage fingers or something else entirely?" He raised one eyebrow at me, his inference evident.

"I'll take the hat trick variety thanks."

Back out on the deck he gazed into the distance, occasionally drinking from his glass, back to his prior morbid state. It was time for me to drag this out of him, like it or not. I climbed onto his lap, which he welcomed me into eagerly, taking me in his embrace and laying his cheek to my chest. "Lorien?"

"Yes Baby?"

"If you don't tell me what's going on, I'm taking the next train home."

"You wouldn't."

"Try me." He sighed, knowing how stubborn I could be, knowing he was going to have to talk about this at some stage.

"It's really hard Ash..." I wriggled on his lap, trying to lighten his mood.

"Not at the moment and how very rare that is." He smiled weakly at me and told me to behave. "Come on, out with it. Do it like ripping off a band-aid."

"I want us to live together." Hell, that band-aid was a ripper! I didn't know what to say, what he meant exactly, when and where. I certainly didn't have a problem with it and when I opened my mouth to tell him this, to refine the details, he spoke quickly, possibly because I had taken too long to comment. "I know we're together all the time Ash, but I love you so much and want to cement this relationship more. We're too young to get married and too involved to be apart - this is the only middle ground I could think of... Ash, will you say something!"

"When you give me a chance," I laughed and he looked at me, smiling slightly. "Firstly, yes, let's live together." His reaction was immediate, and it warmed me no end, knowing this response had made him so happy. He kept forgetting I loved him just as much.

"Secondly?"

"Is this what you've been mulling over all morning?" He looked at me sheepishly and broke into a broad grin, nodding his head. "Why was it so difficult to discuss with me Lorien? You're usually the diarrhoea of discussion."

"Nice analogy Ash," he laughed. "I don't know, it's a pretty big step and I'd rather not have asked you than have asked and you said no."

"Have I ever said no to you before?"

"All the time!"

"Have I ever meant it?"

"No, you're a big tease usually, when you're saying no to me."

"There you go then, decision reached."

"I love you," he whispered, and drew me down to kiss him, so slowly, so deeply. I smiled at him, tracing the shape of his face with my finger.

"My Lorien, how I do love you." His grin was my response. "Now tell me about this. What have you been considering?"

"That I wanted to live with you."

"That's it, no plan, no reserve plan in case the original plan fell through, nothing like that?"

"Nope."

"Have you spoken to your parents about it? Elijah...?"

"Nope." He was still grinning at me, knowing he'd simply thought of the idea and acted on it. But, it was nothing we couldn't fathom out together.

"So, you were thinking of maybe getting a flat or a house somewhere closer to the Uni next year."

"Yeah, that sounds good."

"Do you care if we're living in a cardboard box on the side of the road, just as long as we're together?"

"That pretty much covers it."

"When you have your feet back on the ground again, we can discuss it further OK?" He nuzzled into my neck with his forehead and pulled away slightly oiled.

"Let's make use of that spa."

We took a bottle of champagne in with us. I was really starting to love the stuff, and I lay with my back against his chest, happier than I'd ever been in my life. "Are you having a good time Ash?" he asked, locking his arms together under my breasts, holding me tightly.

"It's been a wonderful birthday, thank you Lorien. I don't think I've said thank you this weekend."

"You don't have to thank me, and it's not over yet. What do you want to do tomorrow?"

"Not sure yet, it's a toss-up between the zoo and the aquarium, not that anything could compare to Swan Lake... it was spectacular." I sighed, thinking back to the beautiful ballet, the bittersweet ending for the two lovers.

"That sounded like a sad sigh Baby..."

"I was just thinking again why so many beautiful stories have to end so tragically, why the lovers always have to die."

"Maybe for love to be represented in the Arts it needs something to be compared to, something to make it shine in the face of adversity." He fell silent. I lay there full of love for him, considering his words when he said quietly, so very quietly, "I'll never be able to forgive myself for what I did to you Ash..."

"Hey," I turned to face him, "don't do that Lorien, please." He gave me a watery smile.

"I think of it every day Ash, every single day. I don't believe I deserve to have you, to be with you."

"You made a mistake."

"One mistake I didn't make was falling in love with you Ashlyn."

"I'm yours Lorien." I kissed him lightly and turned back around to lie against him, holding each other until the water was cold.

We were eating in one of the restaurants downstairs that evening, dressing up in our formal clothes again. I was given the choice of which one and I picked the French restaurant, delighted that I could read the entire menu. "They have poison on the menu?" Lorien asked incredulously.

"That's pronounced pwa-sonne. It's fish," I laughed, for once the holder of the cards. "And there's two S's in there you'll notice."

"Zut alors, quelle idiot!" I laughed at his self-derision, knowing he'd sucked that one out of the bowels of Year 8 French classes.

"You have a good memory, I'm impressed."

"*I'm* impressed. You order for both of us."

"What do you feel like?"

"Surprise me."

I scanned the menu and thought I'd order two simple dishes. That way we could share if we wanted, and it would escape the 'cuisses de grenouilles et escargots' he'd probably want to try. When the waiter approached, I said, "Parlez-vous en Français?"

"Oui Mademoiselle."

"Très bien. Je voudrais de foie d'oie pours deux et le plat principal ... Comment le boeuf est-il ce soir?"

"Excellent, ce sera à votre jouissance, Mademoiselle."

"Et le poulet?"

"Excellent aussi."

"Bonne, nous aurons le coq au vin et le boeuf bourguignon, s'il vous plaît."

"Quelque chose pour boire?" At this stage I looked at Lorien and handed him the wine list which he considered for a moment before replying,

"Le Beaujolais my good man, merci," and grinned at me.

"Très bien," he said and walked off. Lorien was staring at me.

"That was really hot!" I laughed. "No seriously, I've got a rager happening here and it's all because of you speaking French. Why haven't I tapped into this wealth before...What did you say to him?"

"I ordered pâté for entrée and asked him how the beef and chicken were this evening, which of course are excellent."

"I could hear a few 'excellents' being rattled off... continue..."

"And I ordered the chicken and beef dishes, which we can share if you like Lorien. I'm sure you'll enjoy them both."

"OK, and…"

"And then I asked him if I could have a French kiss for dessert." His mouth dropped open in surprise, a smile widening across his face.

"You did not!"

"You'll find out at the end of the meal, won't you?" He raised an eyebrow at me, and I let him sit and sweat it out. His French wasn't too bad, and I was sure he knew I hadn't asked for a kiss from the waiter. He was still staring at me.

"What?"

"I told you, it was a real turn on."

"So you can't stand up?" He shook his head.

The wine arrived and we ceased our conversation, the attendant waiting for Lorien to taste it before pouring us both a glass, leaving the bottle in an ice bucket beside us.

"Cheers Princess," he said and clinked his glass to mine, watching me over the rim as he drank.

"Some Prince you are, sitting there with a roaring hard-on after listening to me sprout out a few basic French menu selections."

"I'm no Prince, Baby."

"Michael has referred to you as my Prince Twin," I laughed, and told him the conversation we'd had at the beach over the Easter long weekend whilst he was in the sin-bin.

"We have a lot of great friends, don't we?" he said.

"The greatest. Speaking of which, Elijah and Keren seem to be back on track again."

"He finally came out with it."

"What does that mean?" I laughed.

"He told her he loved her and that was all it took apparently."

"Does he?"

"How would I know? I can't imagine him throwing it around lightly." I had my suspicions... He chuckled, "Prince Twin...Oh Michael, what a classic."

"I need a nickname for you, you have so many for me and I call you Baby or Sweetheart on such a rare occasion."

"I'm not stopping you Ash, and what is the lengthy list of names I have for you?" he asked.

"Baby, Baby Girl, Sweetheart, Princess, Scrumptious, Gorgeous Girl, Little One, Bashful Angel, Embarrassed Girl, Sexy Boxers..." we both laughed.

"I didn't know I was so gooey."

"Gooey is good," I confirmed, my eyes flashing at him.

"Gooey is *very* good."

I changed into the babydoll in the bathroom and when I came out, he was standing on the balcony, looking down into the street. I climbed onto the bed, waiting for him. His face lit up when he turned, and was inside within seconds, drawing the blinds as he kicked off his shoes. "You're dressed for dinner I see," he purred, climbing over me. "And my favourite is on the menu, a sexy near-naked woman in sexy red lingerie, my *absolute* favourite." He licked his lips, lowering them to mine. "Hey!" he sat up. "You never got your French kiss for dessert!"

"I'll take it now lover..."

"Are you trying to seduce me Miss Mercy?"

"Oui."

"Well, that's OK then, I just need to know where I stand," he said primly and then settled in next to me, teasing my lips gently with his own.

"Where's my French kiss?" I pouted.

"I'll give you a French kiss my little tadpole," he growled, snaking his way down my body, feathering his tongue over my bare stomach as he slid the wisp of a G string down past my knees. "You are *so* going to get it...," he murmured as he buried his face into me. "Oh ho Baby, we've got a little erection going on down here," he moaned and worked me softly with his tongue, making me echo his moan in return. His words alone were enough to drive me, and I wasn't going to get it for long, I was almost there already.

As had become his habit of late, he didn't draw back when my rapid breathing betrayed my tormentous arrival, my thighs pressing tightly to either side of his head, my fingers locked into his hair. "No Lorien, no more," I begged him after my second; his response was to look up at me, his dark eyes silently conveying that this was just the onset. He was in control of this painfully exquisite torture and I was his prisoner. I fell back to the bed weakly, unable to fight either him or my desirous body. Neither of them paid me any mind, doing to me what they agreed between them, taking me further and further. It was all I could do to raise a whimper as the next skyrocketing force hit me. My breath was shallow, my pulse threatening to flow from my pores across the bed and onto the floor, leaving me a victim, slain.

When I came back into focus after the constant onslaught I'd been forced to endure, Lorien was kissing at me tenderly, nuzzling me lightly, making silent promises through his now soft lips that the energy and fire he compelled through me was slowly retracting, from an inferno back to a flame. His eyes were still locked on mine having watched all of my reactions, them being to blame as they drove him to the frenzied state he insisted on taking me to with him. I was still shaking slightly, my body having held a rigid state for such a deliciously long interval now screamed at me to let it be. Lorien was gently stroking my thighs, trying to calm and soothe them although his throaty moans made them nervous, not trusting him to be conveying the truth. He moved up slightly and laid his cheek to my pubis, his hands crossing over my stomach, his fingers lightly caressing. "I know how much you love me when your body tells me so," he whispered, looking up slightly to be able to see my face more clearly. I was smiling down at him, now running my fingers softly through his hair, the prior gripping urgency abating. His face broke into a mischievous grin, "I lost count..."

"I don't think I can count that high," I sighed and sat up slowly, my arms open to him, needing his smooth skin against me.

I kissed him softly, teasingly, and he was like granite under my hand. The kiss slowly deepened, his breathy moans growing in their intensity until he pulled back saying, "Ash, let go of it." He was on the brink, this giving me a wicked idea.

On previous occasions, he had tormented me to the brink and back before finally letting me have my satisfaction and this time it was going to be his turn. I released him for a minute, reining in the kisses and his hands responded by slowing their trek over my body. Then I built him again, moving my hand back to encompass him, forging the heat through a longer, deeper kiss, continuing this circuit as his breath started to catch in his throat, stopping before he had a chance to tell me. "What are you doing to me Baby?" he whispered, his mouth at my throat, caressing his lips up to my ear. "You're not playing fair..."

"Do you want me to put an end to it?" I asked, smiling down at him and he nodded slowly as he took my breast into his mouth. I sat up, moving my leg across him and eased myself down, an appreciative groan escaping his lips as he hit full tilt within my body. I sat motionless for a few seconds, flexing my inner muscles against him only, curious whether he could feel them. Of course he could.

"Please Baby...," he moaned, his head starting to move from side to side on the pillow, his eyes closed for once. His face looking pained. I drew my hands across his chest. His nipples were as hard as the rest of him, and I tweaked them gently, starting to rock.

His eyes flashed open and his hands drew like magnets to my hips, trying to make my force against him harsher; he was ready. I stopped again, smiling down at him. "Baby pleeeease..." It was now him begging. However, when I begged I wanted him to stop. He on the other hand wanted to go, and I felt a little cruel to be putting him through this, not that I hadn't suffered at the point of his tongue in this fashion previously. He looked at me, his face a grimace, pleading with his eyes as he tried to buck under me, my internal muscles still caressing him unseen.

I raised my hips a little, giving him enough room to thrust from beneath and I told him to go for it. He grabbed my thighs, dragging me to him and away as he counterbalanced the energy from below, rushing into his orgasm. A sheen of perspiration covered his body, making his curls stick to his forehead, "Oh... God... Ash... OH GOD OH GOD...! Ohhhhh..." His hard body relaxed. Through hooded eyes he smiled at me, drawing me down to kiss him as his hands traced across my back once more. "You're a man-eater..." he puffed, his breath still not steady.

"Is that a problem?" I asked innocently.

"Only for you. I never intend on letting you out of my sight. If any other male gets a whiff of this, they'll be attacking me for mating rights." I laughed loudly. He was so silly sometimes. He grinned up at me, "Seriously though Ash, that was amazing... you're amazing... we are amazing together." That we were.

Here Comes the Bride

"All of the anguish that we made, all of the fines we had to pay,
Were all distant winter fugues when you said the magic words
'I do'."

L Standish, 'Ringing Bells'

FRANKIE WAS A MASS OF NERVES when we got to the little church, finding it hard to stand still. Simon was doing his best, as the best man, to keep him occupied and calm but it was pointless. Frankie was wired. "What if she doesn't show up?" His eyes were wild, and he played his two hands together, fighting like untamed ferrets.

"Do I need to slap him Michael?" I asked as we approached.

"Ash! Hey!" he said, capturing me around the waist and hugging me fiercely. He drew me back quickly, "She *will* turn up won't she Ash?"

"Of course she will Frankie, she loves you." He relaxed a little at my words, but this didn't hold long. The twins hugged him, clapping him on the back.

"She'll be right mate," Elijah told him. Frankie sat on the raised area near the pulpit, running his hands over his face.

"I've never been this nervous in my life!"

"Just think of tonight Frankie," Michael said. "It will take your mind off things." He grinned up at him as the bagpipes sounded and we all took our seats, turning to watch the bridal party enter.

Keren came in first, followed by Bree. They looked gorgeous in their gowns, and Elijah and Keren shared a wide smile as she passed. I looked at Simon as Bree drew closer; he watched her with a warm smile on his face. He'd loved her for over five years, and I think a wedding confirmed all couples' love for each other in such a deeply shared emotion.

I knew Cyndi had entered by the change in Frankie's actions. He'd stopped fidgeting and had his hands held behind his back, a loving smile on his face. And, I could see why. Cyndi held a matched expression on her face, only slightly obscured by the long veil. She was breathtaking. Her gown was strapless and fitted to her shape down to her thigh, the train following metres behind her and the lower skirt flowed out with the movement of her small steps; the graceful glide of an ice-skater. A bouquet of native flowers lay across her left arm as her father guided her, his arm around her waist, his right hand in hers.

When she reached Frankie, he raised her veil and leant down to kiss her, even though her father hadn't passed her arm to him yet. The congregation tittered in appreciation as her father formally passed her hand over to Cyndi's eager almost-husband. Frankie kissed her again. "As you can see," the Minister started, "we have two people, very much in love in front of us today."

As always, I was surprised at how quickly the actual ceremony sped by, here they were already going up to sign the register. Lorien handed me the camcorder, grinning at me, as he and Elijah stood up and went to the front of the church; this was obviously the secret he'd been hiding from me. They performed the Boyz II Men classic 'I'll Make Love to you' acapella, having modified it slightly by removing a few of the more suggestive verses, making it a little more gospel. When they were done, the congregation actually applauded and Keren skittered over to Elijah, kissing him, as I stood and did the same to Lorien when he returned. The congregation laughed, clapping again lightly as the Minister went back to the pulpit saying, "It appears we may all be gathered here again in the not too distant future." He smiled at me and I smiled back, dipping my head against Lorien to hide my blush as he circled me with his arm.

Shortly after we were introduced to the new bride and groom. The pipes started again, leading them from the church, and it was all over red rover. They were now Mr and Mrs Oates, at least for today, if Cyndi chose to keep her maiden name of Ashton.

We had three hours to kill before the reception, and as desperately as Lorien and I wanted to spend those hours locked away in our room, it would leave Elijah alone. The rest of our friends were in the wedding party. We all did however go back to freshen up and pick up the wedding gifts. The twins also wanted to take off their jackets. No sooner had I closed the door, Lorien was behind me. "Just a quickie..."

"Selfish!" I said, turning to face him and he drew me against him.

"We can make it all about you Baby!" he grinned at me lecherously.

"Show me your hands," I said. I'd brought a new dress for the wedding and it was a pale green. I didn't want paw prints on me as we walked into the reception.

"Did you bring the cuffs you wicked girl?" he asked, plying his lips against my throat, trying to fire the ovens so he would get his way... again. So strong I was, in so many ways, but not when it came to duelling with the passionate intents of a Lorien.

"I don't want you leaving your handprints on my bum!" I said, wanting to push him away, but the hands that rose to his chest to do just that had their own ideas, feathering across his pecs appreciatively.

"Hmmm!" he lowered his hands to caress me, to leave his handprints. "Best we take it off then," he suggested, starting to draw the fabric up at my thighs. There was a knock at the door.

"Get off her Lorien. I don't want to spend the next few hours stag." Lorien drew back from me laughing and went to the door.

"Ah... we're just about to get in the shower Eli, we won't be long." *You're cruel!* I mouthed, not happy with the lend he was having at his unsuspecting brother. Silence met us at the other side of the door. Elijah was possibly conflicted whether to push this or not. He knew neither of us needed a shower so would have realised it was to be a purely sexual event, if not just a downright lie.

"If you don't let him in I will!" I said, and he opened the door, grinning at his twin. I wondered whether this would end up in a wrestle as it had after Lorien had tricked him that Friday afternoon we all ditched school, unaware of each other's similar intentions.

"You're a riot bro," Elijah greeted him and sat on the bed.

"Get off my workbench," Lorien said, jumping out of the way as I went to smack him. "Want a drink?" We'd brought a few bottles of wine and a six-pack of beer with us, chilled in the bar-fridge.

"I've got some in my room, I'll go get it," Elijah said.

"We've got wine and beer if you want some of that?" Lorien offered, pulling a Semillon from the fridge.

"If you're going to open a bottle, OK." He went to sit back down and noticed our gift. "Hang on, I'll go and get their present or I'll forget."

"Bring another glass," Lorien called after him, "there's only two here." He shut the door behind his brother, the wine forgotten for the moment.

"Lorien, he'll be back in a second."

"That's one second more than we had." He came to me, and when meeting no resistance as he took me into his arms, kissed me deeply.

When the door opened, I broke the kiss and took a step back, lightly slapping Lorien across the face. "And don't you ever kiss me again!"

"Nice try Ash," Elijah said, "but I *will* hose you both off if I have to." He put the gift next to ours and sat back on the bed smirking, holding his glass out to his brother. Lorien was laughing and rubbing his jaw,

"I wasn't expecting that. Talk about turning off the tap." I took him back into my embrace; a little worried I'd overdone it.

"Did I hurt you?" I asked, and he shook his head at me, smiling, drawing in for another kiss.

"You just make yourselves comfortable. I'll pour the wine, shall I?" Elijah asked and we pulled away, laughing. He handed us both a glass. I sat in one of the single chairs, and Lorien took the one next to me as Elijah reclaimed his position on the bed.

We talked about the ceremony and the twins laughed when I brought up their song. "It was so beautiful guys, you did such a wonderful job," I praised them. "How did you manage to practice without me knowing?"

"It wasn't easy," they replied in unison and I rolled my eyes at them.

"You and Keren - what a pair," Elijah said, smiling. I opened my mouth to rebuke him but had no words at the ready for once. "No."

"No what? I didn't say anything." I laughed.

"No, I'm not trading places with your boyfriend who wants me to sit where he is." I'd missed that interchange and looked at Lorien who presented me with an innocent face. "You two stay where you are. I don't need to be a witness to your lewd carry-ons, if I may quote Michael. I could make a small fortune if I started to fine you a dollar each time hey?" He could indeed.

When it was nearly time to go Elijah gave us ten minutes to ourselves, excusing himself for some lame reason or another. I was sure this had been arranged by yet another unseen interaction between them. "Quick, get your gear off," Lorien urged, walking me backwards toward the bed.

"Absolutely not Lorien, you're turning into a real sex maniac."

"I wasn't going to get *my* gear off…" he raised his eyebrows at me, letting me know this *was* going to be all about me.

"I can wait."

"But Baby…" he tried, wriggling against me, already hard. Knowing he could fire off an orgasm within five seconds or fifteen minutes, he would be getting his rocks off too within the now eight minutes we had left.

"Have a wank!"

"Help me then," he said, his eyes opening wide, suggestively.

"I thought this was supposed to be about me."

"It can be about both of us. Come on, jump on real quick; you won't even have to take your dress off." He pulled me to him, and I wasn't sure whether he was joking or not. I was fully prepared to continuing batting off his advances until time was up.

"No," I said sternly and started to wriggle, his fingers pressing into my sides, tickling me. "Noooo, Lorien stop it," I laughed. "I'm going to wet myself." He stopped and was serious again.

"Can I at least have a kiss?"

"You can always have a kiss my Sweetheart," I told him, moving my lips to his.

"I'll remember that when you get all shy at our next public performance," he said and sealed himself to me.

There was a light knock at the door, "Bzzzzzz, time is up people!" Elijah called before cautiously opening the door. "Whew, glad he hadn't managed to talk you into it Ash, it could've been embarrassing."

"She was trying to talk *me* into it," Lorien said, and I smacked him on the bum, unable to get away this time as his arms were tightly around me. "Ooh, later Baby," I smacked him again.

It was less than a two-minute walk to the reception. They were holding it outside in the gardens of the hotel, and we walked across the makeshift dancefloor through a torrent of streamers, balloons and flowers to get to the gift table. Unlike so many weddings of today where a wishing well was in place for cash donations instead of gifts, Cyndi and Frankie had created a registry. There were many things they didn't have one of, let alone two. I picked out the crystal goblets, as I wanted them to have something they would have for a long time. Nothing as mundane as a blender or kettle.

The seating was arranged around the small tables in groups of four, with the three of us being the only ones at ours. There was no formal meal happening. Finger foods and hors d'oeuvres were to be circulated all afternoon by the wait staff so people could move around and mingle with whomever they wished. Elijah went to get a bottle of champagne and an ice-bucket and I saw him slip one of the waiters a twenty dollar note on his way back. The waiter in tow, she put the tray of finger food on the table and left. "Nice one bro," Lorien said, lightly knuckle punching his twin, and I realised Elijah bribed a waiter to leave the food with us. Lorien and Elijah shoved a few into their mouths and then he held one out for me. "Sorry Baby, no green ones today." I laughed as I accepted his offering and he shook his head at his confused twin, having no idea what we were on about. "Sorry Eli, private joke." The microphone was turned on and a brief feedback screeched through the area.

"Sorry about that folks," the DJ apologised. "If you will all be upstanding, we will welcome in the parents, bridal party and your new bride and groom." The DJ introduced them as they entered, Keren looking for Elijah in the crowd and blowing him a kiss when she found him, which he caught and put to his lips, making her giggle.

"Sick-en-ing!" Lorien whispered, and when Elijah turned, Lorien was already grinning at him. Elijah pulled a face and turned back to the now entering bride and groom. Both boys whistled through their teeth as they came in waving then took their seats. The DJ put the microphone onto the bridal table and returned to his station. The emcee turned out to be Michael, which was another surprise, but it shouldn't have been. Who else could do the job any better than he?

The formalities and speeches went by so quickly. Simon did a hilarious best man speech, which included not only Frankie but Cyndi as well, having known them both for the same amount of time. With great enthusiasm, Michael announced the throwing of the bouquet, asking all the unmarried women to move to the dancefloor. I hid behind Lorien to make sure I went unnoticed, but he pointed me out to Michael, and he said through the microphone, "That means you too Ashlyn Mercy. Get your butt onto the dance-floor."

"Thanks a lot Lorien!"

"What if you catch it Baby, just think what that will mean."

"I don't need to catch someone else's bouquet to know I love you."

"Aw, that's sweet, now get out there." He punctuated this line with a light smack to my bum. "Git!" he laughed, and I made my way onto the floor.

"Alright ladies, keep your fingernails out of each other's backs and your elbows to yourselves. We want this to be a clean fight. Go for it Cyndi!" She threw the bouquet and it arced across the dancefloor coming directly for me, whether intentional or otherwise. I stepped aside and Cyndi's Aunt standing behind me caught it, now the next to be married. I looked at Lorien who was watching with an amused expression on his face. *Oh well*, I mouthed, and he laughed. I hugged Cyndi and she whispered,

"That was meant for you."

"No kidding," I told her and hugged her again before returning to our table.

"Now for the gentlemen. Frankie, if you would be so kind as to remove the garter, no hands now..." Michael instructed. Cyndi put her foot onto a chair and lifted her dress to her thigh as Frankie went at her with his teeth; the crowd ate it up, always a favourite at weddings. "Now the same rules for the gents, keep your fingernails and elbows away from each other, no wrestling or throwing punches!" I laughed and saw Lorien getting to his feet.

"I intend to catch this one! Come on Eli," he said, and Elijah joined him on the floor. Lorien stood in behind Frankie, knowing that a garter can't be thrown or catapulted very far. He also towered over Frankie. He was in a prime position for interception, which he did. He sauntered back to the table swinging it around his pointer finger, a smart-arse look on his face. "Check... it... out..." He lifted my foot and threaded it over my shoe, dragging it up my own thigh. I stopped him,

"That's far enough Lorien," and he smiled and kissed me.

When the bridal waltz started a few minutes later, he stood, offering me his hand. "Sorry bro, you're stag on this one," he told Elijah. He was a wonderful dancer and he glided me around the floor, his forehead pressed to mine, his eyes deep. *I love you*, he mouthed, and I smiled, mouthing it back.

After two songs, the DJ started the dance music and Bree, Simon, Michael, Keren and Elijah joined us. Even Cyndi and Frankie had a dance with us for a few minutes when their schedule would allow; so many people for them to socialise with tonight.

We took a break and sat back at our table. Lorien dragged my chair in front of his and embraced me from behind, his chin on my shoulder. We drank champagne and watched our friends having fun, cracking up when Michael danced with Bree - a good rendition of dirty dancing.

Back on the dancefloor, taking in a slow number, Lorien held me gently, looking into my eyes as a broad smile covered his face. "What are you grinning about?" I asked, smiling back at him.

"Let's have a baby," he whispered, and I drew back looking into his face, knowing that mine was set with bug eyes and an open mouth. He mirrored my face back at me and smiled. "What?"

"We're too young Lorien."

"You want to have a family at some stage though?"

"Definitely," I nuzzled back into him.

"With me?" I looked at him and raised my eyebrow. Like there was ever a question about that. He smiled and kissed me lightly, returning to the conversation. "I think having kids when you're younger is an advantage to the child and the parents. We're young enough to have the physical and mental strength it takes to raise children, and the child will have young parents, able to run and swim and play the fool with them." He was right, it had been this way with my parents, and I was always glad they were young when they had me. I doubted they would've been so thrilled about our conversation, however.

"It's a good point, but it's only one point. What about the other issues that effect it as well, like having to work?" I asked.

"You don't have to work."

"I want to work."

"Well then, I can be the stay-at-home Daddy and compose from there, you can be the career girl." I laughed at this but knew it was also a more common thing happening in many family homes these days.

"You're crazy for even entertaining these thoughts now." I kissed him, lightening the mood. However, he was sincere.

"I just want you to think about it Ash and I don't mean having a baby right now ..." I cut him off,

"I takes about nine months to cook properly I believe." He shot me a smouldering glance, wanting me to be serious.

"I think," he glared at me, pulling me closer, "that if we're going to do this, it makes no difference to the bigger picture whether we do it in a year or so, or five to ten down the road."

"A Bachelor of Music takes three years to complete Lorien, assuming we get into Uni next year." I knew he wouldn't have a problem being accepted with his natural ability, but I was certain there were many students who were at my level, increasing my competition dramatically.

"We could do our certificates and diplomas through TAFE. Uni can wait until later."

"Why would you do that when you're already able to knock out jingles? You want to be a serious musician Lorien, not a hack."

"I will be a serious musician Baby, regardless of how long it takes. *As* importantly, I want to be a father. I want to have our own family." I didn't answer him but considered the options he'd put before me. "I'm just asking you to think about it Ash."

"I will."

"I want you to *seriously* think about it Ash."

"I will," I said laughing. "I promise." The warmth and love held in his eyes melted me just a little. "Where did this come from anyway?"

"I've been thinking about it since we came back from our Easter holidays... I love you with all of my heart Ashlyn Diane Mercy and I want to turn that love into a beautiful extension of us, a tiny little person to reflect our love constantly back at each other... With her mother's beautiful eyes..." He kissed me again, slower and deeper.

"So, it's a girl hey?" I teased.

"And then a boy." He smiled at me.

"Twins would be nice," I mused, leaning in to kiss him again.

"Does it run in your family?"

"No."

"Then we won't be having twins, Baby girl."

"But you're a twin... oh right, my eggs." I laughed. He could certainly determine the sex, but it was my fertility that would make it twins.

"If we had a daughter, she would be likely to have her own set."

"Grandparents of twins... that would be special."

"Nanna always thought so," he smiled at me.

"And if you get your way, we'll only be in our 40s, assuming our daughter would be silly enough to have kids in her early 20s." I smiled up at him and he frowned at me, not agreeing with my inference at our own stupidity for thinking of it now. "Where are the twins on your mother's side?"

"Her mother and grandmother were both twins."

"Wow, it's a pretty strong gene."

"That's why I want a daughter," he whispered into my ear. "We'll call her Mercy."

"Mercy Mercy?"

"Mercy Standish thank you Madam!"

"I think the fact that you're at a wedding and have been drinking champagne has clouded your vision a little," I smiled up at him.

"Nuh uh," he exhaled in my ear.

"Uh huh!" I breathed, ready to run back to our room. Aware of my growing intensity, he slowly ran his hands across my stomach, starting the foreplay for the acts that would follow, that always followed.

"Want to go and practise?" I grabbed his hand and we ran through the streamers, waving their fingers at us in our wake.

THE END

EPILOGUE

THE THREE OF US trounced happily down the Standish staircase, huge grins on each of our faces. We'd just received our approval to start at Castlebrook University next year and we were all relieved, especially Elijah and me. Lorien's choice of career was already written in stone; the Uni just didn't know that yet.

We had previously talked about getting a flat or a house closer to the campus, but Nick and Cara had convinced Lorien to stay put and for me to move in with them for the time being. I was more than happy with this arrangement and I picked up another of my boxes to take back to Lorien's room, *our* room. "How much stuff do you have?" Elijah asked, grabbing the next to last box.

"Just this," I threw back.

"I don't know where you're going to put it all," he said, shaking his head at me.

"We'll find room," Lorien said, putting the last box on the bedroom floor. "Thanks Eli, we can take it from here." Elijah smiled at him and rolled his eyes before leaving the room, saying,

"I'm sure you can little bro. Don't turn your back on him Ash."

"Am I allowed to peek in any of them?" Lorien asked when Elijah had closed the bathroom door.

"It's nothing you haven't seen before at my place, knock yourself out."

The first box he opened held mostly books. He grabbed an armful of old magazines off his bookshelf and dumped them into the garbage bag

I'd brought in with me. "Sweetheart, you don't have to throw any of your things away to make room for mine."

"These should've been thrown out long ago Ash, it's not a problem." He stacked my books in the space they'd vacated and moved onto the next box, containing my jewellery box and knick-knacks. He put the jewellery box on the nightstand on my side of the bed and a few of the knick-knacks around on his bookcase and desk. My teddy bear from when I was a child went into the middle of the bed on the pillows.

"You don't have to do that Lorien. I don't want to restyle your whole room on you, although I'm enjoying watching you unpack for me." His answer was a smile as he moved onto the next box, clothes.

When he opened the wardrobe, I was surprised to see he'd already cleared half of it out, as was the case with his tallboy also. He was so very thoughtful and just a little excited I was moving in with him.

Within half an hour he was done; boxes flattened and garbage disposed of. "I forgot to show you," he said. "New," pointing out the locks that were now on the inside of his bedroom door and a latch-hook on the bathroom, which he led me through. "This is for you." He handed me an attachment to fit onto the electric toothbrush the twins shared, a red band around the base to determine it from the others.

"My very own toothbrush Lorien, how sweet." He noted the slight sarcasm in my voice and turned on the cold shower tap, threatening to push me under it. "I'll be good!"

"I don't want you to be good," he growled at me, taking me back into our room.

"So, I guess this makes us a de facto couple in the eyes of the law."

"I guess so," he laughed. "Or do you prefer common law wife?" he teased.

"It has such a horrible sound to it doesn't it?" I said, pulling a face.

"Not when it involves you and me." I went to him and hugged him.

"I'm so happy I think I'm going to burst!"

"Best I don't prick you then," he laughed, and I joined him, understanding his undertones. We kissed our first living together kiss, slow and deep, driving us to the inevitable. Lorien broke away to lock both of the doors as I lay down on the bed, waiting for him.

GLOSSARY OF AUSSIE SLANG

- **501s:** a cool brand of Levi jeans that button down, instead of having a zipper.
- **All over red rover:** to announce the end of something, ie a game, marriage, etc.
- **Bachelor of Music:** Degree given after successful completion at University.
- **Beauty:** as a rule this would mean great, or fantastic. 'We're going to the beach tomorrow. Beauty!' However, if you 'hit your head a beauty', you did it well. It really hurts, I did it so well.
- **Blind:** see 'write yourself off'. I was blind!
- **Boardies:** abbreviation of board-shorts. Knee length quick drying swim shorts, worn by all sexes, but predominantly males.
- **Boot:** car trunk.
- **Bottle-shop:** A place to buy alcohol. Also known as the 'bottle-o' or 'grog shop'.
- **Buckley's chance:** very little chance. A common expression is also 'none and Buckley's' meaning it's not going to happen, give up.
- **Busted:** caught in the act, guilty.
- **Centimetres:** 1 inch = 2.54 centimetres.
- **Dag (to be a):** to be weird, uncool or goofy.
- **De Facto:** to live together as a couple, without being married.
- **Dickhead:** fool, idiot. Never meant in a nice way. A wanker is a 'bigger dickhead' and a 'fuckwit' is the biggest and worst of them all. A smart-arse is of a similar level to a dickhead, but they are usually arrogant, smug and a know it all, moreso than a fool or idiot.

- Dirty big: huge, extremely big.
- Dob: inform on someone. 'I'm going to dob you right in!'
- Dodgy: unreliable, possibly dangerous.
- Down pat: thoroughly practised or rehearsed.
- Dunno: I don't know.
- Esky: portable cooler, cooler box, ice box, chilly-bin, igloo.
- Fanny: in Australia, a fanny is your vagina, not your butt as it is referred to in the USA.
- Finger (give the): flipping the bird. Using the middle finger to give an obscene hand gesture.
- Flushed: as in 'I flushed him'. To be on your knees whilst your head is held into a toilet bowl and then flushing the toilet. This is never agreed to by the flushee, and is a form of punishment.
- Fuckwit: see dickhead.
- Get that into you: an upbeat positive phrase meaning 'here take this, and enjoy it'.
- Getting / get it: as in 'I am getting you' – understand (I understand you). Get it – cop it, as in you will get it tomorrow! To be punished or spoken to severely.
- Get wind of: to find out about something, begin to suspect something, hear a rumour.
- Go for your life: an expression of encouragement. Can be also used with sarcastic undertones.
- Hammered: see 'write yourself off'.
- Hang on: wait. 'Hang on a sec'. Wait for a second.
- Heaps: as in 'heaps of time' – a lot, plenty.
- Jaffle-maker: makes a toastie / toasted sandwich.
- Knock yourself out: go for it, enjoy yourself, make great effort.
- Kodak moment: a rare, one-off opportunity for a photo.

- Lend: as in 'having a lend'. To lie to someone, for your own amusement. It is taken in a light-hearted way.
- Maggoted: see 'write yourself off'.
- Mate: friend, buddy, pal. You can refer to anyone as 'mate', from your best friend to a complete stranger. However, 'a' mate, or 'my' mate, is someone you know and like.
- Mobile phone: cell phone.
- Myer: an upmarket department store.
- No worries: do not worry about that. Also known as 'no wuckers', which is short for 'no fucking worries'.
- Oi!: rhymes with boy. Means hey! It gets someone's attention.
- (The) oval: the school sports field.
- Paro: as in paralytic. See 'write yourself off'.
- Pegged: as in 'I pegged the orange at him'. Threw.
- Perving: checking someone out in an erotic way without their knowledge. Not considered overly crass or depraved, but girlfriends don't like to catch their boyfriends doing it, and vice versa.
- Pissed off / pissed at / pissed: to be cranky or angry. 'He pissed me off'. 'I'm pissed at him', 'I'm pissed that we had to miss out'. For drunk, see also 'write yourself off'.
- Play with yourself: masturbate.
- Ploughing the field: to have sex, with the field being the female sex organs, and the plough, the male.
- Pretty much: just about.
- Rash (all over it like a): excessive attention.
- Reckon: think, as in - What do you reckon? What do you think?
- Reefed: yanked, pulled with great force, even violently.
- Ripped: fairly drunk. 'We went out the other night and got pretty ripped'. See also 'write yourself off'.

- Ripper: awesome, exceptional, great.
- Root / Rooting: having sexual intercourse. Rooted can also mean tired or exhausted.
- Schooner: 375 ml glass, usually containing beer.
- Sec: second. Not necessarily a literal meaning of one second. Hang on a sec could refer to as long as it takes, and definitely not only one second.
- Shits (have the): to be extremely cranky or angry with someone or something.
- Sin-bin: penalty box. Used primarily in sports when a player makes an offence and gets 'time-out' for a certain period of time. The player is not replaced, so the team is at a disadvantage for that period of time, performing with less players.
- Smart-arse: see dickhead.
- Smashed: see 'write yourself off'.
- Smidge: abbreviation of smidgen. A very small part.
- Stewing: to ponder or brood over something over a period of time.
- Stirred: to tease or joke, or to be the victim of the joke – you would then be all 'stirred' up, from being stirred. Can also mean to come out of a trance or begin to wake up.
- Sunblock: sunscreen.
- TAFE: Technical and Further Education – a lesser version of University. Completed with a trade certificate moreso than a degree.
- Take-away: take-out. Place where you buy a variety of ready-made meals such as hamburgers, fish and chips, chips (aka fries), plus an assortment of other deep-fried food. Carries ice creams and soft drinks (soda), chips (crisps) and often lollies (candy), milk, bread, etc. In the USA this would be a 7-11 or an AM/PM.

- University / Uni: University in Australia is the equivalent of USA College.
- Wanker: see dickhead. To wank is to masturbate.
- Washer: face cloth, wash cloth, face towel.
- Wasted: see 'write yourself off'
- Write yourself off: get really drunk, also 'smashed', 'paro' (as in paralytic), 'wasted', 'maggoted', 'hammered', 'pissed', ' blind'.
- Year 8: equivalent to USA final year of junior high (middle school).
- Year 10: equivalent to USA sophomore.
- Year 11: equivalent to USA junior. Year 11 and 12 are the senior years and is mandatory attendance unless you are starting a full-time job, or are enrolling in TAFE.
- Year 12: equivalent to USA senior.

Elijah's phonetic drunken mumblings, translated:

- Cannav a birthey kiss: Can I have a birthday kiss.
- Wanna shee my arsh Babe?: Want to see my arse Babe?
- I luvuu Ash, alluz did, alluz will. But you don't lumme, luv Lori: I love you Ash, always did, always will. But you don't love me, you love Lori.
- I thing I pizzed her off tho, she's crangy wimme: I think I pissed her off though, she's cranky with me.
- Kiss me Ash, nowunce loogin: Kiss me Ash, no one's looking.

This glossary of Australian slang was developed to assist non-Aussies with any terms they find confusing in the novel. This could range from another country having a different understanding of the same word or phrase, to not understanding the term whatsoever.

The glossary outlines the reference to how the slang is used in the novel and is not all encompassing of every use of the word or phrase in Australia. Slang can also vary from state to state, which is why immigrants who have lived here for decades still look at we born and bred Aussies in total confusion when we speak. Who can blame them! ☺

A special thank you to my dear friend Jennifer D McLaughlin, my USA mate and pen-pal since we were 13 years old. Her input into this glossary from an American perspective has been immeasurable. Thanks Jen!

About the author

Cassandra Ann Frew (nee Souter) was born on a July winter's night in Hornsby NSW. At the age of three, the family moved to a dairy farm outside Lismore NSW where she spent the majority of her childhood. At ten years old, the family moved to Lake Macquarie NSW.

Cassie found her love of romance writing during her high school years, and her first several 'novels' were hand-written exercise books, passed around for her friends to read.

Her career in business and administration has led her into further self-education including web design, IT, professional proofreading and editing, creative writing and industrial psychology. She is also a Justice of the Peace and a Civil Celebrant.

Her most rewarding achievement to date is what she has in common with the residents of the Standish household – their love of music, playing an instrument and the 80s. What a decade!

These stories belong to my readers, and to Ashlyn and the Standish family. This is how love should be, can be, is.